THE CLOCKWORK ADVENTURES

PART TWO

CIRCLES OF THE REALM

WRITTEN BY
ALEXA RAYBURN

WITH ILLUSTRATIONS BY
CLARA KAY

EDITING BY

ALEX KAY AND LOUISE D. STAHL

Alexa Rayburn/Ingram Publishing Company

1 Ingram Boulevard

La Vergne, TN 37086

www.ingramcontent.com

Book Layout ©2017 BookDesignTemplates.com

Ordering Information:

Quantity sales. Special discounts are available on quantity purchases by corporations, associations, and others. For details, contact the "Special Sales Department" at the address above.

Clockwork Adventures: Part Two, Circles of the Realm: The Artist's Edition / Alexa Rayburn. -- 1st ed., 2023

ISBN 979-8-9883361-0-5

Your laughter, intelligence, and wit
through the sun and the rain
brings this story to life!
For the two best people I know.
Love always,
Mother

"You gain strength, courage and confidence by every experience in which you really stop to look fear in the face. You must do the thing you think you cannot do."

-Eleanor Roosevelt

Prologue

Well, I see her clearly now, just like I was back home. *She's been crying off and on all night.* I see her waking, rubbing her eyes with her fists. She'll flop back on the pillows, as if by taking a couple of deep breaths she can fall back asleep *and make it all go away.*

She slept in Mom's bed last night. She was probably too scared to sleep in her own room. I never imagined her being scared of anything. I guess I really didn't know her that well after all. Our mother has been gone for a week now, but Claire is *already* sick and tired of running the house and doing the chores.

Oh, don't get me wrong. She's hauled laundry and walked the dog like a champ. She's tutored me so hard that I aced my end of semester exams. She's cooked, cleaned, and lied to the office staff about where Mom is; a full week of misery, even for her.

I used to call her *Miss Pitter Patter Perfect, not-a care-in-the-world-Claire.* That's who I imagined she was. I was way off base about that. I see her grumbling, *finally* getting out of bed like she does in the mornings. She isn't a morning person at all. *She hates mornings.* I see her look at herself in Mom's bathroom mirror and pull out a hair she thinks is gray. I mean, how many gray hairs can an eighteen-year-old pull out anyway?

Claire hates being Mom; it's too much work. I'm not so big on parent-work either, but at fourteen, whad'ja expect? Oh, I can feed the cats, and dump Mom's pricey bottled water in their bowls when I'm tired, but anything other than that, well, best to leave it for Mom. Or this week, for Claire.

All this mess started with the tinydog Pebby, curled up and pretending to be asleep at my feet. She's kept her eye on me through the whole night. I thought she belonged to Naji Najeem, Mom's weird neighbor at her office. He gave me an old backpack that held a widget; address 1426 Wenderling Way, Norwall. Turns out the man and the scruffy dog had accidentally warped through something called the Parallax Contingency. They came from this old-timey town. It's full of steam engines, gears, inventors, and, oh yeah, *Automatons*. Those are fancy robots that will just as soon kill you as look at you, that is, if you aggrevate 'em.

Norwall. It's where me and my best friend Mc-Clure are sleeping on something that smells like the furniture moving pads Mom keeps in the garage. We're sleeping on the floor of a stone cottage belonging to Wassy Wymore and her dad, Wallace. There is only the heat from a little fireplace to keep us warm. There is a crazy old-timey water pump at the sink. I'm still wearing the black pants and shirt I put on last night when I left home. I've got no idea what happened to my backpack through all the confusion of spinning upside-down through the Parallax.

Last night, without waiting for Claire, mostly to save her and me the pain of saying goodbye, I left under cover of night. I didn't plan to take 'Clure, but at the last second he baseball-slid in and grabbed my jacket. He said *I just came along for the ride*. As my best friend you know, he's always got my back. He's got a lot more street-smarts than me. He's probably glad to get away from his parents 'cause their issues have issues. They've got no time for 'Clure, even though he's top of his class.

Somehow, with the help of this tinydog, we kept outta sight of the crazy airships and made it to this safe house. The Wymores' house. We're bedding down here tonight, and tomorrow we start the search for Mom. Don't even *ask* me how she wandered here. Like I said, this whole mess is one huge mistake. Claire, my sister, is alone in a house loaded with our particular, peculiar, persnickety pets. That's not counting one angry-looking green parrot that Mom's friend Nesta dumped on us yesterday. *Friendly, but bites.* Wow.

In my mind, I see Claire making it to the kitchen now, hoping that either me or 'Clure is making the coffee for her. I see the impatient expression on her face as she sleepily moans under her breath.

Dweebs! Can no one make coffee but me? Dweebs! come on dweebs *get up!* I know we left the kitchen a wreck, papers scattered everywhere, dishes piled sky-high. Mom would scream if she saw it.

Can any of you dweebs make coffee? Claire will be calling out in higher and higher decibels. That will probably cause Mom's African Gray parrot, Freddy, to go wild in the front room. His screeching will wake up Naji Najeem, the person I hold accountable for the awful mess my family is in.

Well, I imagine Claire pushing open the door to my room and seeing I'm not there. She'll shout "Phills!" and rip the covers off the bed, as if I'm hiding under 'em. She won't find me. She'll leave my covers lying on the floor, *gross*, and hustle to the west wing of the house looking for 'Clure. He was *supposed* to stay there last night. Out of breath now, she'll make her way through Mom's octagon-shaped office. She'll squeeze through the heavy, sliding bookcase wall into the guest wing where 'Clure is supposed to be. She'll see his bed hasn't been touched and his unopened backpack is on the floor.

Pebby! Pebby! she'll call. No dog. *They must be out walking her.* She'll start calling out for the three of us, all over the house. *DWEEBS! DWEEBS! Come out, come out wherever you are!* She'll call out in her naggy voice, unbelieving, half laughing, half yelling, sticking her head out the front door.

She won't see anyone. Wrapping her robe tight, she'll trudge down the street. She'll get irritated. She'll come to the edge of the park, but we won't be there. It makes me sad to think of her running back to the house now, out of breath running, not want-ing to believe what her heart already knows. She won't want to believe we left without saying good-bye. Maybe he's in my lab?

She'll run down the hall, punch the buttons on the lock, and fling open the door. That's where, only two weeks ago, she taught me to solder wires to-gether. She'll feel the tightness in her chest as she starts to hyperventilate. *Dweebs! Damn those Dweebs!* She'll run back up to the kitchen, hoping against hope that she'll see me and 'Clure arguing. *French vanilla versus hazelnut.* But, we aren't there. *We aren't anywhere.* We left in the middle of the night to find our mother, who we are pretty sure is badly hurt. I *heard* the awful crack of her leg bones, and I saw her hit her head. *Damn! Damn that McClure.* Claire didn't bank on McClure leaving and neither did I. The deal was that he was supposed to stay behind and help her sort everything out and keep the house and Mom's business in some kind of normal. Mc-Clure, with all his level-headedness, was the *perfect* one to do all that.

I can almost smell the heavy aroma of the hazel-nut coffee, my favorite, that I won't be drinking this morning. I look at the tinydog sleeping on my feet and I glance at 'Clure, still asleep on the ratty pallet. I can imagine Claire back home, realizing what has happened. I suffer now, knowing she is crying loudly and bitterly, head down on the kitchen table. She is inconsolable, sobbing for the mother, for the brother, and for the friend that she has lost.

The Dirty Little Girl

Hidden flat against the stones and melting invisibly into the herringbone pattern of the fireplace, an olive skinned girl stepped forward, shocking Phillip. A dark braid hung over one eye and serpentined to her waist. Startled, he jumped back. His left eyebrow was highly arched, as happened unconsciously when he was perplexed. Behind him, McClure gasped, mesmerized as the figure stepped from the shadows.

The girl was as tall as Phillip, but undernourished and scrawny. Her gray calico dress was dirty, tattered and spotted with patches. In a whispering, raspy voice she spoke, fists clenched at her sides.

"What *exactly* are you doin' in my father's house?" she queried, jerking her chin forward and squinting her eyes. Phillip didn't have a second to respond. Head down, she charged at him with toreador-like precision, butting him in the stomach with her head. He lurched backwards and fell onto the packed-dirt floor. McClure jumped into the fray and within seconds, fists were flying as he and the girl wrestled into a tumble.

"I SAID, What exactly are you doing in my father's house?" Wassy Wymore grit her teeth and spit out the words.

"Dude! get her off, she's killin' me!" McClure begged, now near tears as he felt his shoulder ripping.

"Whoa, Whoa, *Whoa!* Look! Miss! We mean no harm!" Pleading now, Phillip clasped his hands as if in prayer and nervously jumped back and forth.

"Please! Let'im go! Please! You got it wrong, we're not qoing to hurt you. No! No! We came here looking for our mother, who's lost and hurt! Pebby brought us here to hide from those airships, I swear!"

He raised both hands up in surrender. The girl cut her eyes at him and let up just a fraction on McClure.

"Let me up, please, leggo my arm!" McClure begged tearfully, certain his shoulder was broken. The girl persisted, twisting it further.

"OOOWWWW!!!" McClure hollered again. The three of them hadn't noticed Pebby scampering out the back door of the cottage. Phillip approached the girl tentatively, fully prepared to push her off of his friend, but not wanting to suffer the same fate.

"Where'youse from? I never seen ya round here, now you tells me, WHERE YOUSE FROM!!!" The girl cut her eyes severely.

The arched wooden back door *slammed* open and a middle-aged man in crusty work clothes and muddy boots stomped in, scowling and pointing an angry finger at the melee.

"Hold it right there Mister, do not, I repeat, DO NOT go near that young lady. Step back, I say, STEP BACK!"

Wallace Wymore was shocked at the sight in front of him. His daughter, Wascilla Wymore, was perched solidly on the back of a thin, ginger-haired teenager, whose arm looked angled as if it had been recently twisted off of his body. Wymore patted the top of Pebby's head.

"Good job comin' to git me, good job girl." She shook her head up and down with pride. The fight had been too vicious for her to stop without help.

Moving toward his daughter and taking her hand, Wallace gently helped her off of McClure, who painfully got to his feet and limped to stand by Phillip. He rubbed his shoulder and muttered under his breath. Phillip could swear he heard a whispered litany of four-letter obscenities.

Putting his arm around Wascilla, Wallace Wymore pulled himself up to his full height and raised his dimpled chin. He let out a long and labored sigh.

"Why don't you boys start at the beginning. Tell me how you came to be in my house, and more importantly, how you came to be in the company of this here dog?"

Pebby had parked herself directly in front of Phillip, and it didn't escape Wymore's notice that she appeared defensive. Stepping forward, Phillip extended his hand.

"Sorry Sir, Pebby led us here, she was tryin' to keep us safe."

"Yeah, Sir," McClure chimed in, "we didn't know where we were, and she was trying to hide us from the flying ships. Sorry if we were intruders, real sorry."

He continued to rub his shoulder, but extended his hand courteously to Wallace Wymore while Phillip interjected.

"Would you know anything about a tall woman who came through here? Might'a been hurt? Tall, kinda' slender, dark-brown hair, wearing black? You know anything about a woman found here? Anything at all?" He parcelled his words carefully and breathed slowly, not wanting to hear that perhaps Abby Weathermore had been found and had not survived her injuries.

"Nope," Wymore shook his head, "I know nutin' at all 'bout a woman. Tell me again, where youse from?" He looked them up and down suspiciously. "And who be this lost woman, anyway?" Unexpectedly, McClure spoke up.

"She's our Mother, and we think she's hurt. Have ya' seen her? No?"

Phillip remained silent and sorrowful, staring at his shoes. Pebby sensed Phillip's pain and brushed up against his leg. Lifting her up, he buried his face in her neck, fighting back tears. *No sign of Mom. No! Maybe she wasn't in Norwall at all. Maybe the Parallax took her somewhere else and I won't ever see her again.*

Softly and kindly now, Wymore asked again, "Come'on boys, tell me how you came to be so friendly with this dog. How'd it happen?"

Letting out a long sigh, Phillip regained his composure and set Pebby down. He slid his hands into his pockets.

"Naji. We came to know her through a guy named Naji. To be exact, Naji Najeem. You've heard of him?"

Wymore's mouth dropped open. Reaching behind himself, he carefully backed down onto a wobbly wooden stool.

"Naji?" He breathed deeply, both hands clasping the sides of his dirty, unshaven face. "You know Naji? Bless my boots! He's alive? When did you last see him?"

A broad smile broke across his face and his eyes opened wide in amazement. Jumping up to his full height, he put his face directly in front of Phillip.

"Com' on! WHEN DID YOU LAST SPEAK WITH NAJEEM? Now tell me, and it better be the truth. If'n you boys is lying, I'll have no mercy on ye's!" He pointed a finger directly in Phillip's face.

"Last night. We spoke with him last night," McClure offered. Frozen in shock, Wymore grinned widely.

"He's alive? *He's alive, that buzzard?* Thank the stars, Naji's alive!" He laughed, tilted his head back and closed his eyes.

Phillip carefully chose his words. "He sent us. Naji sent us here. He told us to get to his tailor shop, and he gave us this." Pulling the widget from his pocket, Phillip produced the key. "He told us about Norwall. We think our mother came here by accident and we've got to find her and take her home. Naji told us all about Norwall. He said we could use the tailor shop as our home base while we're looking for Mom."

Taking the key, nodding his head rapidly in recognition, Wymore held the key against his chest. His eyes closed tightly and he was smiled. My friend, you haven't left us at all. He breathed deeply and continued.

"So, if Naji sent youse, it must be for good reason. And, if youse are knowin' this tinydog, well, youse should know that she is the best dog in all the land. Most respected, most loved, and the hardest working pup on four legs. Why, she's Chief Delivery Dog, Octagon Bakery, that is. Why, she knows this ole' clockwork town better'an any of us, right Pebby?" She stood on her back legs and rested her front paws on his leg. He picked her up and comfortably held her in his lap, grateful that the uproar was over.

"So," asked Phillip, "can you help us get to the tailor shop? Which way should we go? We don't have much time to spend here, we'd just as soon go now."

"Well, youse better not be makin' your way at night, curfew in place an'all. The Automats don't take kindly to movement at night if'en youse know what I mean. No, better to rest here, have some soup and bread, rest tonight and we'll talk in the morning. Just be sure to be quiet, stay inside cause we gotta' keep you under cover. If the Automats suspect a stranger, no tellin' what they'll do, and we'll *all* be in danger." He nodded and pointed to his daughter, who quickly turned away to try and hide the fact that she had been listening to the entire conversation.

Smiling now, Wassy made her way to a wooden shelf, retrieved two mugs and ladled soup from a pot hidden in the embers of the fireplace.

"Sorry, I'm sorry. I dinna' know who youse was, ya know? Sorry if I hurt ye." She hung her head, then looked up and met McClure's eyes as she continued.

"Sorry, really sorry, hope your shoulder ain't too bad, really, I am sorry!" She lifted her hand as if she wanted to touch him, but withdrew. "I'll give ye some liniment I made from Achillea plants, made it meself!" she boasted.

"A ... kill ... what?" McClure looked skeptical, remembering that minutes ago she was twisting his arm out of the socket.

"Yarrow, silly, called *Yarr...ow*," she smiled widely, revealing crooked front teeth that didn't detract one bit from her natural prettiness. Handing him the cup and lowering her eyes shyly, she pulled some worn blankets from a small wooden cabinet and gestured to the floor.

"Go'on, make yourselves comfortable, go'on." She smiled a wide smile, crinkling her eyes. She shrugged her shoulders as she looped the long, dirty braid behind her right ear.

Handing him a small, hollowed out wooden container, she nodded her head. "It's yarrow. I make it by grinding up flowers. We use it on our sores and hurts. Ye kin too, go'on, it's not gonna hurt ye."

Nodding again, backing away, she pulled her worn dress around her, kicked off dirty, brown work boots, and effortlessly climbed a ladder to a loft.

"Gunnight," she softly called over her shoulder. Exhausted, the boys dropped to the floor, unrolled the pallets, and sipped their soup. Only when Mc-

Clure was certain she was not peeking down on him, did he dip his fingers into the liniment and reach under his shirt to rub it on his shoulder. Phillip raised his eyebrows and spoke first.

"Let's sleep dude, we've had enough today. Don't eat that stuff, ok?" Phillip chuckled softly under his breath. Wymore pulled a pallet from the cabinet and stretched out on the floor across the room. He softly mumbled to no one in particular, *"Naji. I canna' believe it. Naji. Of all things. The old buzzard, bein' alive?"* Shaking his head in grateful disbelief, he laughed. "Well, that's just like him to pull sumptun like that." He shook his head.

"But if'n he sent ye boys he must take great stock in youse. I'll help ye all I kin, youse gots to know that!"

Pebby was already curled up asleep between the boys who, likewise, were snuggling down. Exhausted, they opened their eyes wide, when, from the other side of the room, they heard Wymore's soft, but firm voice float through the darkness.

"Waid'a minute. Where is youse from? Where is youse FROM, and Where is Naji Najeem? Where is he right now?"

At that same minute, instantaneously, Phillip sat straight up. Raising his eyebrows and wrinkling his forehead, he exclaimed loudly,

"Wait a minute! Wadda ya mean, Chief Delivery Dog?"

Chapter 2

The Blue Porthole

Her nightclothes were stuck to her, soaked with sour-smelling sweat. She sat up and grabbed the rope pull-cord to call Hilde Hemming, her caretaker. She collapsed back onto the pillow as nausea overwhelmed her and the hateful, warm, bilious stomach acid rose, burning her mouth and nose. Dry heaves racked her body as Abby Weathermore pulled herself up again as gray-haired, stooped-back Hilde shoved a hammered brass basin under her face.

Abby turned on her side and vomited uncontrollably as the room spun 'round and 'round. Two neurons connected for a millisecond and an electrical impulse flashed like a sparkler in her brain. She heard a boy's voice plead in anguish; *NO! OH... NO!!!* Then, she heard her own voice crying out, pitifully weak. *Help ... me .... Help ... me.* She couldn't tell whether she actually *said* the words, or she was *dreaming* she said them. Her mind traveled back through her jaded memory, trying to grab the voice and pull it toward her, to pull it close enough so she could see a face. But the sparkler flamed out and the door to the memory quickly, cruelly slammed shut. Try as she might, she could not reach the voice again and it faded into the black oblivion of a path she could not enter.

But, the room kept spinning, as it had in the dream that awakened her. This was the third time the violent spinning woke her from sleep and left her weak and helpless. *Why do I get so dizzy, and where was I before this? I feel like someone was reaching out to me. Where are they now?*

Her head hurt from trying to remember. Another empty memory; a flash-point scene for a nannosecond, then, fade to darkness. A collage of forgotten things; the unknown source of the scream, the arm of the faceless person, the reaching out that never quite touched her, the lick of a dog on her cheek. *Whose dog? What dog?* People around, but no faces, nothing to grab. Nothing but mannequins, faceless mannequins.

She wiped her face with a rough muslim rag. Annoyed, she shook her fist at a clattering, banging suit of armour sitting in one corner of her room. She saw a puff of steam coming from a small pipe which ran up the back of his head. She rubbed her eyes. *I'm seeing things. But it almost looks like a person, how can that be?*

It was the eyes, the turquoise eyes and the down-turned mouth with vampire teeth that made her shiver with fright. The eyes and mouth gave it a human look; the scowl of an angry human, as if it was angry at her. *But, why so mean?* The arms were pincher claws, the right one grasping something with a flared end, like a toy gun. *Silly, a toy with a nasty face?*

The dizziness was starting to clear. Where am I? She didn't know. How long have I been here? No clue. Hilde's gentle hands cared for her, but everytime she ate anything, she fell back into a deep, dreamless sleep; except for the nights that the violent dizzy spells haunted her. Days and nights melted together like the soft focus of a Renoir painting, her own self barely recognizable through foggy consciousness.

But the fog was lifting a little and she felt able to try and make sense of her surroundings. She pulled the cord at the head of her bed. Instantly, Hilde marched through the door, followed by three assistants, similarly dressed in long, white, spotless muslin gowns, aprons, and hats. Their footsteps were muffled by their muslin slippers.

Supporting her right leg, they lifted her to a commode which stayed at her bedside. Turning their backs until she was through, they ported her back into bed quite mechanically. They never said a word. Whoever they were, they had taken good care of her when she could not care for herself. Hilde stayed with her now, but shooed away the others who then marched robotically out the door.

She was shocked everytime she looked at her right leg. It was encased in white and beige wrappings like a mummy, a constellation of oddly shaped gears protruding on either side. Spiky prongs of the gears protruded through the bandages. *These look wicked!* She strained to touch the gears, but could not bend far enough to reach her ankle. *What happened to my leg?* Hilde would not let her bear any weight on her right leg, so she assumed that somehow it had been badly injured. *So, it must be broken I guess?* Hilde patted her shoulder.

"Good Mornin' to ye Missy, it's time you started wakin' up!" The woman laughed with a sinister guffaw, pushing strands of gray hair back under her kerchief. Resting her fists on her hips she continued. "I see youse more awake today! I know it helped to hold your night medicine last night, you sleep so deep when ye takes it. Course, ye *should* know, I only follow the instructions of the HoNorrable Gleena Glisson, Proprietress and Manager of this Octagon Bakery. You'll meet her soon enough. She's been quite the generous lass, what that we finded ye hurt in the woods and all, got it?"

She had no recollection of being lost in the woods or getting hurt. *What woods? Why the woods?* Hilde continued. "Well lass, is ye remembering anythin' else? Since I've given ye less medicine, is ye remembering who ye is? Miss Gleena wants an answer from me each and every day ye know." Hilde looked down sheepishly, obviously embarrassed. The woman in the bed smiled. *Yes, today I've got a surprise for all of you!*

"Addie!" She whispered very softly, "my name is Addie!" Abruptly, to both their amazement, the suit of armour instantly came to life. It spun three revolutions, puffed a few puffs of steam, and rolled over to the bottom of the bed. Pointy teeth protruded from the mouth with down-turned corners. They vibrated and the turquoise eyes flashed menacingly. The arm that raised did not offer a helping hand, but raised an arm comprised of gears, pulleys, and a claw-like apparatus that frightened her. She nervously laughed to herself. *A joke, this has got to be a joke.* The oval turquiose eyes randomly flashed with a soft clicking, like the shutter of a camera. Hilde quickly stuck her face directly in the face of the metal man, snarled her upper lip and gave him a hiss.

"Now be off wid' ya Mister, I got work to do, now git!" She shook her fist at him. He abruptly turned and settled himself back in the corner of the room as Hilde opened the dresser and fetched a pile of white muslim garments.

"Ready to git outta that bed? Miss Gleena says you're able to git outta this room and come down to the kitchen and give them a hand, if'n you know what I mean?" Opening a small closet concealed in the white paneling of the room, Hilde pulled and tugged out a heavy wooden chair with large wooden wheels on each side. "Com' on now, I'll help ye change into ye work clothes, and we'll git ye into this chair. Gotta keep that leg up, ye know what I mean?"

"Just one thing," Addie asked, almost afraid to know the answers. "Where did you find me? In which woods? Do you know why I was there, or why I got hurt?"

Hilde replied cautiously. "Oh Missy, ye was lying in the dirt o' the Wymore Wheat fields, and ye had the biggest bump on yer head, and yer leg was busted so bad now, that the Medicons thought ye was gonna lose it. They thought they was gonna' have to CHOP IT OFF!" She giggled cruelly as she gestured with her hands, making a chopping action on Addie's thigh.

"They healed it together best'n they could with the gears and they gonna see how it mends. Ye should know ye might not walk on it again, not ever. Here's just hopin' they don' gotta chop ye', no?"

Addie quickly wiped tears from her eyes. She trembled with a combination of shock, fright, and pain. Hilde patted her shoulder, trying to console her.

"There, there, com'on, now, we'll get ya' changed!" Hilde helped her sit on the side of the bed, gently lifting the gown over her head. The mechanical man seemed to be watching her from the corner of the room as she changed her clothes. Addie blushed and he seemed to sense her discomfort. His turquoise eyes flashed several times, then closed. Hilde pulled a white muslim gown over her head; a simple garment with a round neckline and short, puffy sleeves. Slipping the loop of an apron over her head, the woman gently tied it around Addie's waist. Hilde pulled oatmeal-colored socks and white cloth booties on her feet and tied them loosely with strips of fabric.

"Now com' on, up to the chair ye go!" Hilde hoisted Addie up into the chair with her right leg extended in front of her on a platform. Moving her leg hurt worse than she ever could have imagined. The gear apparatus made the leg too heavy to even think of moving it on her own.

"So, where we going?" Addie asked, shifting her weight to get comfortable. The wooden seat had no padding and was already poking her back. Hilde turned the wooden wheelchair around and pulled it toward the door.

"What is this place?" Addie whispered, craning her neck to take in the high, white ceiling and the long clerestory windows bordering the high white walls. One window, looking for all the world like a porthole on a ship, was midway up the wall over the painted white wooden dresser. Its faceted glass in various shades of blue, had eight sides, and the glass looked thick.

"Where are we? Where we going?" Addie whispered weakly, disoriented and off-balance.

"Why Miss, youse going to work, now. Gleena says to keep ye in the chair, but take ye to the kitchen so's ye can be learning to help. Good gracious. I dunno where ye is from, but I know ye better understand where ye is. This is the Octogon Bakery, biggest factory in this ole' clockwork town. Now, ye better be helpin', or they'll have no use for ye and the Council will take ye. Ye better make yourself useful fast as ye can, if'n ye wanna survive, understand? Now com' on, lets see what ye can do in the kitchen!"

Resigned, Addie nodded. Sighing deeply, she leaned back in the chair as Hilde tied a muslin triangle kerchief round her hair to hold it back from her face. She took in the high ceiling and noticed that outside the high windows the sky looked gray and foreboding. It was then, while the woman was wheeling her backwards through the open door, that she focused on the porthole window above the dresser.

The blue glass twinkled and reminded her of something that she had seen before; a memory of twinkling glass as she looked through the window onto the sea. Someone was holding her hand then, and she remembered they laughed at the colored panes of the glass and how they made the seawater sparkle. For the life of her, she could not remember who was holding her hand that day.

Being wheeled out backwards from the room, she noticed for the first time, not the blue glass, not the facets in the window, but the bars on the outside the window; black, foreboding, and terrifying, all at the same time.

The Very Bad News

Phillip opened his eyes. He had slept well, and he felt rested. He felt the cool licky-lick of the dog's tongue and suddenly he remembered where he was. 'Clure was still asleep beside him. He sat up to see Wascilla Wymore filling a kettle with water from the pump at the kitchen sink. She hung it over the smouldering bed of ashes.

She smiled and gave a little wave. He noticed she was wearing the same dress she wore last night, and the same worn-out work boots. She was cooking a brew that smelled like his favorite hazelnut coffee. Her father, Wallace Wymore, was sipping from a carved wooden cup as he rested on a stool by the fire, suspenders casually dropped over his shoulders. His feet, covered with patched red socks, rested on a small wooden footstool. Phillip sat up and rubbed the back of his neck.

"Mornin," he muttered, yawning. Wassy poured a small amount of the fragrant brew and held out a wooden cup.

"Go'on, have some, it'll warm ye," she offered, whispering as she glanced at the still-sleeping Mc-Clure. Phillip slowly took a taste.

"Go'on boy, it won't hurt ya, wadda ya think it is?" she asked daintily, shaking her head in disbelief at his caution.

Her father watched in amusement. Wymore found Wassy's attempt at being a hostess entertaining. It was not often they had company, let alone young men with ties to Naji Najeem. Wymore still was not convinced that no harm had come to Naji, but he began his interrogation kindly.

"So," he began, first clearing his throat. "Kin ye tell me the story of how ye came to know Naji? Where is the ole' buzzard? Did'ja know he used to be Governor of Norwall? Kin ye tell me your story, starting at the beginning?"

Phillip was cautious. "Well," he replied with trepidation. "We met Naji one day when he was walking this tinydog. Me and Mom brought him a sandwich, and we got to talkin'. Naji gave me an old backpack, and that's where I found the key to his tailor shop. We tried to find stuff about Norwall, but it wasn't till later that Naji explained about Norwall and the Parallax. I'm guessing that it's some kinda' gateway from our world to yours? My mom accidentally fell through the port, so Naji helped us come here to look for her. We got reason to think she's hurt, and hurt bad." He looked down and scrunched his eyes shut.

"Still wakin' up ye' are, here, have some more tea." Wascilla gently offered.

"So," Wallace Wymore began, carefully choosing his words and sipping the warm, fragrant brown liquid. "Did Naji warn youse of the danger? Did he tell ye that the Council keeps us as slaves? We work now, every day, and canna' own anythin'. Did he tell youse that? Did he tell youse that most of us canna keep our own children? That the little ones are taken from us on their first birthday?" He started pacing and hugged Wascilla tight as she stood beside him. He kept his arm around her. "The only reason youse sees her standing here now is that she's the driver for the wheat transport. Them that were older than a decade were allowed to stay with their parents, but only if they had a 'portant talent, and by God, Wassy can drive! I taught her to drive, and she been useful to'em, delivering the wheat to Moniker's Mill for millin'." His eyes got teary as he continued. "If'n she weren't one of the best drivers around she'd been working in the garment factory that exploded and killed her mother, 'long with Hannah, Naji's wife, rest their souls."

Phillip interrupted. "Yeah, he asked me to get her picture from his room. He told us to use his shop as our base, said there's food and clothes there, and we should keep the lights off so no one can notice us while we look for our mom. Wadda'ya think of that?"

"Son, I think," Wymore took a deep breath, "I dunna know quite how to say this, but, Mother of God. The chance of finding her is *so* small, not meaning to upset ye or nothin'. If she was found by the Automatons, they likely vapored her on the spot or took her to Council. They've been known to be brutal when they tryin' to git information, if'n ye knows what I mean."

"Are you saying they would torture my mother?"

"Worse, I'm saying, and I'm saying this kindly, that they don't keep prisoners for long. Many of us suspected that there might'a been a port to another world, but we could ne'er prove it, nor could we find it. No one has ever *seen* anyone come through. Although I can say, many a Norwellian has disappeared without reason. We wrote it off to the Automaton Death Squad." Wymore scratched his head.

"Now, wouldn't be something if peoples *knew* about this port, this *Parallax*, and they knew for sure it would take'em to a safer place? Why, folks would be running to find it and get away from the gray-skies and the Automat Army that holds us, right?" Phillip nodded his head in accord.

"What's the 'gray-skies'?" he asked thoughtfully.

Wymore chose his words carefully so as not to scare the boys. "When the Council shut down the Republic and ousted Naji and the Cabinet, they took about half the people and set up settlement up north. They took the technology, the good that we had, and they left the bad. They left the Automatons to guard the people loyal to the Republic. These was the people who got left behind. And, a'fore they left, they took our children, and they killed maybe a third of us in public, bringing fear to us, and forcing us to live in the Habitrons and work in factories. They polluted the skies by pushing the factories and workers to produce and produce, until the town was depleted and left in ruins. The gray-skies with its bad air started to get thick and close in, and with it, the People of the Republic were made sick. Many died, and those that survived had their property taken, their children rounded up, and their food rationed."

McClure shook his head and summerized. "So what you had was an authoritarian takeover? Sounds like something we had in our land. It started slow, them picked up steam. People don't pay attention, right, until it hits them right between the eyes. So there's no fixing the gray-skies? Excuse me, sounds like this is a doomed city?"

Wallace explained. "Well, no one knows why the lungs of some of us can take it. Like me and Wassy. But some, like Naji, *can't* take it and their lungs turn stiff, and gets worser and worser 'til they die." Wymore dropped his head and covered his face with his hands.

Phillip continued. "So you are saying that Naji and Pebby came through the Parallax by accident? Or was he trying to get away and maybe survive?

You sayin' that folks here thought he had been executed by the Army, what'd you call it, those robots?"

"That's right," Wymore added, "the Automatons. The Death Squad." Phillip shuddered while Wallace continued, slowly pacing his words.

"That's what the skuttlebutt on the street was. People were sayin' that Naji and Pebby had been taken down. Gleena Glisson, proprietress of the Octagon Bakery, and mind you, close friend of Naji, was no sooner done speakin' to 'em in the park one day and *poof*, they was gone into a vapor quick as could be. Gleena had set great store by that tiny scruffy, but it won't do right now for youse to make yourself known to her. Gleena has contacts on the Council, so youse better lay low, at least for the time bein', whilse ye figure out where ye mother might be, ye got it? What I'm a sayin' is you kinna trust *no one* now, if there is any chance of seein' your mother alive, are youse clear?"

"Oh yeah, we're gonna be under cover, *totally* invisible." Phillip was anxious to end the conversation and begin the seach for his mother.

"So, how do we get to Najeem's Tailor shop?" Phillip asked, as Wascilla crept up beside him slowly, carrying a light tan bundle in her hands. She spoke softly as she offered him the clothing.

"Go'on, put these on. I gonna take you with me on my snail wagon carryin' the wheat when I head to Moniker's Mill. Youse can jump off at the Five Feathers Falconry and board there. I know Jeeson and Noah will take youse in. For a long while, they been lookin' to try and git Naji to lead us together against the Council. Lucky for youse it's harvest time for the wheat, so I be makin' me route-runs almost twice a day. But, I kin only take *one* of youse though, just one at'a time. Only one will fit in the box under me seat." Wassy shook her head up and down and tugged nervously on her braid. Then she turned toward McClure and pointed a finger at him,

"Ye kin NOT hide under the wheat, the Automats is good about checkin', and if they catch ye hidden in the wheat, they would likely turn us both over to the Council, or vapor us on the spot." She put her hands up to the sides of her face and leaned close to Phillip, whispering and funneling the words directly in his face. McClure, finally awake, quickly leaned in to not miss a word. Wassy stuck her tongue out at him and continued.

"They say ya skins melts right off ya body, slides down ya like slimy, while ya still awake." She picked her teeth with a piece of a broom she pulled from her pocket.

Phillip shuddered, thinking of how they might have already killed his mother. Wascilla continued, quite matter-of-factly.

"Then, when nuthin' but your bones is left, they string 'em up on the Terrible Wall to remind us all what happens if you disrespect the Council."

"Enough, enough already, can't you see he doesn't want to hear that?" McClure interjected harshly, scratching his scalp and ruffling up his hair. Frustrated, he rubbed his eyes with his fists and sighed. "*All* we want is to get to the tailor shop. We want to set up base, find our mother, and take her home. That's *it!*" Throwing his arms up in the air for emphasis, he continued, "We're not interested in the stupid robots, we're not interested in the side stories, we just want to get to Naji's shop! You got that? We aren't interested in anything else that goes on in your weird little town, you understand? We wanna get our mom and get outta here! Shouldn't be that tough to understand." He stood up and stretched, shaking his head and muttering under his breath. He was still stiff from the tumultuous ride through the Parallax. He rubbed his sore shoulder, remembering that Wassy had nearly torn it from his body.

Wymore stood and pulled himself up to his full height, then stooped slightly to look both McClure and Phillip directly in the face. He motioned with both hands for McClure to lower his voice and calm himself.

"Not ta' be scarin' youse, but I dunno what kind of place youse come from. No. Here," he looked off in the distance wistfully, "here they kill at random, whenever it suits their fancy. We used to have a peaceful, beautiful land, but the corruption started with the Council being formed. Fascists they were, and makin' their own army, and pushing their own rules, ignoring the will of the people." Wymore gave a deep sigh and continued.

"Eventually they programmed the Automatons to do their biddin'. We got no say over our food, our clothes, our lives, *anythin'*! Youse ever live like that? You both look to me like youse are well-fed, and well-cared for. I mean, look at my Wassy," he pulled his daughter close and hugged her.

"Wassy can only stay with me in the wheat fields 'cause she's the best delivery driver. If'n she weren't, why, the'd take her to the factories in a heartbeat."

"Well," Phillip interjected, "where we come from, lots of people work in factories. I mean," he stammered, "not really children, but lots of people work in factories, so I don't see how that's so different." Looking at Phillip with sympathy for his naivete, Wymore continued. "Well, the difference is that there is no choice, and no wages. The difference is, here, we wear clothes handed to us. It's the same thing day after day. We eat, sleep, and die in the Habitrons. Lots of us never again see our families. We dunna' have no say in anything, youse get that? If we canna work, we are no better 'an a piece of rottin' garbage, got it?"

Phillip nodded wide-eyed, starting to understand.

"Oh, I'm seeing now. I'm seeing what you're sayin'. And yeah, we had that for a while in my land too. I'm seein' it for what it is. People aren't really free, right? No more the *will of the people*, it's the will of the privileged?" Inhaling deeply, then letting all the breath out, feeling totally deflated, Phillip whispered. "The people are slaves, right? The few at the top makes all the rules, right?"

Wymore dropped his head sadly and nodded in agreement. Phillip glanced at McClure, whose mouth had dropped open. After a few seconds, which seemed like an eternity, he whispered to Phillip. "Mother-of-God, what have we got ourselves into?"

The Unexpected Confession

Claire couldn't believe that her mother had agreed to bird-sit this nasty twenty-five-year-old Amazon parrot. Her mother's friend Nesta had unceremoniously dropped off the massive, lime-green bird with the caveat that the bird was generally quiet, but had a wicked bite. Claire, now left alone in the Weathermore house with its assortment of particular, peculiar, persnickety pets, felt overwhelmed and not much impressed by this large avian with the pinning eyes.

She had sole responsibility for feeding her mother's African Gray parrot Freddy, cleaning the cat litter, and walking the husky Moushka, who was none too easy on the leash. More than once, he pulled her so hard she slipped out of her flip-flops and skinned her knee. The icing on the cake was the angry glare of the newest Weathermore resident, the viscious Gasparilla, a double yellow-headed Amazon. When one of the cage perches came loose, Claire had to take the bird out of its cage. That involved carefully throwing a towel over the bird's head, and wrapping her up so that she could handle her without getting bit. Thick leather gloves protected her hands. When she finally got her to a large wooden perch, she used a spritzer to wash the bird and then push the cage outside to clean it with the garden hose. *Too much work*, she opined to herself as she wiped the sweat from her face.

It wasn't the angry looks of the mean old Amazon that was on Claire's mind this morning as she piloted her mother's car into the office parking lot. Her hands were sweating, and she was shaking. She felt like the time she arrived at the Science Fair and forgot her presentation poster. Her breaths were getting shorter and shorter, and she was starting to hyperventilate, occasionally wheezing as well. Her mother was not here to calm her, and in fact, she realized that it was the absence of her mother that was causing all the anxiety. How could she face opening and sorting the office mail? When her mother had tried to teach her how to write a check, Claire had wrinkled her nose, snickered and joked, *It's all done online now!* That attitude left her mother frustrated and made Claire totally unprepared for taking over the business.

Pulling into the parking space in front of the office, she was anxious to be distracted from the task at hand. Through the window of the dry cleaning shop she could see Naji dusting the counter. She knew she needed to check on him; when she had dropped him off Sunday, he had been more short of breath than ever. *Mom would want me to check on him,* she told herself, prolonging the inevitable meeting with Jaceena and the stack of office mail.

"Naji!" she called, as she opened the shop door and heard the familiar bell-alert tinkling. She was shocked at the change in him. His face looked ashen; his eyes were surrounded with dark circles and he looked considerably thinner.

"Miss Claire, so good to see you! I have not been able to sleep. I worried all night as to the condition of your fine mother and I hope and pray that your brother is now safe in Norwall. I feel so dishoNorrable that I could be the cause of your mother's disappearance!"

He started to sob. "Such a fine woman, and I took her away from her children and perhaps cost her her life!"

He leaned on the counter and sobbed bitterly as he pulled up a stool and put his head in his hands. Claire walked around the counter and wrapped her arms around the old tailor, as he heaved and tried to breathe with great effort.

"Naji, I can't blame you, there was no way you could know that Mom would go through the Parallax, right?" Claire held him as he continued to sob, tears wetting his face. "Right? You didn't know she would be taken, right?"

Claire paused, then asked the question once again. "Tell me please! *PLEASE* tell me you didn't know she would fall through a hole in the universe. Oh, please say it's not so!" She started to shake and she felt her breathing get tight at his lack of response. *"Naji! For the last time, please tell me you didn't deliberately send Mom there! Please?"* Claire felt tears starting in her eyes and she started to sob.

"You are such fine people, and I can't hide the truth. From the first time I saw your brother, I knew he was special. I knew he had the heart of a leader, and just needed time to grow into the wisdom he would need to lead my people to freedom. I saw in him a younger version of myself. I saw in him a goodness and an integrity that I knew the people would follow."

Claire was reaching her breaking point. "So, you had this idea that Phills needed to go and save your city? He needed to be the leader you couldn't be? You had to figure out a way to get him to go? Really? Is that what this all was?"

Naji didn't answer, but continued to weep, his head down on the counter as Claire continued.

"So, you sent Mom, like a sacrifice, knowing that Phills would go after her? It just can't be so!" Claire looked at him wide-eyed as tears welled in her eyes. "You *deliberately* sent her, knowing he would go try to find her? Filthy, dirty thing to do!" She smacked her hand down flatly on the counter, and leaned down to put her face directly in front of his. She shook her fist for emphasis.

"Tell me how you knew that the fireplace was a Parallax? How?"

Naji wiped his eyes on his shirtsleeve. He answered in broken sobs. "Because I've been there before. I've been there, in years past, but only for short times. And one of those times, I saw your brother. I watched from the cover of the trees, and one time I saw him with your mother. I saw them laughing and reading a book together. They were so happy, and I said to myself, these are people with hearts full of love and goodness. These are people with something special. This boy will grow up to be a leader. I could see that in him , even then. I could see a kind spirit that would grow into a man that people would follow."

Naji started to cough in between his sobs.

"A leader, yeah, I can see that, but NOT in another world you fool, you old fool! You mean you *spied* on him? *You spied on us?*" What kind of creepy thing is that to do?" Claire grabbed her hair on each side of her head and pulled it hard. "Oh! Oh my, OH MY! You sacrificed my family for what?"

"For Norwall, for the home that I love, for the thousands of people that slave in the factories and breathe the dirty air. For the great birds that are dropping from the sky, for the hate that has consumed the land, and for my Hannah, who died for nothing! Nothing, I tell you! Just nothing." He wiped his eyes, but the tears continued to flow. Claire couldn't control herself any longer.

"You lied to us, you *acted* like you were our friend ... BUT YOU LIED!" She shook her fist at the weeping old man and stomped out.

Slamming the door behind her, Claire leaned against the wall and let her tears flow at the unfairness of it all. Pulling up her shirt to wipe her tears and dry her face, Claire forced herself to do what she knew her mother would tell her. *Slow deep breaths. Slow breathing honey, come on, slow the train down, that's my girl, you're coming to the crossing, now slow the train down. Choooo chooo! Chooo chooo! Slow it down.* It was as if by looking at the office door with her mother's name, she could feel her mother's arms wrapped tight around her as she slowed her breathing. Gradually the wheezing stopped. After a few minutes, she inhaled deeply and dried her eyes with her shirt.

"Ok, Mom, I got this, I GOT THIS!"

Straightening her clothes, she headed into the office to find Jaceena vacuuming the waiting room carpet.

"Hello little Missy! What brings you here, don't tell me your mother sent you on ahead to work here today?" Jaceena laughed. Everybody laughed when Claire tried to help at the office. Usually she was so distracted by her phone that nothing was accomplished.

"No Jaceena," Claire replied, as she quickly recovered her composure. "Actually, yes, Jaceena.

Two things. First, and I know this will be a shock, but Mom had to go help Uncle Bradley with his office in Colorado. One of his partners got sick, and he needed Mom's help, so she took Phills and left yesterday." Jaceena dropped into the waiting room chair. Her eyebrows were raised, and her mouth dropped open.

"Left? She never done that on her whole life! Why didn't she call me? What I'm to do Missy? We got patients even today! She don't start till noon. What I'm to do?"

"Well, that's why she sent me." Pulling her self up to her full height and trying to sound reassuring, Claire continued.

"Look, *you* call the patients and reschedule them for tomorrow or Wednesday. *I'll* call the staffing company and get someone here pronto. I'll use Mom's office and open any mail, and take care of the business side, ok? You just worry about the schedule. Ok?" Jaceena ran her hands through her hair. She didn't look happy.

"I worried now 'bout your mother. She'd never done that, not to Jaceena, she never done anything like that, noooo. She never in all her life done anything like that! No Ma'am." Jaceena kept shaking her head back and forth as she made her way into the office proper. Claire made her way to her mother's desk, where the mail was stacked neatly in the in-basket.

Claire sighed. *Ok Phills, this misery I'm going through is for you and Mom. I gotta keep us afloat, it's the least I can do, right?* Closing her eyes tightly, she opened the gigantic black ledger book. There, in her mother's neat penmanship, was the total bank balance.

Five thousand, two hundred and forty. Thanks Mom, that's a start! Exhaling and leaning back in the chair, she opened the mail and sorted it. Shaking, Claire picked up her phone. Instead of texting friends, she researched a company that could send a temp doctor to see this week's patients. There was no time to waste.

The Unbearable Ride

Phillip couldn't breathe. He had been stuffed unceremoniously into the dirty wooden bench on which Wassy sat to drive the steam truck. Each breath was a struggle. His shoulder hurt and he was lying on his side with his knees drawn up; he was folded in half. The oversized, wheat-colored clothes were smelly and scratchy. His black clothing was tied into a bundle resting under his head.

He had left McClure behind with a promise that he would be brought to Five Feathers Falconry the following day. All Phillip and McClure could do was to trust that Wymore and Wassy were telling the truth. They were overwhelmed with the fear that once they separated, they would not find each other again.

Phillip wriggled himself into a tighter ball so he could peek out. All he could see was the back of Wassy's boots. He could not hear much; the *whoosh* of the steam engine blocked everything. He could hear the sounds of the steam as it pushed the sprocket-gears to drive the massive metal wheels. The cab of the truck resembled a giant snail with the steam engine attached to the rear. The flatbed wagon pulled behind held freshly harvested wheat headed to Moniker's Mill for processing.

He could see Pebby under a small blanket by Wassy's feet. The tinydog trembled with anxiety. The toots and puffs of the steam machine and the rough ride on the gravel road were making her nervous. She had run this route a million times before, hooked to her delivery wagon. But now, running the road independently was out of the question. Pebby had been reported missing. No one was sure what her status was with the Council, so she needed to keep a low profile for the time being. Wymore promised to speak directly with Gleena Glisson and find out the skuttlebut on the streets.

Earlier that day, the boys poured over a quick sketch of Norwall that Wymore drew in the fireplace ashes. They all agreed that the safest journey to the tailor shop would be in stages corresponding to the concentric Circles of the Realm. The Five Feathers Falconry, Wymore's wheat fields, and Moniker's Mill were all located on the Outer Circle. This Circle was typically the least traveled, allowing more mobility without much risk of intrusion of the Automatons and the Council. It was Wassy's home territory, and she was free to travel The Outer Circle of the realm unfettered. They all agreed it was the perfect place to start both the search for Abby Weathermore, and the movement toward Naji Najeem's Tailor Shop.

The plan was for Phillip, hidden in the wagon seat bench, to jump off near the Falconry. There, he would take refuge with Jeeson and Norra Jevity until he could reunite with McClure, who would arrive in Wassy's next-day delivery. After that, they were to travel to Moniker's Mill, where they could negotiate a trip to The Middle Circle. Wymore assured them that the Jevity family would protect them until safe passage could be arranged. Wallace Wymore was certain of their loyalty to Naji Najeem, as Jeeson Jevity had been a Cabinet Loyalist when Naji was Governor. His wife Norra, was a noted scientist, with expertise in artificial intelligence and robotics.

Bumping along for several hours was all Phillip could stand. Just as he was unable to take another second of the suffocating box, the wagon lurched to a halt and Wassy flung open the hinged top of the bench.

"Hurry, boy! Come quickly, *Come on!*" She yanked his shirt and pulled him, showing no mercy as he tried to stand and orient himself. Wassy wrapped the tinydog in her dirty blanket and jumped down from the wagon platform. She ran, head down, arms encircled around the blanketed tinydog, her face set in grim determination.

Phillip followed, stumbling on his oversized pants which dragged the dusty ground. He pulled at them with both hands, trying to hold them up. He tripped and fell on the dirt path which serpentined around the back of the enormous structure.

"GIT UP NOW!" Wassy commanded, shaking her head. Massive, horizontal gears of different metals were spinning on top the structure. Phillip thought he saw two giant lacy metal wings over the front door. Wassy was pounding on the half-moon wooden back door with her flat, opened hand.

"Jeeson, Jeeson!" she was croaking in a whisper, "Open up! Open up, it's Wassy! Hurry!" She continued to pound as Phillip caught up to her. She turned around and made a sour face at him. "Don't think ya be keepin' this dog. She gonna be mine! I had me eyes on her for some time now, and don't think ya can jus' steal her. See? She wants to be with me! So, ya can keep her till 'morrow, but when I be bringin' yer friend, I gonna take her for me own, got it?" She jerked out her chin at him.

Before Phillip had even a moment to acknowledge her words, the half-moon door was opened by a pale, slender, black-haired man.

"Wassy! What the devil, what's this?" Jeeson Jevity stepped back.

"I gotta go 'afore the Automat sees the wagon, it's headed down the other way, but he'll turn any moment. This boy is from Naji, and I be bringin' his friend on the morrow, *keep'em safe! I gotta go now!*"

She gently set the tiny scruffy dog down inside the door, threw the blanket over her shoulder and ran around the side of the house, boots kicking up dirt. Phillip heard the puffs of the steam engine as Wassy engaged the gears and drove away, clattering loudly down the crater-filled road.

Jeeson ushered Phillip quickly inside the falconry and bolted the door. A slender, dark-haired woman with pixie-cut hair and a heart-shaped face came hurrying in. She came closer and peered directly into his face.

He stammered, "I come from Naji Najeem, who ... *I guess*, you guys know. You know, fat little guy, gray hair, all poofed out, coughs, a lot?" He gestured wildly with his arms.

They weren't listening. They ran to the front window and watched Wassy safely pull away as three nine-foot tall Automatons hurried down the dirt road behind her with weapons pointed. Try as they might, the Automatons failed to catch her. Marching in cadence, they stopped. Abandoning the chase, they swiveled and paraded in synchrony back down the dusty road. They took up residence in the guard booth by the rusty old gate.

Jeeson let out a huge sigh of relief and spoke first. "Whooowe! She made it! Thank Heavens! I think she acted like she was relieving herself in the bushes, clever girl! Well, that's our little Wassy. That's all the excitement I can stand for one day! Norra, let's welcome our guest. Wassy said you ... you ... *you came from Naji?*"

Norra slowly approached Phillip, as if stunned. Slowly, deliberately she chose her words. "Naji? You were sent by Naji? Jeeson, this means he's ALIVE! *Naji's alive!*"

She clasped her hands in front of her, prayerfully looking up to the sky. Then, she grabbed Phillip by the shoulders with both hands.

"You bring us much hope and joy today, do you know that? Much hope!" Tears were running down her cheeks, and Phillip was taken aback. For a moment he thought she might hug him. Then, in the next second, she did. She squeezed hard and he could feel her sobs shaking her skinny frame.

"Oh Naji, you sent help! If you couldn't do it yourself, you sent help!" Norra whispered.

"Come Norra," said Jeeson, separating her iron grasp from Phillip's shoulders and lowering her onto a small stool.

"Come, let us welcome him properly. Look, Pebby is here too! She's safe!"

Bending down, Jeeson scooped up the scruffy tinydog and nuzzled her neck. "We thought you were vaporized! I knew if there was any way Naji could protect you, he would do it with his very life! And, *HERE YOU ARE!*" Setting her down carefully, he provided her a bowl of water from the large siphon system in the center of the room.

Norra guided Phillip from the foyer through an elliptical archway. He gave an audible gasp as he took in the room with its cathedral ceiling. In amazement, he gazed upwards as he watched three gigantic horizontal gears of different colors spin in opposite directions on top of one another. He thought they looked like giant pancakes with sharp, pointy gear edges, stacked and spinning in the gray sky of the dome. The copper was high contrast to the silver, which was separated by a gear resembling tin.

Phillip could not believe what he was seeing. Sixteen ornate cages formed a semicircle around a black marble laboratory counter with a fifteen-foot tall water purifier system. The convoluted tubes bubbled water through a series of filters and hoses, all run by a small steam engine chugging along effortlessly under the laboratory counter.

"Whoa, oh I wish Mom could see this, would 'ja look at that!" He circled around the room, taking in the majestic, multicolored birds who eyed him skeptically.

"These are almost *all* that is left," Jeeson instructed sadly as he followed Phillip around the room.

"Their species are dying. We're here to save them, and the Council has mandated we use our technology to construct a mechanical bird; one that can still exist in the decaying environment. But how does one imitate the exquisite beauty of these creatures? How does one create what is only divinely made?"

Phillip nodded in agreement and roamed freely around the room. He stared in awe at sixteen cages housing the most amazing creatures he had ever seen. The birds were so large and so brightly colored he could not believe his eyes.

The profound beauty of the birds took his breath away. Not only were the colors overwhelming, but there was a quiet grace and dignity about the birds; a sense of calm and safety. Phillip sensed that the birds knew their fate was safest in the hands of Jeeson and Norra. He began to feel that way as well, and some of his fear subsided. These creatures, with their calm and regal bearing, could sense the kind and gentle heart of this new stranger, and they instinctively knew that Phillip was no threat.

There were deep coral birds with jet-black eyes and beaks, bright yellow birds with green and red tipped wings, and pure white birds with huge plumes on the top of their heads. There were deep aqua birds, and two birds who were the most majestic deep-indigo color he had ever seen. There were two of every kind, paired side by side in separate cages. Reaching into one cage with his gloved arm, Jeeson brought out the most beautiful snow-white bird Phillip had ever seen.

"Good boy, good boy! Phillip, meet Romeo. Romeo, meet Phillip!"

Phillip was in absolute awe. "I've never seen anything like this. I mean, we've got Freddy, Mom's parrot, and her friend Nesta dropped off the meanest Amazon you've ever seen, but *nothing* like this, *nothing*." He shook his head. The gigantic bird turned his back to Phillip.

Romeo was three feet tall, with long, pointed gray tail feathers, a majestic gray plume, and a massive black beak. Pale aquamarine circles surrounded both his enormous black eyes, and he lowered his beak submissively to allow Jeeson to pet him. The falconer placed him on a tree branch perch in the center of the room. Stretching, and flapping his wings once or twice to his six-foot wingspan, the bird settled as Jeeson lovingly rubbed his head feathers. "Go on Phillip, he wants you to pet his back. It's a sign of submission and trust. He is showing he trusts you. It is an honor, indeed. *You must not disappoint!*"

"Ok, ok," Phillip stammered. In slow motion, he pet the satin-soft pure white feathers. Romeo replied by lowering his head even further.

"Oh look!" Jeeson exclaimed, "he is acknowledging you as an honored guest! Amazing, I have never seen him respond to someone so quickly! Look Norra, look!"

As Phillip gently withdrew his hand, a gigantic stainless steel door burst open, and another tall, pale, dark-haired figure emerged.

"Noah, come! Look! He comes from Naji!" Jeeson offered.

"Well, well, well, comes from Naji?" Noah inquired haughtily, raising his nose in the air as he dried his hands on his white lab apron.

"And *what*, may I ask, brings you here? What business do you have with us? Even on behalf of Naji Najeem? How do we know he sent you? Tell me, and tell the truth if you know what's good for you!" Phillip could see his hands were clenched at his side.

"No, really, I come to look for a lost woman. Tall, medium build, chestnut-colored hair, and she might be hurt. We think she came here by accident. You know anything about a hurt woman wandering around?"

Clucking his finger ascerbically, Noah motioned Phillip to the front window. Phillip noticed several rings he wore, each a different colored metal gear. *"Come on man,* look at what sits in front of our house. You think a hurt woman wandering the streets would have a chance? No way, *no way in hell!"*

Phillip made his way to the front window. To his disbelief, a nine foot metal man was patrolling the guardhouse, cruising the length of the gate. Gears on his head and back were spinning wildly and smoke puffed out the tube on its back.

"Notice anything sinister about those blasters on its arms?" Noah asked mockingly. "You're lucky you got to jump from Wassy's wagon and make it unnoticed before he steamed your flesh from your body. He could eat you alive if he wanted too, or report back to the Council and you would be steamed in the public square, then hung on the Terrible Wall an left to rot. Just think, you were saved by ole' Wassy pretending she had to pee-pee herself!" He threw his head back and laughed disparagingly.

The Fine Laboratory

"Noah," Norra pleaded, "can you be just a *little* bit kind to our guest? Don't take your frustration out on him. I think Naji sent him here for a reason, don't you? He seems to have good intentions, so let's at *least* be kind Noah, he doesn't know everything going on here, OK?"

"Ok. Sure Mom, I'm sorry," Noah extended his hand to Phillip amicably.

"Come on, let's talk," Noah added as he pulled up a lab stool to the counter and motioned for Phillip to do the same.

"Now, this missing woman, first, who is she? How did she go missing?" Noah picked apart a crust of roll that remained on a small dish and bit off the end, chewing loudly, looking at Phillip directly with his ink-black eyes.

"She's my mother," Phillip said solemnly. "She came here by accident and we have reason to think she's hurt. Naji sent us here to try and bring her home and he told us to take Pebby to show us the way.

"Well," opined Noah slyly, "whatever the reason, I'm glad that you were able to bring our dog home as well, right Pebby?" Winking all the while at his mother as she shook her head in amazing annoyance.

Phillip pulled himself up to his full height and looked the older teenager straight in the eye. With courage springing out of fatigue and exasperation, he spoke clearly and distinctly with all his heart.

"I was with Naji just yesterday. I know he is sick, and I know that he cannot come back here and survive in this nasty air. And, I know that the chance of finding my mother alive is growing smaller every day. But, I have hope. I have my best friend 'Clure here with me, and I have an *amazing* sister taking care of everything at home. And I know, as sure as

I am sitting here, that this is *NOT your dog*, and she will *NEVER be your dog*. Now, you and I have a lot of talking to do so let's see how we can help each other, ok?

Smartly, with reduced arrogance and an attractive asymmetrical smile, Noah gave a curt nod of his head. Smiling, Norra watched them, tall handsome teens dressed all in black, carrying their food through the stainless door into the laboratory. Pebby trotted not far behind.

Clearing space on the counter, Phillip found himself surrounded by an unbelievable laboratory that Norra and Noah had constructed from purloined, primitive equipment. There were flasks, beakers, and glass tubings intertwined with pots of chemicals and small boxes of gears and metal pins. There were dozens of mechanical-bird prototypes in various stages of completion. Some were hung with wire from the high ceiling, giving the room the appearance of an aviary, with the mechanical birds in various stages of flight. Although it looked to be quite the high-tec lab, the artistic beauty of the projects stunned Phillip. The blackboard scrawlings reflected sophisticated intuitiveness beyond even what Claire produced in her lab. Phillip was highly intrigued. These were obviously skilled scientists.

No telling how the information would help him in this new environment.

"So, why such a push for this mechanical bird?" Phillip asked. "And, why Norra? Why would they expect so much of her?" Noah learned back in his chair, closed his eyes, and debated whether he could trust this stranger. He spoke with a sarcastic edge. "While she may nag me everyday to pick my clothes off the floor, she was the one scientist that could figure out the aerodynamics of flight. She was the one, years ago, that figured out the trick of getting those heavy airships off of the ground. Yep, all done with mathematical formulas devised by my mother. She is one of the most decorated scientists of her generation, but those medals and awards mean nothing now." Noah lowered his head sadly.

"Even with all the prosperity, the inventions, the discoveries, all indicators of a real *Age of Enlightenment*, still the government changed." Noah sighed deeply and continued. "First, rule by the people faltered. Our democratic government was dying, but people weren't paying attention. Kindness and empathy became ideals of the past. There was a threat of invasion from the people of the Westward Islands who are skilled mariners and boast a fleet far superior to ours. While there grew a moral vacuum, there rose up a group and their leader purported to know what was best for everyone. *Whoosh*, in marches the Council, offering to be the solution." Noah crossed his arms protectively as he continued. Phillip could feel his anguish, and he listened intently, hanging on every word.

"Propaganda became rampant and Norwall rotted from within. Best for everyone? You see the sky. You see what breathing that foul air did to Naji. If my father hadn't risked his life, hadn't risked all our lives by bringing our family out into the open, those birds in there would now be extinct!" Noah pointed toward the atrium, where they could hear gentle squeaks and squeals and rustling of feathers from the treasured flock.

Noah continued. "The takover by the Council began with propaganda that Norwall could only be victorious by takedown of intellectuals and a push for a hierarchy; ruling class versus townspeople. Decency didn't matter; life became cheap. The Council insisted that they were the voice of the people, and soon, no other voice could be heard."

Noah strummed his fingers on the black laboratory counter, then, looking for all the world as if he would could speak no more, he jumped up, shook his head, and stood in front of the massive chalkboard. He grabbed two erasers and started clapping them together like a child, releasing a cloud of chalkdust. "About that time, my mother met my father, who was a curator at the Museum of National Antiquities. They had a substantial aviary. Fearing the suppression of the universities and the takedown of intellectuals, they went into hiding. Shortly after that, I was born and they had even *more* reason to hide."

Phillip was aghast. "You mean they were killing off the scientists?"

"Yeah, they were calling them traitors, and the people who had invented the technology were suddenly and *accidentally* stepping out fifth floor windows of the labs. They were being found in the streets, run over by the steam engines. My mother and father wanted the government to forget they even existed.

"Doesn't seem like that happened?"

"Nope. Not at all," Noah's shoulders sunk. "They came and searched for her. She couldn't hide from the Council, especially since she was married to my father. His knowledge base of avian health, coupled with her engineering skills, was the perfect combo to build the mechanical bird that they were hoping to use against the invaders as well as the population." He erased the board, saving the few equations at the top.

"So now, where are you?" Phillip asked as he stood up from the lab stool and stretched. "Are you close? What's your timeline?" Noah tossed a piece of chalk up in the air and caught it expertly.

"Well, our timeline is as soon as possible. The islanders have backed off for the present. But, it isn't just a matter of making something fly, my mother was able to do that with the airships that patrol us. It's trying to make a miniature steam engine so small that it doesn't interfere with the flight patterns of the birds. We are afraid that when we complete the project, the Council will be finished with us, *and* those birds. My father would give his life to save Romeo and give him one chance to live free again."

Phillip went silent, thinking carefully before he replied. "So, if you don't produce the mechanical bird, you are doomed? But if you *do* produce the bird, they have no further use for you? Is that it? That sounds like no win, no way out?"

Noah picked up the wing he had worked on through the night a few days ago. "Yep, I guess aren't we're both trying to figure out how to save our mothers from an unimaginable fate?" Noah gulped hard and rubbed his eyes. Then he pointedly directed questions to Phillip.

"What about *you*? Why are you *really* here? Who are you really? You are so young, I can't imagine that Naji would expect much from you, would he really? Tell me, Phillip, what drives you? Are you searching for your missing mother, *or is it a wee bit more?*"

Phillip straightened his shoulders. He was shocked. "Me? Whooaaaaa. Really now, *me*? I'm here to find my mom and take her home. That's it, nothing more, nothing less."

Noah replied thoughtfully. "Well, that's a simple answer, but there's got to be more to it. Especially since we know you were sent by Naji Najeem. He wouldn't have allowed that unless he saw that you had the knowledge base to help us. He would never have abandoned us here, and I know what was in his mind; if he could no longer lead us, if he couldn't save us, then you would become the answer we've been looking for."

Tossing the eraser in the air, Noah added, "Unless all you can do is think about yourself."

"Myself?" retorted Phillip, feeling his emotions boil. "I got a broken-down mother and a scared sister at home, never mind McClure whose life is on the line too!" Phillip started to pace, and worked his way to the chalkboard, where he drew a triangle, with circles in each corner. Taking deep breaths, he calmed himself and then continued.

"See, it's been me, Mom, and Claire, for a long time. We have each other's back. When one needs help, the others jump in headfirst, no questions asked."

Noah interrupted him.

"Phillip, look. I know your family is close. But now, instead of just taking care of each other, you have a chance to change our world. You have the chance to save countless lives, stop an infinite number of deaths, and stop the destruction of our society. You have the chance to bring all of us back to living in freedom. Together, as free people, we can stop any invasion and hold our territory. We're all on the line here. Just think how you will feel when you find your mother, and you go home safely, and tell Naji that more people are dying and his beautiful city is no more. Think of that while you are lying in your comfortable bed, Phillip."

Noah sighed deeply before he continued. He proceeded to quickly sketch what appeared to be a large gear. He added several rings, and it took a minute for Phillip to see that it was a crude drawing of a map, a crude schematic of The Republic of Norwall.

"Phillip, you can be more than you thought possible. Naji had faith in you, and so, the people will have faith in you too. They will follow what you say. You bring knowledge and experience that can help get our city back. Surely you wouldn't go back and tell Naji you did nothing?"

Moving to stand directly in front of Phillip, Noah looked him square in the eyes.

"It's no longer about finding your mother. It's no longer about getting you and your friend home, and it's no longer about keeping this tinydog. It's bigger than any of that. It's about finding these people that need you. They need you to step up and bring them together. This is your calling Phillip, and Naji sent you for a reason. He saw something in you that you can't deny."

Phillip remembered the day Naji gave him the backpack. *"Be a leader,"* he had said. *Maybe this is what he expected all along. Maybe he picked me for a reason.* Phillip was remembering the events that led to this point, and all the times that Naji was prepping him to be more than he could ever imagine.

Suddenly, the door to the lab flung open and a breathless Norra, eyes wide, whispered frantically, "The Council! They are here for inspection! Hide him quick, Noah! Quick! Quick Phillip, hide Pebby too!"

The Sweetberry Smile

The work was hard on the production line of the bakery. Her leg hurt terribly, even though they allowed her to keep it elevated on a wooden platform extending out from the seat of the wheelchair. She was not allowed to stand up, except briefly, to dress and to transfer. She was tired and exhausted from the long hours sitting at the counter. Oh, it was an easy enough job, checking the cinnamon rolls coming off the line, making sure that the icing was perfectly swizzled on the top. If any of the hot rolls did not pass inspection, she had to lift them off with her giant wooden paddle and put them on another conveyor where they were boxed for delivery to the middle level managers. If they were of a lesser quality, they were reserved for residents of the habitrons.

She had a tray of dried berries in front of her, and when a red light was blinking, she had to decorate the top of each roll with three dried sweetberries, just three, no more, and no less. This was boring, and she was expected to keep up with the pace.

"One, two three, one two three, one two three," she voiced in cadence, as she dropped the sweetberries on top of the hot rolls.

"Keep up the pace Addie. *NO talking on the line!*" The burly supervisor pacing behind her showed no mercy, and she noticed for the first time that he carried a wooden baton and kept smacking it against his thigh. The pain in her leg still bothered her. It was difficult to lie flat in bed; it felt better to be propped up. Every other day, the bandages were changed, and she could see pins coming out of each side of her leg just below the knee. The pins were fixed to metal gears. Every time they changed the bandage she would ask when the gears were coming off, but no one would answer.

Twice during her workday, another worker wheeled her to a large meeting room set with long wooden tables. Most had benches, but one table in the front was reserved for those unable to negotiate benches. Her gear-chair was wheeled to the table where a small plate of bakery bread, one small cooked egg, and slices of some sort of fruit was set in front of her. There was a shaker of dark-brown spice on the table, which she gingerly sprinkled on the slices of fruit. There were no utensils, so she ate with her hands. She watched lines of workers, all garbed in the same bleached-white muslim uniforms, stand in line to pick up a similar metal plate. Everyone got the same, no matter their age, nor their size. They too, ate the food with their hands.

Curiously, there was no laughter or friendly banter. The workers stood with their backs perfectly straight, in line, not making a sound. Another worker, like the one from the line, carried a smaller wooden baton attached to a rawhide cord on his belt. *Strange. Lines of people, but no one speaks.* It was difficult to tell the women from the men, as everyone was costumed the same, with the exception of the sleeves; straight on the men, puffed on the women, all ending above the elbows.

The women's hair, as well as the men's was concealed. The women had white kerchiefs tied at the base of their necks, but the men wore white caps, tight to the skull, with a stiff semilunar brim in the front. No one mingled, and all took their places at the tables, staying in perfect line order. The only thing different was the speed at which they ate, some gulping down food, others picking at every morsel.

They finished eating at the same time, and as if by signal, the man in the front of the room held his baton high in the air and all rose, as if they had practiced staying in synchrony for years. They stood regally, pushing back the benches, picking up the metal plates, and leaving in the exact line in which they had entered. They dropped their tin plates into receptacles at the front of the room.

As they walked past the door, they stopped at a round, metal tub, which had water flowing freely from a stainless pipe at the top. As each group of eight people gathered around, they cupped their hands and drank the water, serving the double purpose of drinking and cleansing their hands at the same time. As each group finished, another took their place to perform the same ritual. She watched them walk away in silence, all with the same frozen countenance. The man with the baton kept his arms folded across his chest as he monitored the behavior. No one even flinched.

After the room was evacuated, another worker, but not the same worker who had wheeled her in, came to collect her. He did not say a word to her, but wheeled her to the round fountain, where she braced herself, filling her cupped hands with water.

Strange, it has such a sweet taste, she thought, as she drank greedily. She washed her hands in the water and dried them on her apron, as she had seen the other workers do. Finished, she was pushed back to her station, where she spent the afternoon inspecting the food production on the line. She added sweetberries when the red light flashed. The hours seemed endless, and she lost all track of time.

Whoooshmph! Whoooshmph! The stainless steel chute reflected her face as it dropped one perfect cinnamon roll every ten seconds. Addie felt sweaty and filthy. She had no idea how long she had been working, since clocks were forbidden at the Octagon Bakery. She looked deep into her reflection in the shiny tube, touching an ugly scar above her right eyebrow. She knew her name was Addie, and she knew she had been in an accident. Every movement of her leg reminded her with scorching, shooting pain.

What did she look like before the accident? She didn't know. All she knew was that her job, day in and day out, was to decorate perfectly round cinnamon rolls with a perfect layer of white icing. When she had exactly ten rolls iced, she had to dot the icing with exactly three sweetberries. No more, no less, in a perfect triangle pattern.

Funny thing, memory. She could remember the bean soup she had on her afternoon break, but she could not remember much more than that. She could remember that yesterday, and the day before yesterday, and the day before that, she was escorted to her position on the line by a man who looked like a machine, or maybe it was a machine made to look like a man? It didn't really matter.

At night, they escorted her and the other workers back to the Habitron where she had a thin, flat mattress and a single bureau drawer for belongings she didn't have. Every day was the same. Every roll was the same. People expected uniformity from the Octagon Bakery. Three sweetberries it was. No more, no less. Day in and day out, the beautiful cinnamon rolls dotted with three perfect berries were boxed and bagged by the next worker on the line. Day in, day out. *Icing, sweetberries, box and bag. Icing, sweetberries, box and bag.*

On this day, perhaps because she was tired, or perhaps because some receptor in her brain fired and suddenly released serotonin at exactly the right moment, a synapse connected two neurons. These neurons connected quite serendipitously to the next neurons, and she stared at her handful of sweetberries. She then looked at the white, smooth icing. She didn't know what made her do it, but she placed one, then another berry on the icing as if the icing was a face and the berries were eyes. Suddenly, without warning, neurons ignited and reflexively fired. She placed a row of sweetberries in an upside-down smile. It was a frown. A frown of red sweetberries on a silly, icing-face roll. She felt woozy, as if she was under the influence of a drug. She remembered the sweet taste of the fountain water. *Could there have been something in it? I don't feel right.*

Her eyes opened widely, then closed tightly as she suddenly imagined him, a teenage boy, as a memory tape unexpectedly played in her cortex, The boy was perched on a stool in a kitchen somewhere far away. There were shiny silver bowls filled with sugar and flour on the counter, and a butcher-block island holding a mixer. And the oven? It was a shiny, stainless steel oven, not in any factory, but in a home. Could it have been her home? The boy sitting on the stool was frowning, eyebrows knitted tightly together. His arms were crossed defensively in front of him.

"That's not funny, Mom, not funny at all!" she heard him say, his voice somewhere off in her distant past. Without any warning, without any intention, the word tumbled out of her in a raspy whisper. She opened her eyes wide.

"Oh, com' on! Seventy-two on the math test? Com' on, you can do better than that!" As soon as she spoke the words, she plastered both hands over her mouth, realizing that she had no control over the words spilling out. But the boy was fading away. At the last second, before he was no more, she heard him painfully scream out words that made her heart hurt as though she had been kicked in the chest.

"NO mom, no! Please, NOOOOOO!" Tears ran down her face as she saw the shape of him fade, but for the life of her, she could not make out the details of his face. She could not hang on to him. It seemed for a moment that he was reaching out to her, trying to grab her and drag her back from a dark place. But, try as she might, her memory would not bring him back; she couldn't not see his face, and worse, try as she might, she could not grasp his outstretched hand. Tears ran down her face, and she leaned out of the wheelchair with her arm raised, trying to re-

connect with the unseen boy. *He had called her Mom. She was a mom?* A loud crack of a baton on her counter brought her quickly back to reality.

"Missy!" the supervisor shouted, stop daydreamin' or ye be dreamin' of my baton across yer back!" He sneered sardonically at her, as another worker came by to retrieve her. It was the end of her shift. She shivered and cowered with fear. " Ye is here to work, and work ye shall!!" He laughed uproariously, with his head falling backwards, as he slapped the baton against his leg. "Now be off witch'ya!"

Her chair rotated easily enough, and the slight, young girl who pushed her got her quickly out of the way of the supervisor who returned to patrolling the shift change.

"Let's get you outta here afore he makes an example o'ye," the skinny girl stated matter of factly. "I never seen him discipline a hurt person, but there's a first time for everything!" The girl, who could not have been more than sixteen, huffed as she pushed the heavy chair out of the bakery proper. They traveled down a hall lined with brick half-way up the wall, and stainless steel panels which glimmered. There was no view of the outside, and Addy had long ago lost all sense of time.

"Is it day, or is it night? Do you know?" she asked.

"Sorry Miss," the young girl responded, "I ain't seen outside myself, I haven't. But, I knows that you're staying in my pod, along with eight others, and maybe one of them knows. Best not to worry about things like that, cause you kinna do anything about that. Best to worry about that leg, and gittin' your rest cause tomorrow comes soon, and it'll be another day just like today, another day just like every other day! Now easy, we're moving onto the lift."

She winced in pain as the gear chair moved into a square cubicle, as wide as it was long, as it was high. A crude, primitive wooden box, there were wooden slats set wide apart that acted as doors on the front. Two workers dressed in bakery gear, but colored gray, motioned to each other, and started turning matching cranks. Addy felt the cubicle rise as she watched the brick wall in front of her change colors from dark red to golden yellow. The cubicle came to a halt so bumpy that she cried out in pain.

"Oh my gosh! Ouch!" she grabbed her leg to stabilize it. "Oh, it hurts, it hurts!"

"Ok, Ma'am, we done with this ride, com' on now, we'll get you situated better in a few minutes, I promise!" The girl had to push hard to get the gearchair out of the cubicle. They exited into a dark metal tube, at most eight feet across, and Abby noticed a damp smell. Occasional small puddles of water could be seen on the floor. The tube stretched in darkness as far as she could see. The girl heaved the chair down the cylinder, so fast that she was afraid the girl would lose control. She *did not* however, and expertly she brought the gear chair to a screeching stop. She was out of breath as she touched Abby gently on the shoulders. She leaned close, and whispered in her ear. "Ye are home now, this is yer home."

Taking a deep breath, holding her throbbing knee with both hands, the exhausted, dirty woman in the wheelchair leaned back and closed her eyes. She could see him again now, perhaps not just the shadow of his face, and the outstretched arm, raised, reaching for her, and the words he said again chilled her to the bone. *"NO mom, no! Please, NOOOOO!"* Those words, pleading, sorrowfully pleading, touched her in a way that nothing had in such a long time, perhaps, never before so deeply. It was then that she opened her eyes wide, and sharply, without hesitation, responded to those around her.

I'm Abby, yes, my name is Abby, *not Addie.* I'm sure of that. Abby. *Just what is this place?* Where am I? WHAT IS THIS PLACE AND WHERE AM I!!!" Abby screamed in a terrified high-pitched voice. The skinny girl who had pushed her wheelchair leaned over and touched her lightly on the shoulder.

"Abby, I am Dottson, Dottson Diggins, and Abby, *this place be the Habitrons. This place is your home now!*"

Chapter 8
The Terrible Foe

There wasn't time to run anywhere. Phillip grabbed Pebby as Noah pushed him to the back of the lab and hustled him to a back wall. Noah struggled to slide open a small three-foot concealed panel at the base of the wall.

"Come on, come on, COME ON!" Noah gritted his teeth as the panel finally gave way and opened. Phillip saw old, rotting, rickety wooden steps leading to a dirt-floored basement room.

"Go, go, GO! You'll be safe! It was my hideaway when I was little! Go, go!" Noah was breathless as he shoved Phillip and Pebby down the steps.

"Oh, and DON'T touch anything, and don't be snooping! Now, git! Quick!"

Phillip lost his footing in the darkness and slid down the stairs on his back. He held onto Pebby for dear life. The musty, rotting wood smell was overpowering, and he cupped his hand over his nose. There was no light there, but a small crack in the floorboards emitted enough light that Phillip could just barely see his hand in front of his face. He set Pebby down, but was afraid to move. The stomping of boots, as well as the *whirr* of mechanical men pounded the ceiling above him. A nasal, brash voice spoke first.

"NOOORRA, how is our favorite scientist? Tell me, tell me! Come'on, feed me the information you know I want! We're here for the update on the mechanical bird. So, how is it coming? When shall we see a test flight? Quick, quick! Give us a status report now, please! IMMEDIATELY!"

Jeeson answered for Norra, who was speechless with fright.

"We *are* working hard, Sir, we are using the birds as prototypes. You must know that she will get results!"

"Never you mind, no one requires your input Jeeson, you're nothing but a glorified zookeeper, poop cleaner-upper if you really must know. Norra is the one with the expertise, and she is the one we are looking to. You Sir, are only a worker drone to clean up after her, is that clear?"

"Oh, yes Sir! Yes indeed. Drone, that is what I am, drone, nothing more, Sir, I got it!" Jeeson flushed beet red.

"Now Norra, an update please! Hurry, I haven't got all day. Now, where are you, and where is that assistant of yours. Isn't it No…ah? Where is No… ah?" Norra spoke timidly and slowly, realizing she needed to stall for time. She chose her words carefully and delivered them measuredly.

"He is in the lab, working, let's just go see! Noah! Noah, are you there?" she called out, her voice shaking, trying her best to hide her fear. "Noah, Council's here," she shouted, walking *very* slowly to the massive metal door. She grabbed the circular stainless handles, and gave them a quarter-turn, pulling the doors open slowly. Thankfully, there was no sign of Phillip or Pebby. Noah was intently working on the filigree wing at his lab table. Looking up, he lifted his safety glasses.

Pebby, under the steps, lay perfectly still, flat to the ground, the dirt feeling cool on her underbelly. She wrinkled her nose; the basement crawl-space smelled stale and moldy. Phillip glanced to make sure she was safe but then his eyes focused on a shape under the stairs. The metal contraption was dotted with gears like those he had seen on Pebby's vest. *What the heck? It kinda looks like some toy gun, doesn't it? No, it can't be. Looks like a tin-foil prop for some school play. Say nothing, say nothing.* Then, against the opposite wall, a small arsenal of similar contraptions, twenty or so, looking for all the world like hand-made toy guns.

Frightened beyond belief, Phillip was shaking as he peered through a crack in the molding. He got only a partial view of the leader of the group, a tall, slender man, garbed in solid black. His tightly-fitted, tunic-length coat was adorned with dark medals of tarnished brass. Several of them sported looping chains. His sleeves were adorned with stripes which Phillip supposed had military importance. He wore a satin hat, not a high hat, but a bowler hat. The hat sported red goggles in the front. Embellishments of feathers were anchored by tarnished sprockets and gears.

Phillip's eyes settled on the man's face. He would never forget that face. What appeared to be a tattoo covered the left side of his face, starting at the left temple and extending all the way to his chin. A series of inscriptions of burnished gold sprockets and gears extended in a giant curved "C" shape to the corner of his mouth. Behind the gears design, gray stippling covered his skin from the middle of his forehead to the left side of his chin. A bridge of dark gold stippling covered the bridge of his nose. He was clean-shaven, save for one tuft of dark hair protruding from the middle of his chin. Underneath the hat, his head appeared to be shaved or bald. He held himself erect, and in the few seconds Phillip was permitted to take it all in, he felt himself sweating profusely. The terror this man inspired was palpable. Noah was stuttering now.

Ah, ,... YYYes, ... YYYes, I have been working day and night on the wing, so you can see, I have just the right angle that Norra asked for. I have built it *exactly* to her specifications, and I have yet to attach it, so I would think by next week, we should be ready for a test flight. Norra, can you weigh in?"

The tattooed gentleman, without moving a muscle, replied sarcastically, "Yes Norra, why *don't* you weigh in? The question simply is, will you be ready for a test flight next week? Tell me now, don't disappoint me, you know how I *hate* to be disappointed!"

"Yes, Councilman Crashus, I would think that next week would be perfect for a test flight. We are putting finishing touches on the circuits and wings, and will be producing a bird who is everything you want it to be!" bowing her head submissively, she backed up a few steps.

"Not me, Norra, the *Council*. Everything the *Council* wants it to be, so don't blame me for the pressure they bring to you. The Council wants the bird as a warning to the Westwards that we are supreme in our flight power, remember? Remember that, and remember, I only am here to do their bidding, You have been reasonably warned, correct?"

"Yes, Councilman Crashus, yes indeed. We shall be ready, you have my word," she replied meekly.

Crashus walked straight up to her, grabbed her chin and cupped her face in his leather-gloved hands. He grinned sardonically. "You know, maybe we should just take your poop-cleaner of a husband with us. You might be persuaded to work faster if you knew he was sitting in Trinity Tower, instead of scurrying around here doing your bidding, no? Such a weakling, Norra. I really don't understand what you ever saw in him anyway, do you?" Crashus turned to see Jeeson standing watchfully in the doorway. Norra answered him timidly. "Councilman, he had nothing to do with the trouble that came between us, you know that!"

" Still, I would like to see you do better than that fancy poop cleaner, no?" Crashus pushed for an answer.

Norra answered, more bravely now. "Crashus, you have my word that I will push forward on this assignment with all due haste. I give you my word!" Crashus looked sharply down his nose at her in disgust. "Just remember, my love, my precious engineer, if they are disappointed, I shall *not* be able to dissuade them. Likely, you will *not* be given a second chance! Oh, I should so hate to see you and that magnificent son of yours dragged through the streets to face the Terrible Wall, no? Question would be, who would get strung up first? What a day that would be for a boy and his mother, no? Some spectacle?"

Winking, he pointed his walking stick directly at Noah and grinned, then shook his head up and down slowly to affirm his threat. He sharply turned on his heel, and the three Automatons in line behind him also rotated. Without any further fanfare, they exited behind him in a straight, marching line.

Just at that instant, Phillip heard a rumbling and a hissing noise he had heard before. For an instant, he could not think of what it was, but it sounded familiar. Then, he threw up his hands, and covered his face completely. He was more afraid than he had ever been in his life. The sound was familiar. It was the sound of Wassy and her wheat delivery wagon, headed with a load of wheat to Moniker's Mill. But, most likely, Phillip knew, folded up inside the bench seat, unaware of the danger he was being led into, unfortunately, would be McClure.

Chapter 9

The Strike-light Signal

Wassy was singing a silly tune to herself as she piloted the snail-wagon along the dusty road, kicking up a cloud of smoky dirt as she headed for Moniker's Mill. She was in a good mood and she piloted the gigantic vehicle skillfully without much effort. Certainly, she was in no hurry. She was rightfully proud of her recent accomplishment.

Shrewd Wassy had saved the day, recognizing the steam-powered chariot parked in front of the Five Feathers Falconry. It belonged to Councilman Crashus, the foreboding, brutal, and dangerous dictator. The square tubular front showcased gold-toned metal ring decorations and housed a compact steam engine. A six-foot high smokestack in the front glittered in the evening twilight. Wooden wheels with yellow spokes turned on a short wooden axel. Behind the main engine apparatus, larger wheels carried a black chariot with a black canopy roof rimmed with copper filigree metal.

While Councilman Crashus was threatening Norra in the Falconry, Wassy had quickly, without drawing the attention of the Automaton guarding the chariot, hurredly sequestered McClure in the woods, instructing him to lie flat on the ground. She had covered him with dry brush, and made her way back to her snail-wagon, just as Councilman Crashus stomped out the front door.

"Evenin' Gov'nor," she had called respectfully. "Just taking a little relief behind a tree, I am."

She curtsied quickly, keeping her head down, which was just as well. She didn't see him wrinkle his nose at her patched dress and dirty, worn boots.

"Evenin' Wassy, how is the wheat crop this harvest?"

"Oh, it's profound Governor, real profound!" She nodded her head up and down several times, making him detest her all the more. Whether it was her dark skin, her femaleness, or just her dirty appearance, he turned up his nose and had no problem pretending she was invisible. He hurried to his steam-chariot, pulled the starter cord, and revved the motor, leaving Wassy covered in a cloud of dust. She laughed sardonically, not only at him, but also for her quickly contrived trickery.

Phillip crawled up the wooden steps on his stomach while Pebby bounded ahead, nosing her way outside to rescue McClure, who was terrified and had not moved. Working as fast as she could, without regard for keeping her coat clean, she tunneled under the brush and quickly dug him out.

It was a more relaxed but focused Phillip that introduced McClure to the Jevity family. He rapidly brought his friend up to speed. Norra and Noah perched on chrome lab stools on one side of the lab counter, facing Phillip and McClure. Jeeson stood at the blackboard, where he had cleaned the bottom left quadrant, leaving Norra's and Noah's formulas and calculations intact. Pebby sat attentively near Jeeson's feet, and he addressed the group.

"OK, since you may not be too sure of the lay of the land, let me sketch a quick diagram of the Circles of the Realm that surround the town center. It's, well, think of it this way, the layout of the town is a gigantic gear. The town center is the center of the gear, and that's where most of the people lived before the take-over. Most of those row-houses, called Rainbow Ridge are deserted now, and they make up the Inner Circle of the Realm. Former leaders that could make a deal with the Council could open shops and live better lives than at the Habitrons."

McClure interrupted. "Habitrons? What the heck is that? Sounds like something we'd buy at the pet store to keep a hamster in." He shook his head and gave a little laugh.

Jeeson continued. "Except, I'm dead serious. The Habitrons are attached to each factory. They are sterile, dark structures with cots set into the walls. This is where people spend their lives, that is, when they're not working the factories. They're given rationed meals, one or two sets of uniforms, and not allowed to have belongings. Every person is just like the other, and after years in this environment, their individuality is lost." Jeeson looked down, but sadly continued.

"It's basically a hybrid of a workhouse and a prison; they are not permitted to leave. Ever. And, if they *do* leave, they are put to death when captured." Phillip and McClure looked at each other, and remained silent. Jeeson sat down, and it was Noah's turn to address the group. Drawing a series of ever-enlarging concentric circles, Noah sketched a gigantic gear, and then began to explain.

"OK, so this is where you landed." Picking up a chalk stick, he marked a small x near the wheat fields, "and here's where you are now. Naji Najeem's Tailor Shop sits in the Inner Circle of the Realm, at about the seven o'clock position on a clock.

McClure now chimed in. "What about going on the crossroads? Wouldn't that be the quickest way?"

"Yeah, why not take the most direct route? Why not just go through the crossroads?" Phillip asked. "All this seems like a waste of time. We don't know if Mom is hurt and we shouldn't be wasting time."

"It's not wasting time," Noah replied matter-of-factly, "we want to keep you guys alive."

"I agree," added Norra. "The Automats are constantly on the lookout for any unusual activity on the crosroads. If they see the two of you strolling along those roads, you won't be strolling for long. No telling *what* they would do, but if you mysteriously disappear, there will be no help for your mother. Think of it this way. Her only hope is us keeping the two of you safe so you can find her, right?"

Phillip nodded his head in agreement, but continued. "So, what you were saying yesterday about needing our help? I don't understand how we can help you. Seems like the Council is ruling with iron fists and a horror show. Not much we can do about that, right?"

Noah nodded in agreement then added. "We have to believe in Naji Najeem. He *had* to have sent you here for a reason. I have to believe that he *deliberately* gave you the key to his shop for some reason, we just don't know why at this point. Think, think, *think*. He is a smart man. He was one of the greatest inventors of his time. He knew he was ill and the gray-smoke sky was killing him. He gave the key to you, and lured you in with the promise of this dog. I have to believe that he saw things in you that would save us. I have to believe, that somewhere, in that tailor shop, there is an answer. He is too brilliant a scientist to have let this happen by chance."

Noah paced nervously, continuing his tirade.

"You know, maybe there is nothing for any of us. Maybe we will die, one by one, just like the birds are dying. But, I have to believe that there is a chance. Even if there is a one-percent of a chance that the people can find their freedom again, we have to try. I believe in Naji Najeem, and I have to believe in his decision to send you here. He gave you that key for a reason, and we have to get you there without question. You, unknowingly, have brought us a mandate directly from our leader."

McClure interjected, "Well, that's all well and good. We can sneak over the next few weeks and get to the tailor shop. We avoid the Automatons, right? How do we keep looking for Abby Weathermore in the middle of all this intrigue?"

Holding up both hands, as if to say STOP, Noah continued. "I've already thought of that. There is one, and only one, part of this broken society that has free run of the town. That's the squad of delivery dogs. Pebby had free run of this entire clockwork town, and in fact, we were able to send a note to Naji in the band of her hat, remember, girl?"

Pebby nodded her head up and down in agreement, but her mind drifted. *Wonder, where is my hat? The one with the flower?* Sadly, she remembered that the last she saw it, it was on the ground at the park as she and Naji were pulled into the Parallax. She had no way of knowing that when she did not show up for work the next day, Gleena Glisson had trudged back to the park and found the little black hat at the edge of the stone fireplace. Cradling it lovingly, Gleena had sat on the rough edge of the fireplace and sobbed tearfully for the little scruffy dog and tailor who were lost to her. She placed the miniature velvet derby on her nightstand, where it remained still.

Phillip was adamant that Pebby not be put at risk. "We can't have her on the loose playing messenger until we know it's even safe for her to reappear, got it? I won't agree to anything that puts her in danger."

"OK, fair point," Noah nodded in agreement. "Look, I'm able to go to the Hydroponics Lab twice every month to get fresh fruits and vegetables for the birds. Of course, the good stuff goes to the Council, and we get second-rate goods, but it's better than starving," he muttered softly under his breath and pointed to the map again. "Hydroponics is located here, on the Middle Circle of the Realm." He placed a mark on the map. The Council and the Elites are way to the north, and to the west, the Westward Islands, our greatest foe. The Hydroponics Lab is a safe haven where you can plan your next moves."

Norra added, "Ok Noah, I get your plan. Lee Anna Loo has the trust of the Council, and she can give us an idea if Pebby has been reported as missing. If not, Pebby can head back to the Octogon and keep contact with *all* of us until we can help them get to the tailor shop, right?"

"Ok, ok," added McClure, "just remember, the main focus is on finding Abby Weathermore, not taking chances with our lives, and not solving the puzzle of what Naji left at the shop. Right?"

Phillip was intrigued now. "Yeah, I guess so, but Noah is right. Why did Naji give me the key? Why is he wanting us to go to the tailor shop? I think it's more than just using it for a hiding place. He told me, *be a leader*, and maybe that's what he meant. I agree, *no* chances should be taken with Pebby. We move to the next safe place with her until we know she's in the clear, right?"

"Absolutely." Noah was definitive. "I am permitted to go next Tuesday, so until then you should shelter at Moniker's Mill, where you will be safe. We never know when the Council will come here to check on the mechanical bird. Moniker is an old friend of Najeem, and you two and Pebby can be safe there. Not much chance of the Council coming to see him. He's old and so efficient that they just let him be."

"So great!" McClure added, "It was an awful ride, but when can Wassy take us there?"

Noah shook his head. "Sorry, that won't be possible. The loads of wheat are thoroughly inspected just before the mill. And, at least on the outside,

Moniker's Mill is swamped by Automatons. There is no chance that you would not get caught trying to sneak in there. I already have a plan. The only way," said Noah shaking his head back and forth, "the only way, is if you crawl on your bellies through the Rastadon Woods. Pebby can show you the way, and I know Moniker has a trap door in the side wall of the mill. Wassy can let him know to be on the look-out. I will give you something I call a *Strike-light*, which will flare for a few seconds. You light these when you are close and he'll open the door for you to scoot in. Got it?"

Norra scratched her head. "What has my little scientist been cooking up in the lab?"

"Nothing Mom, just a little potassium chlorate, antimony sulfide, and a little gum. Just a little rec-ipe I mixed up in my spare time!" Noah chuckled.

Phillip reached for the Strike-light, a stem of metal gears housing a wick. A lever on the side was leveraged by a spring, and when Noah flicked it, the flare lighted. It extinguished after a brief five seconds.

"After it lights, it needs a recovery time of about ten minutes before you will be able to refire it, so use it carefully," Noah admonished.

"We don't want you stuck out in the Rastadon Woods for any longer than necessary. There's vile creatures roaming about," warned Norra. "Fire the Strike-light as soon as you are close to the back door to the mill. You'll see, it will be a small, semicircle hidden in the sidewall, just before the mountain."

"Enough talk of saving the world, com' on everyone, I'll fix us some food, "Norra offered, as Pebby, high-tailed, led the procession into the dining area.

"Better start filling those bellies" Noah added, "you guys are in for two days, *if you hurry*, of crawling through some pretty dense terrain, so this may be your last good meal for a while!"

Phillip and McClure turned, and both looked each other straight in the eyes, while Pebby hurried ahead of them. McClure grinned, and whispered to Phillip, "Look, no matter how *bad* this is, it sure beats having dinner with my old man, right?"

Phillip picked up the tinydog. He held her close-and laughed, burrowing his face into her curly black coat as he nodded in agreement.

The Intruder

Claire slept fitfully. For the third time this week she awoke from dreams about her mother, seeing her as an apparition dressed in flowing white clothes. In her dreams, she thought she saw her mother standing before an oven where she was taking out baked goods. Her heart silently prayed that she was not seeing the ghost of her mother, who could already have died. The idea that her mother could be dead seemed so unthinkable that she could not even entertain the thought.

It didn't appear that her mother was working in *their* kitchen, but whose kitchen? The oven was large and unfamiliar. *Everyone* knew that her mother loved to bake. But in the dream, Abby Weathermore wasn't smiling. In the dream her mother was solemn and quiet and her eyes looked glazed, as if she could not focus well. She moved stiffly and robotically, as if she were in pain. Claire missed her mother *much* more than she cared to admit and the dream frightened her.

Even worse, Claire sorely missed the younger brother she had tormented for years. When she teased him mercilessly, both had laughed; or at least *she* had laughed. But Claire was now appreciating how her brother could have felt intimidated by her silly digs at his shortcomings. She had touted her own achievements. Were they really achievements? Claire shook her head and ran her fingers through her wild morning-hair. Things, academic and otherwise, came to her easily. She was an acknowledged whiz at math and science, and inventing naturally followed. Her mother had set her up with on-line classes when the schools could not keep up with her curiosity.

Now, she was seeing for the first time the distinction between her "achievements" and her natural abilities. Perhaps Phillip, who was not similarly gifted, had truly been the one to achieve. She saw her actions in a different light now and it was not particularly flattering. At the very least, she saw her behavior as self-promoting. It was too late to apologize to him now, and the chance that she would never see him again broke her heart.

She remembered her classes in wind turbines, electrical circuitry, hydrostatic equilibrium, and bacteriology. Hadn't her mother always made sure she was challenged? Had she truly made the most of her talents? She dropped into her mother's rocker, which Claire had taken the liberty of pushing into her own bedroom. Her mother's fisherman's knit sweater was still draped over the back. It gave Claire a measure of security, as if once again she was nestled in her mother's lap and they were reading a story, like they had done so many times when she was much younger.

Strange how often she resisted her mother's hugs, as if they somehow jeopardized her passage into adulthood. Now, she would give anything to have those arms wrapped her, making her feel that things would turn out for the best. She wished things had never changed. After her brother met Naji Najeem and Pebby, he had matured too quickly. He had become obsessed with the scruffy tinydog, and the events of the past couple of months had tumbled down, leaving their lives in chaos.

Pushing herself out of the comfort of the rocker, stretching, she heard Freddy and Gasparilla screeching at each other in the front room. Some of their loud chattering had interrupted her sleep throughout the night.

"What's wrong with you guys? Can't you let me sleep?" She groaned, trying to force herself awake. The angry green Amazon she nicknamed "Gassy" was clinging to the front of her cage and pinning her eyes at Claire.

"Yep, thanks Nesta," Claire retorted, referring to her mother's friend who operated a parrot sanctuary. "Nice bird, bad bite. Is there such a thing, Gassy?" Claire put her finger up to the cage gingerly, and the bird lunged and tried to bite. Startled, backing away quickly, Claire turned her attention to Freddy, a twenty-some-year-old African Gray with an attitude.

He related to Abby, and only to Abby. He looked sharply and critically down his beak at Claire, and angrily threw the dried pepper rings out of the cage the minute she fed him. A few plucked feathers were on the bottom of his cage and his usual animated imitation of household sounds was subdued. Ever since Abby vanished, he sat sullenly on his perch and barely touched his food. Looking into his cage, Claire pulled her thick robe tightly around herself.

"I know little guy, I miss them too, but, *one*, you gotta let me sleep at night, and *two*, you gotta eat more. Wanna come out? Let's try some sunflower seeds. Let's put you on your perch, ok?" Reluctantly, he blew her a kiss. That gesture didn't fool her. He would bite the fire out of her as sure as he was looking at her. He had lured her in before with a smooch which resulted in a painful chomp on her finger. Wrapping her arm in a thick towel, she extended it into his cage.

"Com' on, step-up Freddy, com' on. Mom would want you to come out!" Reluctantly, the little bird hopped up on her arm. Unloading him off onto his wood perch, she filled his cup with sprigs of millet and sunflower seeds. Slowly taking a nibble, Freddy watched apprehensively.

"Enjoy, ya little canary, I gotta get coffee!" Wandering into the kitchen, she looked with disgust at the dirty coffeemaker. Forgetting to clean it last night wasn't a great idea, she thought. A collection of empty pizza boxes sat on the counter in a stack, towering over stacks of clean dishes that she had never put away. Baskets of clean, unfolded laundry sat like unwelcome visitors in the straight-backed chairs. Yellow food stains discolored the white porcelain kitchen sink and crumpled papers littered the kitchen table.

She cleaned the coffee maker, wrinkling her nose at the old grounds. She set the pot to brew and dropped into a ladderback chair, covering her face with her hands. *Gotta clean up this mess. Come to think of it, Phills could bring home Mom any day. She'd scream if she saw this. What am I thinkin, What the heck am I waiting for, and why am I letting it go? Not good Claire!*

Hitting her like a ton of bricks was the realization that, after cleaning, she still had to go to the office and check the mail, address the bills, and placate Jaceena as to why her mother had not called. Snapping her headphones in place and sipping her coffee, she turned up the volume and danced around the kitchen, singing. She reached in the broom closet and snapped a large black trashbag off the roll. First, she cleared the trash off of the table, then carefully folded three baskets of laundry. Singing kept her from the sadness of folding clothes belonging to Phillip and Abby. Moushka, lying on a small rug beside the kitchen fireplace, raised his nose in the air and started to bay. It made Claire laugh and she sang even louder, believing that he was accompanying her. He stayed close by her side, so close that she nearly tripped over him. He seemed skitterish.

Between her singing and Moushka baying, she couldn't possibly give attention to the sinister turquoise eyes that watched her from the edge of the doorway. She couldn't possibly notice the small robot that was the focus of Moushka's attention. The vampy style teeth of the robot chattered. The metal parts, inactive for years, clattered, but Claire didn't notice the noise. From the front room, perceptive Freddy squawked even louder than ever. As if to join in the frenzy, Gassy proceeded to scream "Hell … o! Hell … o! Hell … o!" in the loudest parrot voice possible.

The melee continued. After putting away the clean dishes, mopping the floors, and walking Moushka in the park, Claire settled him in his crate and resolutely got ready for work. She wasn't looking forward to seeing Dr. Jarvis Jamison at her mother's office. He was fresh out of internship, and agreed to take over the practice for a week or two at a dirt-cheap hourly rate. He watched her in a way that made her uncomfortable. Twice, he had invited her out for coffee, and twice, she refused.

Claire very reluctantly felt like his boss. Although she had Jaceena to manage the day to day problems, she was still responsible for paying the salaries, paying the bills, and ordering the supplies. *I don't like being Mom at all!*

Stepping from the shower, she dried her hair and shunned her usual acid-stained T-shirt and baggy pants. She dressed in her favorite Halloween themed shirt and black shorts. Black fish-net stockings and black boots completed her outfit. She carefully applied a tiny bit of eye makeup to complete her look. A bowed headband held her hair in place. *Mom would think I'm a bit Goth for the office, but what'da heck, I'm a professional now!*

Her music was loud, and her headphones canceled any ambient noise. If she had been paying attention to her surroundings, she would have noticed the whirring noise emanating from her lab. If she had been paying the least little bit of attention to anything other than her music, she would have noticed that the robot she had set carefully on the laboratory counter was now sitting upright on the floor, having toddled back from the kitchen after he aggravated Moushka and the parrots. If she had been paying the *tiniest* bit of attention, she would have seen the gears on his back spinning wildly and his turquoise eyes flashing rapidly, almost as if a camera was snapping pictures. She would have undoubtedly noticed that the sharp vampire-like bicuspid teeth were vibrating. She would have seen that it looked for all the world as if the robot was preparing to launch himself at her.

She had her back to him as she grabbed her purse and keys. Stashing the vacuum in the hall closet, she made sure Moushka, who was now confused and standing at attention in his crate, had fresh water. Lastly, she grabbed her favorite black hoodie and headed toward the front door.

"What's wrong, Fred?" she asked as she quickly went to his perch. In the front room, the little gray parrot was screaming shrill, ear-splitting sounds and rapid beeps. In the next instant, Gassy also began shreiking uncontrollably. Claire offered Freddy the end of a broomstick and transported him back into his cage. She headed quickly out the door just as Moushka began to howl and bay as though his heart was breaking.

Guess they miss Mom really bad, but I'm trying the best I can. She frowned in frustration as she climbed into the car. She turned up her music and couldn't know, wouldn't know, that Moushka had stopped baying and was barking wildly. The turquoise eyes of the robot flashed, while his pointed, vibrating teeth pressed flush against the bars of the husky's crate, as he banged into it again and again. She couldn't know, wouldn't know that it would be another hour before the two parrots would stop screeching. Seriously upset, they watched the robot cruise the entire house several times while it made other-worldly clicking sounds. It finally settled itself back in the corner of the lab, and eventually, finally went into deep sleep mode.

Chapter 11

The Creatures in the Woods

The torrential downpour started exactly one hour after they left the Five Feathers Falconry. They were crawling, then walking head down through the underbrush with Pebby in the lead as the rain began. Her gear-vest was folded neatly into the black backpack on loan from Noah. Phillip's camouflage backpack that he had packed so carefully with supplies had been lost during his trip throuugh the Parallax Contingency. Other than a few containers of water, a few rations of food, and a dark-green tarp, they had nothing. The widget remained in Phillip's pocket, the link to his family; the reminder of why he had taken this trip.

The rain, first soft and gentle, then hard and cold, pelted down on them. Phillip wished he had let well enough alone and not been so stubborn. But for his interest in the key to the Wenderling Way Tailor Shop, and his refusal to let it go, his mother might still be safe at home. He could be sitting in his room right now chasing enemies in *Revolutions of the Ages*, his favorite first-person shooter game. Instead, his hair drooped and rainwater dripped into his eyes. He shook with chills and tried to forget that his clothes were soaked. He looked ahead at Pebby, who, above anything else, hated getting her feet dirty. Her long, silky ears were dripping with water and her matted mop-top hair covered her eyes. There was an odd musty smell to the rain.

"OWW... owww! Burning, it's burning me!" McClure cried loudly as he wiggled and squirmed, swatting raindrops away from his face. Phillip realized, as Pebby ran to him for comfort, that the rain was acidic. Boils were popping up on McClure's face like the worst case of acne they had ever seen.. Phillip picked up Pebby and held her close as he grabbed 'Clure by the arm.

"Come on, Dude, we gotta' find shelter quick. Stay low, stay low!" Phillip whispered as he covered Pebby, who was whimpering. He held her close as he ran, head down, toward a rock ledge where he set her under the overhang. Quickly unzipping the backpack, he unrolled the dark-colored tarp.

"Move! Quick! My arm is burning!" McClure begged frantically. "Move over! Move over! I can't fit! Com' on man!"

"Ok, ok!" Scoot closer, man, SCOOT IN!" Phillip draped the tarp over the rock ledge to make a small hut, but it was barely enough shelter for both of them as they sat side by side. Pulling their knees up to their chests, they cradled Pebby between them. McClure, face red and blotchy, took off his hoodie and smiled as he wrapped it around the tinydog.

"We keep her safe, right?"

"Yeah, gotta' protect our guide," said Phillip, smiling lovingly at the tinydog. Sacrificing precious water, they rinsed Pebby and dried her with their jackets. Phillip was silent as he rubbed her dry with his hoodie and pushed her mop-top out of her eyes. He scrunched up his face as the acid odor burned his nostrils.

Sighing with resignation, he continued. "This is nuts! No wonder the birds are dying, ... battery acid fallin' from the sky! What the heck? You'd think they could'a told us?"

McClure nodded in agreement. "Yeah. I've got this feeling that there is a *lot* we haven't been told. I mean, Naji sure didn't say anything about giant birds and acid rain, although I gotta' give him cred-it, he did mention the gray-sky, probably because we saw he could hardly breathe, *duuh!*"

"You're right," Phillip added. "We weren't told what we were getting into, but after Mom was gone, I guess it really didn't matter, we were gonna'come here and try to find her, right?"

"Yeah," agreed McClure, "I just didn't think I would be getting my skin melted off doin' it, ya' know?"

Phillip laughed. "Hey, Dudeness, looks like you got the worst case of zits I've seen all week. How do I look?"

McClure inspected Phillip's face.

"A few pink spots, mostly on the cheeks, nuttin' a little make-up won't hide," laughing, he nudged Phillip in the ribs.

"Dudeness," Phillip nudged him back, "we gotta' laugh or we'll cry like babies!"

They laughed and looked at the little tinydog. The hood of the jacket draped over her head and her small face peeked out. Most of her fur was dry now, but the inside of the hoodie was covered in white crystals, much to McClure's dismay.

"Crap man, you owe me a freakin' hoodie too!" He leaned his head back on the rocks. "Mind if I close my eyes? Just for a few?"

"Go ahead. I'll keep watch." Phillip shook water off the heavy cloth and peeked out.

"Like, whose gonna' be out in this?" asked Mc-Clure through shuttered eyes, as the whirring of a steam engine dirigible came directly overhead.

"Funny you should say that. DON'T MOVE!!!" cautioned Phillip as he squeezed the tinydog closer, "Don't move!" he whispered, keeping the fabric over them. Mercifully, the dirigible moved on toward the Falconry.

After several hours, the heavy rain stopped. Stiff and barely able to stand, ravenous, they dug into the backpack and divided the rations that Norra had generously packed.

"Great. Beans and stale bread?" Phillip chomped down on the rations.

"Hey, man, at least you had cooking back at your house," McClure added. "I would give *anything* now for your mom's cinni rolls. Remember the icing?"

"Yeah, don't remind me. Just don't remind me," added Phillip, not wanting to think he would never see her again. Then, he remembered the question he had been afraid to ask.

"Hey 'Clure! I don't mind, nothin' like that, but you keep sayin' *our mother* to these folks. I mean, you're as good as any brother could be to me, and Mom says you're welcome anytime at our place, but what about your own mom? What's that all about?" McClure looked down, and answered thoughtfully, afraid to meet Phillip's gaze.

"Well ... well, you see, I read a lot, and I talk to the counselors at school, *a lot*. I know I got two real messed-up people raisin' me. And, ... no matter how I try, they always let me know I'm *not* what they wanted. Dad calls me a loser all the time. And Mom? Well, ... Mom stands by quiet and lets it all happen. She never says a word to the old man. She wanted a girl instead of me, you know, someone she could dress up like a little doll. She told me that herself. I'm a disappointment to them, no matter what I do."

Phillip looked down too. It was as if he had always known, but they had never spoken of it. It was always the crouching tiger in the room, waiting to spring on a day like today when their defenses were down.

"I know, 'Clure. I know. You always like to come to our house, and I really like that. But my mom's not perfect either! You know how she goes on about the old house and she uses us for free labor. You know how she can be the *most* annoying person in the entire universe, right?"

McClure chuckled, then added, "Oh, I know, I know. But I gotta' tell you. When she looks me straight in the eyes, I know she's got my back, no matter what. No questions asked. When she looks at me, she likes me for who I am, and I never had that at my house, no, never. Maybe you don't see it, but you and Claire are at the head of her parade. You're lucky, Dude, *real lucky*. Yeah, I'm here to have *your* back, sure. But, if there is any chance I can help your mom, I wouldn't miss it for anything in the world. Got it? I owe her that. A million boxes of movie candy says I should be here for Abby Weathermore, right?"

Phillip sighed, fondly remembering all the times his mom had taken them to Friday night movies. "Yeah, I guess. I know Mom would want us to look after each other, and I think we got enough craziness in our family that we can share it. I think she would want that. Right, brother?"

"Brothers," McClure added softly. "Brothers. Let's find her and bring her home, waddya' say?" Sighing deeply and hugging Pebby tightly, Mc-

Clure continued, "Come on, let's move. We got lots of ground to cover, and we can't move much in the daylight. Let's go!"

With Pebby leading the way, they crouched and moved forward the best that they could. By morning, they were both exhausted. They slept and hid in the daytime when the risk of being spotted was high. Several patrol ships churned overhead during the night, but when they heard them in the distance, they spread the dark tarp over themselves and were still. Pebby was careful to not move during those times too, lest she give away their position.

She fretted about both boys. *Their clothes are still all wet and the food is almost gone, water too.* She knew better than to let them drink from any of the small streams they encountered or eat any berries; Rastadon Woods was known for poisonous plants and water.

By the evening of the second day, they were at their breaking point. Pebby too, was tired. They took turns carrying her, letting her covered head stick out as she rode in the backpack. If they strayed off course, she gave a low growl signaling them to right their way.

As the gray-sky turned to black. Phillip could not go another step. He dropped down onto a log, took off his shoes and shook out the dirt. Rubbing his foot, he shook his head and sighed.

"Ohhhh, ... I don't think I can make it much longer, 'Clure. I've got the biggest blister and my stinkin' bandaids are floating somewhere in the Parallax." McClure, who had dropped down beside him, also pulled off his shoes and socks.

"Hey, my feet got wet with that acid rain, and they stink! Look, I got spots on my feet too. Damn, I'm allergic!" McClure shook out his socks and twirled them fiercely in a circle, trying his best to dry them.

Pebby was filthy. Her paws were sore, and her mop-top hair was a damp curtain over her eyes. Without warning, a rattling sound could be heard in the distance. Her ears perked up. Ssswwwiiissshhh came the swishing sound, as if a gigantic snake was sliding through the brush. She jumped to an alert stance, growling a slow, steady growl. Within minutes, Phillip and McClure heard it too.

"NOOOOOOO!!! *What's... com...ing?*" McClure whispered, as he put his socks and shoes on as fast as he could. The sound was getting closer and closer, louder and louder, *SSSWWWWIIISSSHHH!!!*

"Shhhush! Keep quiet!" urged Phillip, struggling to get his own shoes on quickly. McClure was frantic. "Should we climb a tree? Wadda' we do?" He covered his head with both hands.

Panic filled them both. Before they could climb to higher ground, the swishing was upon them in the darkness. A hundred or so baseball-sized bronze-colored crabmetals, each with a set of turquoise, piercing eyes and vampy teeth formed a fierce line as they scurried in unison. Not one broke formation as they created a circle around the trio and froze, all clicking their front pincers and chattring teeth in unison. The echo of the metal clicks resonated through the woods and magnified so loudly that Phillip and McClure covered their ears. The first crabmetal, the ringleader, stood directly in front of the boys. His deep turquoise eyes penetrated the darkness of the night and flashed, not once, but three times slowly as Phillip and McClure trembled with fright.

The Moniker's Mill

All the forest was silent as the chief crabmetal held her right front pincer high in the air. The entire contingent of metalcrabs froze in silent attention. She stared menacingly at the boys, then snapped her pincer slowly twice, followed by three times in rapid succession. The sharp sounds echoed through the dark, misty forest. She flashed her turquoise eyes twice slowly, and then three times so fast that Phillip missed seeing it, but Pebby bobbed her head in recognition. She turned and looked directly at Phillip, giving three sharp barks to signal her approval. Phillip understood immediately what she was tryin to tell him.

"Com' on, this is friendly fire! Let's follow, com' on!" Phillip urged, as he tossed on the backpack and grabbed Pebby. The cavalcade of metalcrab creatures proceeded through the underbrush, moving quickly and silently as the boys followed. They could barely keep up with the serpentine line that led them quickly and safely through the gnarled vegetation. Dawn began to break.

Suddenly, the underbrush ended. The boys and the tinydog froze. The crabmetals slithered away silently into the last vestiges of the darkness and were gone. Towering in front of them, a majestic stone structure protruded from the side of the mountain. In front of the four-story stone edifice, a massive wooden water wheel turned slowly, silently. The only sounds were the flowing of the water softly falling over the wheel, and the hissing from silver metal pipes rising from the top of the building.

Phillip shivered, pulling his hoodie around him. His clothes were damp and they smelled stale. They had been told to flick the strike-light as soon as they saw the stone wall and the half-door. There it was, dead ahead. But unexpectedly, they heard the hissing of a steam-powered dirigible overhead.

"NOW!" whispered McClure frantically, "NOW! Quick, Phills, they're coming!"

Phillip set Pebby down and dug in the backpack. He shook as he fumbled for the strike-light. He tossed the folded tarp to McClure, who rushed to open it. As fast as Phillip could, he raised the strike-light high above them and flicked the lever. The stick flashed for a few seconds before Phillip dropped to the ground. Simultaneously, McClure launched the tarp over them. They froze as the airship cruised above them, sailing low in the sky. As it passed, they peeked out. They saw a arched, half-sized door open in the base of the wall. From inside, a lantern flickered for three seconds.

"Come on! Let's go! Come on 'Clure, before they see us! NOW!" Clutching the tinydog in his arms, Phillip ran, head down. McClure, out of breath, followed closely, huffing and puffing. They crouched and made their entrance through the waist-high, hidden arched door as the steamship's searchlights flashed on the clearing they had just crossed.

Out of breath, cold from the dampness, aching from the two-day crawl through the brush, they found themselves facing a portly old man with wild shoulder-length silver hair and beard. He wore an immaculate white shirt, brown sailcloth breeches, and silver buckles on his boots. He looked for all the world, Phillip thought, *like a pilgrim. Santa Claus gone Pilgrim.*

"Welcome friends, your loyal servant Mendaleus Moniker here. Welcome to The Mill!" the man exclaimed in a low, husky voice as he opened his arms widely.

"You're safe!" he laughed. "Well, at least for now!" Throwing his head back, he chuckled with a deep belly laugh and continued, "Any friend of Naji Najeem is a welcome guest here! Come now, not a moment to waste! Hurry! Come in, come in, tell me everything you know. What instructions do you bring from Najeem?" Rubbing his hands together in anticipation, he smiled and continued.

"I stand ready to receive me marchin' orders!" Smiling warmly, and enthusiastically, he ushered them into the vestibule. The light and warmth from a roaring fire in the adjacent room relieved their worries, but they were still chilled, shivering in their soaked clothes. Phillip extended his hand, as did McClure.

"Pleased to meet you," Phillip offered. "We were with Naji yesterday before we came. He gave us the key to his tailor shop, and told us that everything we need would be there. That's why we're here.

You know anything about a lost woman wandering around here?"

McClure added, "We're looking for our mother, who came here by accident. We think she might be hurt. You heard of anyone like that? Tall, dark-brown hair, black clothes, name's Abby? That ring a bell?"

"No, no, certainly not. Not at all," Mendaleus replied dismissively as he shook his head. "Come to think of it, not a word about any strangers. I *have* seen the airships come over a wee bit more, so maybe there is something I don't know. Me an' the wife live a quiet life here. Why, we're the only industry in Norwall that has barracks instead of those rat-infested Habitrons! By God! I'm more than a little proud of that!"

He continued, "If youse must know, or care to know, I was second in command to Najeem, and I stand ready to carry out his orders! By God, I've been waitin' for this day, so don't keep a man waiting!"

Phillip stammered, "Yeah, we're a little cold and wet. Mind if we clean up first?"

"Oh sorry, rude of me it was. Yes, ... yes, come now fellows, follow me! Let's get you right as rain. Maybe that's not the thing to say now, but let's get you made right! Yes, we'll get you made right again!"

Grabbing both their hands, shaking them vigorously, he muttered under his breath, *"Naji. Naji, ye rascal! Naji Najeem, I knew you couldn't desert us! Ol' rascal, ... ol' rascal!"*

He motioned for them to follow him. They hiked down long hallways lined with knotty, gnarly wood planks. Phillip thought for a moment they had entered an underground mine shaft. Moniker trudged ahead with his wide-based swaggering gait, lighting the pathway with a rusty lantern swinging in his hand. Both boys stayed silent as they followed silently behind him through the dark, cold passages, giving each other worrisome glances. Moniker continued to mumble barely perceptible musings peppered with the name of Naji Najeem. He seemed to be speaking to the ghost of his old friend. Phillip shivered from the cold, wet clothes sticking to his skin. McClure, who hadn't yet recovered from the acid rain wash, was itching horribly. Pebby, still dirty and damp, trudged faithfully behind.

Finally, they reached an perfectly round wooden door. Moniker turned several gears on the wall, and the door slid silently into the wall as the path opened. Inside, for as far as they could see, stainless piping coursed through the middle of both sidewalls. There was a damp freshness to the air, like freshly-washed clothes. The hall was lined with vertical metal capsules of distressed, pounded brass. Across from the capsules, crude wooden benches held stacks of beige-colored cotton towels and sets of beige-colored muslin pajamas.

Moniker gestured to empty baskets beside the benches. "Now, here's where ye'll put yer grime-ees!" he instructed, with a nod of his head as he folded his arms across his chest. He stood watchfully while they each grabbed a towel and pajama set and entered adjoining capsules. Dispensers on the wall marker "washee" held soap. The fragrant, warm water poured out at a comforting temperature. Both boys were relieved to clean their skin and rid themselves of the sticky crystals from the acid rain. After they dried and dressed, they ventured out cautiously.

Mendaleus, still standing guard with his arms crossed in front of him, continued to softly mutter one-sided conversations with Naji Najeem. He led them back to the small room adjacent to where they had entered the mill. Two low, wooden stools were set in front of a small fire, and despite the earthen floor, the room was cozy. Warm red and black plaid blankets were quickly tossed over their shoulders, and Pebby found her place on a brown braided rug close to them. A tin pot bubbling with fragrant-smelling stew hung over the fire. They warmed their hands and feet and breathed a sigh of relief.

As the boys and Pebby relaxed and filled their bellies, Moniker continued his focus on retrieving messages they might be bringing from Naji Najeem. "Feed me the information, best you can of course, from Najeem!!" Moniker directed, as he watched them devour the stew.

"Well, Sir," Phillip replied with trepidation as he slurped, "he said, *Be a leader, organization is the key!*"

"Yes, yes, you see," Mendaleus replied, pointing and wagging his finger, "he's sending the signal that the time is right. He has sent you as a sign that the time to organize is now! He must'a seen that if'n we wait, we will only grow weaker and sicker, and the time, like it or not, must be *now*. Yes, yes! He sent youse to bring the message, and to inspire us with your knowledge, and to lead us to victory! *God save the Republic!!!*"

Moniker stood, raised a fist to the sky, and choked on his words. He coughed for a few minutes and rubbed tears from his eyes. Collecting their bowls, he quickly regained his composure and showed them to an adjacent room. It was sparsely furnished with wooden bunks, straight-backed chairs, and a small desk. A fireplace warmed the room. Phillip noticed it had an evergreen smell like his Christmas tree back home. It saddened him, as he remembered opening Christmaas presents with Claire, knowing now that she was light-years away, depending on him to find their mom. Hw shook his head, as if to shake away the memories of what he left behind. Moniker's instructions brought him back to reality.

"Now, here ye's can rest, and don' ye's be worrin' about that tinydog. Me wife knows her well, and she'll care for her properly. That doggie needs a good washee to get the acid off her, and she be back soon enough! Now, you boys rest easy, we'll speak in the morn', got it?"

He picked up Pebby and tucked her neatly under his arm. He left without further admonitions, making his way down the short hallway. He exited and locked the door behind himself.

It was McClure who spoke as they heard the sounds of the sentry steamships overhead, still searching for intruders. "Wait a minute! Did he just lock us in?"

Phillip sighed in resignation. "Aahhh...yep!" he replied, as he threw himself on the bottom bunk and promptly fell into a deep sleep.

The Bedtime Story

The rickety elevator lurched to a halt. The chestnut-haired woman squirmed in the wheelchair; there was no getting comfortable. She winced as the quick stop jostled her. It had been a long shift today at the Octagon Bakery. Her right leg was supported on a platform, but when the chair moved, it pinched her. Sharp pain cut through her like a knife and took her breath away. The bandages on her leg were dirty and dusty with flour. Her gown and kerchief were stained, and her head itched. The wrappings on her leg had not been changed in three days and they smelled sour. Brass-colored gears protruded from the bandages and kept her leg from flexing in the least.

The woman called Abby could not bear weight on her right leg. Even so, she worked on the bakery line daily. Each night, she followed the line of women back to the fifth floor of the Habitron under the watchful eyes of several Automatons and guards. Behind her, the woman pushing her chair sighed.

"I *think* it's our day to take a wash, Abby. At least, I pray it is. I stink, and you're not so fresh either, Missy. Let's get back there quick so's we can be at the head of the line. Come on, hang on!"

Clarice Constants could only push the chair so fast. She was skinny and frail. She was twenty-one years old, pale, with long blonde hair that she twisted into a knot high on her head. She kept close to Abby ever since that first day, when Hilde had wheeled in the broken, confused new resident. *There's something very different about her*, Clarice had thought. But, as usual, she kept her thoughts to herself. Perhaps out of pity, perhaps out of the kindness that was second nature, Clarice kept close to Abby. It helped that their bunks were in the same row. It helped that Clarice, abandoned by her mother long before the Council took over, longed for female companionship. At least in the Habitron, she had food, clothing, and the chance for female ca-maraderie. Her life here was better than wandering the streets as a beggar, as she had done in the early years of her life.

Day in and day out, she pushed Abby along as the others only watched. No one else ever offered to help. The worn, misshapen gear-wheels of the wheelchair had carried many a disabled resident and the chair was far from new. It was hard to push. As she hurried them back to their bunk-space, her feet kept slipping out from under her and she leaned her whole weight to push the chair forward. Clarice huffed and puffed as she maneuvered Abby down the long hallway. Row after row of metal bunks were inset in the wall; three bunks tall, three-feet apart, each six-feet long, covered with the same white coverlet with light blue pinstripes and the same flat, thin mattress. A small pillow complet-ed each bed. Opposite the beds, drawers were set into the walls, two drawers for each resident. One drawer was marked for clothes, and the other for personal items. Any items not in the proper loca-tion were confiscated. Workers from the laundry division restocked the clothing drawers daily with clean uniforms and pajamas.

"Ok, Abby, we made it!" Clarice exclaimed. "Let's wait 'till we hear if we gonna' shower a'fore we git you outta' that chair, ok?"

Abby nodded in agreement, then sighed. "I'm so tired, I just want to lie down. But, you're right, it hurts too bad to move. I better stay in the chair 'till I can go to the shower." She grabbed Clarice's hand and patted it. "Thanks for helping me. I'm too weak to move this chair, with the platform and all."

"Oh, it's nothing Abby. I was hurt when I came here too, and someone helped me. She ain't here no more, bless her heart, she took sick one winter and passed on. But we gots to help each other, it's all we's got, you know."

Abby remembered her first day at the Habitron. She had depended on Clarice to make her introductions. They sat together on the edge of the thin, paltry mattress as women filed by to meet her, as they always did when a new resident came. It wasn't often someone new came to the Octagon Habitron, unless it was a transfer from another facility. The women had shuffled by, their exhaustion palpable after the arduous shiftwork. They had no reason to hurry, there was nowhere else for them to go. Many sported burns on their arms from working the ovens, and many were gray-haired and pale, having not been in sunlight for years. Some were hunched-back, some limped, some could not focus well; neither eyeglasses nor medical were provided to them. Each of these women had suffered the incomprehensible loss not only of their family, but their freedom as well. Most had no more fight left. They trudged by in identical, bleached-white muslin smocks and aprons, hair held back by identical white hair-kerchiefs, skin dirtied with flour and scarred by healed burns.

Graciously, each of them offered their hand to Abby as they looked deeply into her eyes. Most said little, the offered hand saying more than words ever could. Some offered a small ribbon tie for her hair. Others offered a small square of muslin. One gave Abby an extra pair of socks *to wear at night when your feet git cold, 'cause they turn off the heat.* The elder of the group, a withered, tiny, silver-haired woman, sat on the bunk and raised a finger to her lips, as if telling Abby to be silent and listen as she told her the story of how they came to the Habitrons when the Council took over the city. All the women kept still and kept silent, as the story of their bondage was told by the old woman, as it had been told so many times before.

On that infamous day, the day we call The Day of the Broken Hearts, well, on that particular day, the Automaton army came a'marchin' through the streets, dragging people from their homes and capturing or killing all who were in their path. Metal wrist-bracelets were snapped on us, and they connected each of us woman to the next woman in line by a piece of a chain. Our children was all rounded up and they was sent to Council-run boarding warehouses, where their heads were shaved and their clothing taken. Some children had cloth bags placed over their faces and were carried away from us mothers screaming and thrashing their arms wildly. This why we call it The Day of the Broken Hearts. The men were herded off to separate Habitrons. Adults who wouldn't submit were steam killed on the spot. Most of their skin peeled off and it pooled in a puddle 'round their feet. We saw it took thirty minutes to die that way, and the screams of pain filled the air, and the unbearable, stinkin' odor of melting flesh. None of us women ever forgot that smell, as God is my witness. Clarice here, had been sent to the Habitrons that day, lucky, because she was tall for her age. The pictures of folks bodies half-cooked, some still squirmin' and hollering littered the street. This picture was burned deep in all our memories. Nothing was ever the same after that, everything was different. Everything would be different for us forever...

Seeing the Automatons leading another line of women approaching her and Abby, Clarice felt her pulse quicken. They were all covered in flour and dirt from their long shift in the bakery. Abby seemed lost in a daydream.

"Com' on, lets git with 'em, we gittin' showers!!" she whispered to Abby as she heaved the heavy chair into formation as the line passed. The first few women smiled wanly and helped point the heavy chair in the right direction. One of the woman, slow and rather old, had a dirty wrap around her forearm. It was littered with dirt, and her arm below the bandage was swollen and streaked with red. Abby turned her head and paused. She looked sharply and analytically at the red arm, cutting her eyes.

"Wait, wait ...WAIT! Come here!" she urged unexpectedly, as instinct took over. Motioning the old woman to stand beside her chair, Abby gently took the woman's hand and examined the reddened arm closely. Deep within her middle brain, dendrites suddenly, unexpectedly, joined hands with other neurons. Transmitters popped open from vesicles, and oozed their fluid across nerve channels, making electrical connections between the cells of Abby Weathermore's nervous system. The neocortex fired ever so briefly, as the memory of others who were injured jolted her so hard that she grabbed her head with both hands. She pounded her skull lightly with both open palms, and suddenly, memory jolted through to the hippocampus. She began to unwrap the woman's arm fearlessly, as if it was the easiest thing in all the world. It was as if she had done it a million times before. Expertly removing the bandage, she stated very clearly, simply, and authoritatively, "You're going to need some medicine for that burn, you know that?" The woman nodded, eyes wide open. Then, as if a part of Addy's brain rewired itself and reconnected the regenerated neurons, she slipped seamlessly into another place and time. In a trance, speechless, she stared straight ahead as the women took turns pushing her along toward the showers.

The short, friendly man was speaking to the small group gathered around him on the upper floor of a mansion. The house overlooked a large body of calm, turquoise water, which sparkled in the sun. Most remarkable of all were the window panes, each a different colored glass square. Some were pink, some light blue, some yellow, but all glistened in the sun and cast watercolor hues onto the bay. It was as if a painter had splashed a million sparkling colors of the rainbow across the water nd the sky.

The man named "Volunteer" told the group that the owner, John, had the windowpanes colored so that when his wife looked out at the water, different colors reflected, like a prism.

The house was so elegant, and so beautiful. I held the hand of someone small, someone who kept fidgeting. I squeezed the hand tightly so they wouldn't pull away. For the life of me, I can't see what they looked like. I remember the smell of the house, very clean, but very old. I remember the wooden plank floors, so smooth and shiny.

There were fancy gardens outside. I sat on a bench in the garden with the little person sitting on my lap. They were getting heavy on me, but I squeezed them tight, as if I could hold them close forever. The little person spoke quietly, "I no like clowns, I ... no... like... clowns!" The voice is a child, but who? Who are you, and ... where are you now?

She grit her teeth, squinted her eyes, and tried with everything in her brain to force the picture into focus. She could clearly see the woman sitting on the bench, surrounded by flowers in an exquisite garden. Watching herself from a distance, the picture became more clear. She could see herself, and if she could take her a few steps closer, she could perhaps, just maybe, see the little person. There! Closer. There! *It's a girl. Yes, it's a little girl. She's kicking her feet now and saying it again. "But, I no like clowns, I NO*

LIKE CLOWNS!!!" She saw herself hug the little girl even tighter, as if she would never let her go. But, let her go she did, as the little girl, unknown, unnamed, faded away into darkness. Abby couldn't hold on to her tight enough to keep her. She just couldn't. The little girl was lost, and the tears, so many sad tears, came once again.

The Flying Skee-bots

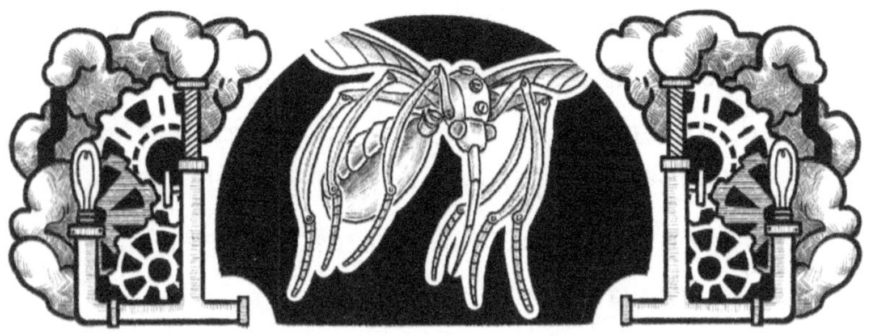

Phillip jostled McClure, who rolled over and sunk deeper under the coverlet. Phillip tried to rouse him. "Wake up, Dude! Wake up!" He had no idea what time it was, or how long they had slept. Phillip kept jostling McClure, who rolled over and sunk even deeper, pulling the coverlet over his head.

Phillip, now fully awake, remembered that they were locked in this small cluster of rooms. Front paws up on his bed was Pebby, now clean and brushed to perfection.

"'Clure! Wake up! Moniker must've opened the door and let Pebby in last night. Look, she's all clean!"

"Yeah, yeah, give me a minute, just a sec," mumbled McClure, as he turned over and yawned.

Warming his hands by the fire which was now starting to flame, Phillip pulled up a straight-backed chair and warmed his feet too. The scruffy tinydog jumped in his lap and licked his face. She was, indeed, quite clean. Her fur smelled like lavender. Her ears and coat had been brushed to a shiny luster with not a tangle in sight. Her teeth were clean and her breath was fresh.

"Wow! They did an amazing job on this dog! Someone knew what they were doing. Her grooming is perfect! Com' on 'Clure, get your butt up!" McClure sat up in bed, rubbing his eyes.

"Oh, I forgot where we were. I thought I was at your house and your mom was fixing pancakes. Wait, what is that smell? I smell food!!!" McClure was right. As they looked down the dark hallway, they saw a covered tray sitting just inside the door. Approaching it cautiously, they found their dirty clothes now washed and neatly rolled up into two bundles along with their shoes, which were also clean.

"Man, this door is still locked, darn it!" Phillip pushed and pulled, trying to jimmy the door open, but to no avail.

"Hey, quit making noise, I'm still trying to wake up. My feet are freezing!" McClure yawning, stumbling, and reaching his arm out to keep from falling, caught himself on the sidewall.

"Hey! What the heck? Crap! Door on the sidewall! Door!" he whispered, noticing the outline of a door hidden in the wood, framed to be invisible.

"Gotta' be a way to open it! Com' on Phills, your eyes are better than mine, there has to be a latch somewhere. Put the food tray down and help me out here!"

"'Clure, this food is hot. What say we eat, and change into our clothes first? No sense trooping around this place in jimmy-jams, no? Come along son, let's dig into this. How long since we had a hot breakfast?"

"Too long, man, too, too long!"

They pulled the braided rug near the fire and set the tray down. Then, both cross-legged, they devoured the cakes. They delighted in small slivers of a fruit that looked like apples but tasted like fresh bananas. Round ceramic bowls of oatmeal completed their feast, by far the best oatmeal they ever had tasted. It was not too sweet nor too runny, with a delicious maple flavor. Unfamiliar, small, sweet, red berries dotted the entire surface, adding crunch. Beside each bowl sat the freshest, flakiest cinnamon roll they had ever seen. The white, creamy, sugary topping was melted into a supreme glaze, which melted in their mouths.

"Oh, OH this is SO GOOD!" Phillip exclaimed, wiping his mouth and breathing deeply. "If you thought my mom's cinnis were good, you're gonna' die for these!"

McClure shook his head. "Well, I kinda' expected something like this, I mean, we are in a wheat mill!" Cramming spoonfuls of oatmeal into his mouth, and talking while chewing, he continued, "Ya know, I would give anything to be sitting in your kitchen eating your mom's cinni rolls, but here we are in some forsaken fortress. Don't forget, the moron has us locked in! Eat up quick, I am dying to get that door open. Don't you think we just *might* want to find an escape route? I mean, just in case we need one? Waddya' think Phills? Had enough of his hospitality?"

"Yeah, I get it, if it looks like a duck and quacks like a duck, blah blah, blah, ... I get it, I don't trust him either. Com' on, let's get dressed and see what's behind door number three."

Calmly, slowly, they quietly made their way down the long hallway. The wood planks were rough and the molding between them pure white. At the end of the hall to the right of the outer locked door was the outline of another door, three-quarters the height of the main door. After almost an hour of searching and feeling the wall around the door, they discovered a tiny gear, measuring no more than one inch, which blended seamlessly into the log. It did not turn, but when they pushed it in, they heard a series of gears turn. More clicking and turning of gears could be heard, and not too long after that, the door popped open slightly. Pulling and tugging together, they were able to force it open enough for each of them to slide through sideways.

'Com' on man, squeeze it in, squeeze it in Phills," McClure urged, chuckling.

"Hey, man, tryin', I'm trying," Phillip replied as he inhaled deeply and squeezed through. Then, he noticed the tinydog trying to follow him.

"Pebby, stay here. You can't come with us! Not this time girl, not this time!"

Pebby whimpered softly for a few minutes, but then dropped to the floor, head between her front paws, back legs t-boned, and she proceeded to wait.

The door drifted ominously shut behind them and they heard the latch lock. Everything went black. The brief glimpse they had of the platform in front of them told them it was slime-covered stone.

"Smells like your stinky gym locker!" whispered McClure, as they inhaled rancid air. Feeling their way cautiously, they felt the edge of each step with their feet. The boots they wore didn't help; Phillip found it hard to bend his foot and feel for the edge of the step. Behind him, McClure was grasping the cup-sized depressions in the sidewall to keep from slipping on the slimy rocks. The steps spiraled downward. As they stepped judiciously, they had a sensation of going lower, descending into the dark unknown. The smell of dark secrets engulfed them with each step they took.

Phillip dusted his hands on his pants. "Man, what is this sticky stuff? I can hardly hold on!"

McClure felt off-balance, and he grabbed Phillip's shoulder in an attempt to keep from slipping.

"Dude! The stink is gettin' worse! You hear water running? Dude, this is creepy! Should we keep going?" McClure's voice was shaky, and he was holding onto the wall as they made their way down steps that twisted into a tight spiral. There was no railing.

"Dude!" McClure whispered again, "The walls feel like rock, but kinda a real porous rock. It's kinda' damp. And sticky. You feel that?"

Phillip's whisper was a bit shaky, "Sure you didn't just forget to wash your mitts after eating those rolls? Keep moving, just keep moving. Is that water I hear? Sure smells like there is water down here, kinda' damp, ya' know?"

"Dude, the steps are gettin' smaller, and this wall is gettin' more and more sticky. What are we in anyway? Oh, wait ... listen!" McClure warned.

Suddenly, they heard the same hissing sound they had heard in the woods. At the same moment, they realized that the staircase stopped. They were on a landing of cold, damp stone. Coming from nowhere in particular, dozens of crabmetal creatures flashed deep, iridescent turquoise eyes and clicked their front pincers while they chattered vampy teeth. They were following each other, and they all appeared angry to have been disrupted. They continued to swarm faster and faster, building up momentum.

"Oh man, *may ... be* we better head back up to the top? I think we're in over our heads here, man.

Remember, the guys with the greenish eyes are the leaders, so there must be a million more followers, I mean, I wanna' get outta' this place, and NOW!!!," McClure pleaded, starting to turn around. "And by the way, I do hear water falling somewhere, this place is too dark and too creepy! Let's skee ... daddle, OK? They got them mean lookin' pinchers in the front!"

Leaning back against the sticky wall to get his balance, Phillip inhaled deeply and caught his breath, his nose burning from the acidic air. "Yeah, I hear it, I hear it now! Freeze!" he whispered. Phillip reached into his pocket and brought out the strike-light that Noah had given him. "Ya know, I can light this, so we can see what's really goin' on, no?

McClure's voice trembled as he shook. "Maybe I don't wanna' see what's really goin' on, didja think of that?"

"Watch and *learn!*" Phillip lit the strike-light and held it high over his head. For several seconds only, it illuminated the massive underground cavern with a two-story waterfall coursing down the back wall. A river ran not even ten feet in front of them. The water was pea-green, with nauseating yellow foam adorning the top like melted icing on a badly decorated cake. Debris of different shapes and sizes floated past them. Then the strike-light went dark.

"Creepin' Crap!! I swear I saw a freekin' arm floating by!" McClure's voice shook with fear.

"You're right, Dude, I saw it too! Mega retreat, and I mean NOW!" Phillip turned and started back up the slimy steps, stepping off an edge and grabbing onto the wall as he slipped but caught himself. The lines of crabby-creatures seemed very aware of the presence of the water and avoided it with a series of twists and turns, swarming together on the landing, turquoise eyes blinking and pincers clicking all the while. Suddenly, Phillip heard an agonizing shriek come from McClure, who had backed up several steps in front of Phillip. McClure began to scream.

"My eyes! My eyes!!! They're on my eyes! AAAhhhhhhhh!!!"

Phillip whipped around to see McClure clutching his face with both hands. Mechanical metal insects, numbering in the hundreds, were fkying out of the honeycomb crevices in the wall. The strike-light had attracted their ire and awoken them. McClure was surrounded and Phillip could see them lighting on his head and face.

"'Clure! Hold on, I'm comin'!!!" Phillip crammed the strike-light in his pocket and ran up the steps, brushing the flying metal insects off of McClure and swatting them away from his face. He kept sliding on the slippery, wet steps.

"Can't see! Can't see!" McClure was now batting at them too as they put their heads down and made their way back up the spiral steps. Phillip could feel them biting his back through his shirt and landing on the back of his neck. He was too busy protecting his own face and swatting them off of McClure to care. When they reached the top, the door would not open.

"On my count!" Phillip shouted, "one, two .... *three!*" Both boys shoved their shoulders against the door, and it burst open. McClure dropped to the floor, hands covering his face. He cried loudly and bitterly as Phillip cradled his head in his lap.

Chapter 15

The Secrets of the Mill

Pebby ran to them, trying to see what was wrong. "Lemme see 'Clure, lemme see. Com' on, lemme help!" Phillip gently pried McClure's hands away from his face, where there were several sting marks just below his right eye.

"Can you open your eye? Com' on, try, 'Clure, try!!!" Phillip gently pulled open McClure's eyelids, and McClure opened his eyes and blinked rapidly as he squinted.

"Man!!! That burns! What happened? I got bit so fast, after that I didn't see a thing!"

"It's better that you didn't," Phillip cautioned. "It wasn't something you would have wanted to see. Scared the crap out of me, really! Com' on, let's get back to the room. You gotta' rest, and I want to wash off those bites."

McClure hugged Pebby tightly and the tinydog licked his neck.

Helping him up, Phillip let McClure lean on him as they hobbled back to their room as Pebby followed dutifully behind.

"This stinkin' room's got no door! I don't want those things coming after us again. How come we never noticed that?" 'Clure asked, holding his eye closed.

"Here, man, lie down on my bed. I'll get some water." Grabbing the pajama top still on the clothes hook, Phillip washed the wounds several times as McClure complained bitterly.

"Easy, man, easy! I'm worn out after that! Industrial-strength mosquitos! Damn!"

Throwing himself on the floor, leaning back against the bed, Phillip sighed. Pebby stretched out beside him and licked his hand to comfort him. She gave a deep sigh.

"Here, girl, you must be hungry. I got a little left-over breakfast wrapped up in this napkin. I'll share." Phillip smiled at her tenderly. *So, this was her life before she came through the Parallax? She must have had to fight to survive here, just like we're doing now.*

Suddenly, without warning, the door to the main hallway burst open and Wassy Wymore, out of breath, hurried in, followed by Mendaleus, who was himself quite out of breath trying to keep up with her. Shaking her head from side to side, she waved her index finger back and forth as she admonished them.

"Wah, Wah, Wah, the skee-bots got'cha! Cry little babies! Wah, Wah, Wah! No, no, no, you babies better learn to listen if'n you want to survive. Right Mendi?" Mendaleus Moniker nodded his head in agreement as he brought out a tiny jar of salve and dabbed it gingerly on the spots all over McClure's face. The red boils were starting to swell, and McClure winced as Moniker dotted each lesion. Phillip could not hold back his frustration any longer.

"Well, this wouldn't have happened if we had a plan! I mean, what do we do next?" Wassy was snickering at him, covering her face with her hands to try and hide it. McClure propped himself up on the floor, still in shock from the stings that left his face dotted with swollen, red, pointy lumps.

After a few seconds, he finally spoke. "Yeah, com'
on, you've got to help us with the plan. We don't
have time to waste. Abby Weathermore probably
got hurt coming through the Parallax, and we've
just *got* to find her. Naji told us everything we would
need could be found in his tailor shop, and that this
little dog knows her way around. We gotta' move on
this! You guys aren't understanding that we gotta'
have a plan! Help us out here, please!!!" Moniker
stood up to his full height.

"Well then, gentlemen," gesturing to Wassy,
who was still shaking her head, rolling her eyes, and
trying not to laugh at McClure's discomfort, "and
ladies," sweeping his arms to include the tinydog,
"let us assemble properly! Follow me!"

Pebby shook her fur, as Phillip readjusted her
gear-vest. Mrs. Moniker had cleaned it thoroughly
and brushed Pebby until her coat shined. Helping
McClure to his feet, Phillip noticed that Wassy continued to blush and giggle at them, and he crossed
his arms defensively.

"Look, let us re-group here a minute, would'ja?
Everyone, just wait in the hallway please. Give us a
few minutes, com' on now, please?" Realizing the
boys' discomfort, Mendaleus ushered Wassy out of

the room, and reassured them. "Of course, lads, of course."

Huffing in indignation, Wassy followed. On her way out of the room, she grabbed Pebby and squeezed her tightly in her arms. "I mean to have this tinydoggie for me own," she whispered, putting her nose in the air as she marched past Phillip. She giggled again and squeezed even harder. Pebby was powerless and she bore the indignation bravely. Phillip patted her head as she was carried by, trapped tightly in Wassy's arms. Pulling the door shut behind him, Mendaleus Moniker exhaled sharply and shook his head. He had little tolerance for petty grievances, and no patience for teenage drama.

Phillip helped McClure stand up and squarely faced him. "Look," Phillip said, "we gotta' be careful. We don't know who to trust. We know Pebby. *Her* sincerity has never been questioned. *But everyone else*, we gotta' be careful. Heck, we got crab-creature metal spiders, and killer wadda' they call it, *skee-bots*, so what else? What else? I mean man, you should get a look at your own face. Remember Noah and the huge robot bird? All these things look like weapons to me, like this isn't something that just started yesterday. These people have been putting together this collection of stuff for a while, right?"

"Yeah," replied 'Clure, "we dropped into a freakin' mess didn't we? Just look at me! Giant-sized pimples, and gooey crap smeared all over my face!" McClure dropped his chin down and looked for a moment like he might get teary. Phillip patted his back as he had seen his mother do when his sister had anxiety attacks.

"Ok, ok, just stay calm. We learned a big lesson. No more chances. No more opening doors when we don't know what's on the other side, Ok? Deal?"

"Deal, man, deal!" McClure rubbed his eyes and composed himself. "Freakin' nut case, that Wassy. Why does she always turn up at the most awful times? Did you see her? She knew about that grotto. She knew those flying crap-bots or whatever they're called were just waiting for us. She knew it!"

"Dude, we walked into it on our own without any help from Wassy! But, no more. From here on out, we protect ourselves, right?"

McClure nodded. "Right. No more Lewis and Clarke." He sniffed a few times. Slinging the backpack over his shoulder, he motioned to Phillip. "Come on, let's pick their brains, and come up with our plan. Finding the tailor shop and Abby Weathermore can't happen soon enough for me. I wanna' get outta' this place, it gets more creepy by the minute!"

Outside in the hall, Pebby was squirming to get down, so Wassy reluctantly let her go. Putting her nose in the air, Pebby sniffed, and sniffed. There was something more than the smell of the cinni rolls. There was something more that was calling her. She stopped, planted her feet, and turned her head to look squarely at Moniker. There was a silent communication between the two of them that no one else could appreciate. He nodded his head.

"Yep, you can. Go on now, girl, go find 'im!" Giving a quick nod of her head at Moniker, she turned, and sprinted away, ignoring Phillip and McClure who had just joined the group.

"Hey!" Phillip called out. "Wait for us! She's going! No Pebby, No!"

Mendaleus placed his hand gently on Phillip's arm. "It's alright, she's alright, remember, she's home now my friend, she's home. She'll be waitin' for youse at the end. She's got her own business to do. Now com' on!"

He marched ahead and stepped up the pace. They coursed through several long tunnels, some requiring them to stoop, some lit by tiny portholes. They

climbed flights of rickety, rotting steps patched together with rough pieces of hardwood. Each staircase evolved deeper and deeper into the earth, like
a mine shaft deep into the subterranean earth, and
the sound of falling water became so loud that the
echo drowned out any their conversation.

After the last flight of steps, which curved on
itself in a sharp downward spiral, they were out
of breath and sweating. The air was damp and the
smell was of pungent, unclean water. The final door,
a wooden circle studded with gears, was locked.
Moniker produced a long, rusty skeleton key and
handed it to Wassy, who opened a series of three
gear locks with the same key. Mendaleus turned a
large gear crank on the wall. It did not take much
effort, and as he turned the crank, the round door
slid open with a loud, deep thud.

Before them stood a laboratory, as sophisticated as the one they had seen at the falconry. Wassy
waltzed in, spinning her dress out around her and
making herself at home. It was as if she had been
there a million times before, an effect not lost on
both boys. A round conference table sat in the corner of the room, and behind the table, blackboards
lined the walls. Against the far wall and running
the length of it was a lab table, complete with glass

containers of gears of all sizes and colors. Pipes and glass tubing connected to small motors under the table, and ominous-looking green and orange iridescent fluid flowed through the tubes. Skee-bots in various stages of assembly dotted the counters.

Phillip immediately thought of Claire's laboratory at home. He had not given her much thought since their journey began. But now, he remembered with a touch of sadness, the days they had laughed together while he perched on one of her lab stools, and she critiqued his soldering techniques. Those days seemed so far away now, and he remembered, looking downward, that their mother had been safely asleep on the couch in the front room. Those days seemed light years away now, and he felt McClure jostle him with an elbow.

"Hey Phills! You falling asleep? Look at those chalkboards!" Mathematical equations peppered the boards and McClure wondered just how much of those equations Wassy actually understood. Realizing that both boys were staring at her, Wassy grabbed two erasers. Laughing uproariously, she clapped them together right in McClure's face. The powdery assault made him sneeze and itch from the irritating dust settling on his pox-marked face. He waved her away and addressed her sharply.

"Get outta' here with that! What are you, a nut case? I'm hurt, man, can't ya' see?"

"Sor...*ry!*" Wassy curtsied gracefully, still holding the erasers as Pebby suddenly raced into the room. She was followed by a white tinydog who resembled her, but as a smaller version. Still, their faces were the same, and their eyes, clearly identical. An over-joyed Pebby romped and raced around the room with the tiniest white dog Phillip had ever seen. There was an unmistakable kinship between the dogs. They romped with reckless abandon.

Oh, Linus! I thought I'd never see you again! I got so much to tell you about everywhere I been, I want so much to know about Gleena and Treena, and Deen, and all the delivery dogs, just EVERYTHING!

Wassy dropped to the floor as both dogs tumbled in her lap and licked her face. Phillip watched amazed, as Wassy turned to him and announced, "This here is Linus. He's Pebby's brother, and she be mighty glad to be seein' 'im!"

Phillip and McClure both dropped to the floor as well, and they formed a perimeter with Wassy as the two dogs charged each other and tumbled. The dogs growled and feigned attacks on each other as the three of them laughed, joined hands, and kept the tinydogs within their protective circle. Watching the scene with interest, Mendaleus smiled to himself as he pulled at his beard. Things were getting interesting.

The Dark Places

The tall, thin man slammed the office door behind him, peeled off his military jacket and flung it carelessly on his chair. He took off his black derby and tossed it on his desk. That is, if you could even call it a desk. Rather, it was an oversized wooden table with claw-legs, heavily lacquered, and covered by a three-dimensional map with miniature flags marking key locations.

Councilman Crashus, the authoritarian ruler of Norwall and its surrounding territories, smirked and turned to look out the massive portico window that overlooked the City Center of Norwall. Dawn was just breaking, and the sky was pink. The gray clouds did not yet cover the three suns, and the buildings glittered in a breathtaking display. Most all of the Eliticon residents lived north of the concentric Circles of the Realm that defined the city proper. But Crashus, along with his cadre of engineers, stayed in apartments connected to his laboratory and warehouses on Wenderling Way, the main thoroughfare of the Inner Circle of the Realm.

The laboratory was the birthplace of the Automaton army. It was where they were produced, programmed, and repaired. His children, his fleet of executive mechanical soldiers, were born here. It was the place to which their observations were relayed and monitored by a small band of his most trustworthy followers It was the military stronghold of his operations.

The majority of the pretty, pastel row houses in the town center had long since been abandoned and their occupants indentured in the Habitons. Their facades, unkempt and worn, showed signs of neglect. That didn't bother Crashus one bit. He was energized seeing the remnants of the ruined lives of the residents that had called Rainbow Ridge their home. Dilapidated shops remained open for the convenience of the upper-level managers and the Eliticon residents, who could freely travel into the City Center on select days. Most of the shops were maintained by the previous Republic of Norwall's cabinet and legislators, who had been given the choice to run their own merchant shops rather than be contained in the workhouses which became known as Habitrons. Many chose to become merchants rather than sacrifice their families to the indentured labor of the Habitrons.

This location in the City Center enabled Crashus to keep a close watch on the commercial productivity in the town, and better yet, stay close to the army of Automatons he created and controlled. He smirked again, a smug, twisted smirk, as he remembered the past forty years since the development of the prototype. *Forty years* to rise in power. *Forty years* to slowly take control of the populace with his rhetoric of ethnic and racial division. Oh, it had all worked to his advantage. Creation of panic in the masses by the threat of invasion from the northwest was the key to his meteoric rise as he won election after election, and finally, several years later, booted out his main competition, Governor Naji Najeem.

His speechs had increasingly, over the years, incited fear in the citizens of Norwall. He had to admit, as he scratched his head, it had taken some time to disrupt the republic and sow the seeds of division. It had taken time and work to discredit the scientists, banish the experts, and convince people to believe the truths he had contrived. He laughed out loud. Especially effective was the propaganda that Norwall was facing extinction from an invasion by the neighboring town of Ochinclast, capitol city of the Westward Islands.

That brilliant move garnered even more financial support for his army of Automatons. His long-game had been successful. He had disrupted the politics of democracy and slowly, over time, fed propaganda, discredited and shamed the intellectuals, and dehumanized entire groups of people. He smiled with delight as he remembered the days of marching citizens out of their row houses and into the Habitrons. Of course, he had argued, it was purely for their own protection.

The ace in his hand was always the Automatons. Convincing people that Norwall was under siege was the key to displacing Naji Najeem, their much-beloved leader, increasingly portrayed as inefficient and weak. Pulling on his white coat and spectacles, Crashus snapped on shoe covers. *Oh, it was a most brilliant move of mine, wasn't it, convincing the fools that the Automatons would be used to protect them from the rebellious minorities and the invading Ochins.*

Punching his code into the heavy, metal door, he entered an elevator controlled by a gear-driven apparatus. But this was not like the primitive steam powered system that ran most of the mechanics of Norwall. No, this was an invention of his own making. A clean, efficient energy cell he nicknamed *The Titan* smoothly allowed the mechanism to run on a shred of energy he cultivated from special rocks that glowed deep-turquoise. The rocks came from the mines of the Outer Bank Islands, far past the outer Circle of the Realm. Swooshing him quickly down several floors into the enormous warehouse and storage facility, the elevator bounced as it stopped. He marched out into the darkness with the requisite pomp of a leader, even though no one was watching. He insisted on keeping the lights down low to effect a twilight aura, and the sconces mounted on the high concrete walls of the fortress gave just enough light to see head.

He grinned to himself. His technology was years ahead of anyone elses, and he refused to share it. He smiled cruelly as he thought of his former partner Norra, struggling with the bulky mechanics of the flying bird prototype. It pleased him greatly to think of her struggles, as well as the impossibility of her assigned project. Pity, her life was on the line.

Pity, she had betrayed him, and found company in that idiot Jeeson.

"Oliveio, where the hell are you!" he shouted, looking for his chief deputy.

"Here, Boss, I'm here," softly replied a short, rotund, balding supplicant who scurried up close to him, but thankfully, not too close. Everyone knew to keep a distance from Crashus. Not one person would dare to offer to shake his hand. Oliveio had been with Crashus since before the insurrection, and he served with blind devotion. Bowing several times as he approached Crashus, his flushed face was afraid to smile. His lips were pursed and his gray eyebrows knotted together in a unibrow look of consternation.

"Sir! What doest thou want?"

"I want the weekly report, you fool! What do you think I want? Silly, unbelievable nonsense! Now, what's the report from the Outer Realm? Be specific, man, come now, tell me! It's not so much the peasants in the Habitrons that vex me, it's the aristocrats that would rise against me, and you know exactly what I mean. If Petraeus Palova for one lousy minute could take control of the Automatons, he'd bring a rising against me, don't you know that? Why am I *always* the one who knows everything?"

"Well, Sir, I suppose he could, but how many of the aristocracy would follow him?"

Crashus spun on his heel and replied sharply, "Perhaps none, perhaps everyone. Who knows. Remember the uprising three years past, led by that band of merchants rising up to put Najeem back as Governor? Maybe I should have killed him outright, but, in my usual show of mercy I gave him a position and a tailor shop so he could prove his loyalty. Didn't the people support me giving him mercy? No one could have blamed me if I had hung him from the wall, you know? The people loved me even *more* for that show of mercy, now, didn't they?"

Oliveio rubbed his chin and nodded in agreement.

"Sure, sure, Sir, no one would have blamed you, but you showed mercy. That got you the approval of the populace, after all, didn't it? And, Sir? I heard the ol' vagrant got steamed by the Automatons a couple'a weeks ago, so's he won't be making no more risings against ye!"

"Interesting!" Crashus rubbed the top of his shaved head. "Interesting, he finally gets what he deserves after all. Any news about the wheat crop?"

"Well, Sir," Oliveio began with trepidation, "There's some possibility that vagrants escaped from Wymore Wheatfield Habitron. The Automats suspected someone was runnin' through the woods around the Wymore Cottage during restricted hours. No one got caught, but it was reported as suspicious activity."

Crashus perked up. "Increase the security runs over the wheat fields and take a census. Specifically, target the Octagon and Gleeful Garment, got it?"

"Yes, Sir. Right away, Sir!" Oliveio bowed several times and backed out the door, returning to Central Command where feed was collected from the new prototype of Automatons. The old rattletrap Automatons still sent coded messages with a series of dots and dashes. But now they were obsolete, and slowly being replaced.

Crashus headed to the warehouse, where rows of Automatons stood at attention in near-darkness, as if waiting for his command. He thrilled just to look at them, and his skin tingled. Forty years of prototype after prototype, all to replace the rattletrap boxed robots he constructed early in his career.

After building hundreds of smaller prototypes, he finally brought the Automaton to life. Secretly, silently, he had persuaded the government to fund their development, believing that they would be the key to food production and manufacturing. The gradual modification of the program was slow, and over a long period of time, the machines morphed from servants to vicious killing machines.

As his gaze moved to the display wall in the warehouse, the collection of featured prototypes demonstrated their evolution through the years. He wrinkled his nose at the primitive versions, with their flashing turquoise eyes, vampy teeth, and obsolete steam pipes running up the back of their heads. Leaning now on the lectern, he pretended he was addressing the army of humanoid Automatons as if they were faithful followers. These supremely efficient specimens were the final answer. It was easy after he discovered the Titan energy cells. Small, efficient, powerful enough to provide energy for the Automatons for months at a time. Powerful enough to energize his army of obedient, violent robots who never questioned him. And, it was all so easy to direct them from his center of power here in the City Center. Pity, the three engineers who had discovered and helped him harvest the Titans had all been quickly tried as traitors and silenced forever.

"Gentlemen!" He laughed at the suggestion of a female Automaton. *Ridiculous!* he had said when it was suggested. *Women were innately inferior. They were soft and they were treacherous. They were not to be trusted, they were only there to be used and controlled.*

"Gentlemen," Crashus repeated, clearing his throat. "Soon you shall be ready to protect and defend those ideals we hold dear. We know, there is *us*, and there is *them*. Never, I repeat, never, shall those two survive as equals. One must always lead the other! And you my good fellows, are the key! *You* are the key to maintaining the social structure on which Norwall thrives! *We are the farmers, and they are the mules!* And, if they do not work as hard as we say, *if they are obstinate, if they refuse to move, we shall only beat them even harder with the sticks!* And, my beautiful creations, YOU ARE THE STICKS!"

He applauded his own soliloquy, and his solitary applause echoed in the cavernous, dimly room. The Automatons, silent, stared at him unflinchingly. Tired, he sat on the edge of the stage, swinging his legs encased in knee-high military boots. *Authoritarian*, that's what they had called him; a *Dictator*. But wasn't he the greatest inventor of his time? Had he not found a way to convert the rattletrap boxes into humanoid machines?

What had begun as a humanitarian venture had morphed and twisted over the years as his mind had morphed and twisted. Fingering the buckles on his boots, as one-hundred-and-twenty Automatons stared straight ahead at him, he blinked several times. In an instant he was back in the Gallegon Village just north of town, back many years before. His daughter was three and she played in his laboratory, as she had done so many times before. These were good years, happy years, while he constructed the prototype of the first Automaton. As he worked on the lab table, she babbled incessantly and imitated her mother, his beloved Catrianna, a dark-haired beauty.

"No, no, no!!!" the baby babbled, parroting her mother, as she tottered up to one of the prototypes and gave it a hard push on the center of the chest.

"No, no, no! Bad Woobot!" She pushed a little harder, and sent the robot crashing on its back, one arm disjointed and lying in pieces.

"WHAT ARE YOU DOING!!! Crashed screamed, as he jumped up, grabbed pieces of the robot and screamed at the three-year-old child, who was cowering in fear.

"NO... no... no... on you Missy! No, no, no, on you!" He said through gritted teeth as he picked up a small wooden dowel stick from the workbench and struck the little girl swiftly and mercilessly across the legs.

"AAUUGH!!!" she screamed, running out of the laboratory. "Bad, bad, bad Daddy! No, no no!!!" She ran, and he started after her. In her running away from him she tripped and fell on the stone cold floor. She lay there screaming wildly, and terrified, he saw that she could not move.

"Bad, bad, Daddy, no, no, no!" She continued to scream wildly and bat at him with her tiny fists as he picked her up and carried her into her mother. The welt from where he had struck her was red and raised, and her leg twisted into a grotesque shape. The next day when he awoke, Catrianna and their daughter were gone.

He didn't see them leave, and he didn't get to say goodbye. He didn't get to say he was sorry for the pain he had caused; didn't get to say sorry for the strike on her tiny baby leg. He would never forget the primal screams of his wife when she saw her daughter's leg. He would never forget that she took the baby in the middle of that night and left without so much as even a note. He would never see them again after that day, and he would never know what happened to them. When they vanished without a trace, his heart was dealt a mortal wound that would never be right again.

Over the years, he became immune to suffering. Over the years, Manipulation and control of the populace had comforted him. He created more Automatons and refined their design so now they were almost human. They were loyal to him, and best of all, they would never leave.

Touching his face now, he remembered the pain of the tattoo. Shortly after Catrianna left him, he ordered the multicolored tattoo burned into the left half of his face. It didn't really matter anymore that she had left, useless woman and her baggage baby, he was better off with them gone. The wide grimace, complete with teeth, made him look as though he had a permanent sneer. He smiled to think of them leaving. Many, many years had passed, and still, to this day, he was not filled with much regret. Their leaving had changed him from a man who had made a grevious mistake, into a monster who could deliberately, thoughtlessly make horrendous, cruel decisions without the baggage of guilt. There was no turning back now. His wife and child deserved what they got; a life without him, precious leader, inventor, genuine genius. What did it matter now? A million dark regrets would not bring them back. Not now, not ever.

The Blood Print

The dogs growled and tumbled as Wassy threw her head back and laughed at their antics. She stopped suddenly and frowned severely.

"Com'ere Linus, let me take a look atcha, com' on boy." She grabbed him roughly and inspected his bandana.

"Will ya look at that, Mendi, he's got a spot on his bandana looks like a blood print, don't it?" She frowned and continued, "I mean, he took over some of Pebby's runs after she was gone, but Deen always gives him the shorter runs in town. Don't know where he'd get a blood print, do you? You got an idea on that Mendi?" Mendaleus leaned over the white tinydog and inspected the kerchief.

"Looks like a blood print to me, and a human one at that. I got *no* idea how it happened, and Linus, you canna' tell us. What've you been up to?" Wassy untied the bandana and slipped it into her pocket.

"Just the same Mendi, I gonna' keep it and show it to Pa. Maybe he kin' make sense of it. Real strange ye know, and I don't want Linus to have the Automats thinkin' suspicious, like tying 'em to a crime or something." Mendaleus nodded his head in agreement.

Linus and Pebby sat side by side motionless as Wassy patted each of their heads. Then, she jumped up effortlessly to take her place at the conference table. With the sharp clickity-clacking of stiletto heels, a middle-aged woman with sharply chiseled facial features, a slender but well-toned figure and silver-white hair entered the room. She made her way quickly to the table, grinning widely and opening her arms to greet Wassy. The two women hugged as if they had not seen each other in decades. Cradling Wassy's head in her hands, the woman looked straight into her eyes. Her staccato tone commanded attention.

"Now tell me *exactly* what you have been doing with yourself today, Missy!" She smiled widely, showing perfect teeth, then continued, "I know you *too* well Wascilla Wymore, and you dare not hide *anything* from your Auntie Maribel. You've *got* to tell me, in *greatest* detail, what you've been plotting and planning this fine Trifecta Day. I shall expect nothing less than an *absolute*, thorough accounting! Go on, tell me, tell me at once!"

Shocked, the boys watched in amazement as Wassy whispered in Maribel's ear, and the women both giggled like schoolgirls. The two women laughed and hugged as if there were secrets between them; some private story that only the two of them understood. Mendaleus, exasperated, cleared his throat.

"I'm wondering if we may kindly interrupt your amusements ladies, AS WE HAVE WORK TO DO!!! Now, let's take our places!" He gestured widely to the sturdy wooden chairs scattered around the table. Pointing at McClure and Phillip, then pointing to the chairs, Moniker dropped his bulky frame into one. His wife daintily slid into the seat beside him, squeezing his arm affectionately and grinning so hard her eyes squinted.

Maribel Moniker's thin, athletic build was in sharp contrast to her husband's portliness. Her silver-white hair was smoothly knotted on top of her head, and haircombs shaped like clockwork gears held wisps back from her face. Her long fingernails were painted a matching silver-white, and her skin pure alabaster. Her enormous light-green eyes twinkled proudly as she watched Wassy take her place not at the table, but at the front of the room where she furiously erased the chalkboard. Wassy was giggling to herself the entire time, although there was nothing particularly funny.

"Go ahead!" Moniker threw his hands in the air. "For the love of all that is holy, PROCEED!"

"Why is she always laughing?" pouted McClure.

"You'd be wise to never underestimate Wascilla, Mr. Clure," Maribel admonished in a whisper. "If you have any hope of getting to the tailor shop, she's your best chance. She knows every nook and cranny in this town, and every place ye's might hide."

"Nothin' worse than a giggly mastermind if you ask me," McClure spit back, and the names McClure, not Clure, thank you!"

"SILENCE!!!" Mendaleus Moniker buried his face in his hands.

"Gentlemen, and *la ... dies*," Wassy began in earnest, as she began to draw on the chalkboard.

"Gentlemen and *la ... dies*," she repeated as she began to draw a series of concentric circles. "Norwall, as we know, is a series of three decreasing circles, named The Circles of the Realm. The outer circle begins just north of Wymore's Wheat fields, swings around to the Five Feathers, and loops at the bottom through the Rastadon Woods to Moniker's Mill, which ye have the pleasure of sittin' in now! *Watch and learn!*" She directly aimed her remarks at the two boys who were sitting quietly, now mesmerized.

"Now, according to my father, the goal is to get ye's to Najeem's Tailor shop, which sits squarely in the Inner Circle of the Realm, a*nd to get ye's there alive.*" Throwing back her head, she rolled her eyes and shook her head from side to side, giving a short chuckle.

"See that? See it again?" whispered McClure, "there she goes again. See what I mean? Why is she always laughing?" He threw up his hands in exasperation, then crossed his arms in front of his chest as he huffed and pouted out his lower lip.

Pulling herself up out of the chair, and rising to her full height, which was actually only a few inches taller than Wassy, Maribel Moniker placed the full weight of her body on the dark lacquered wood of the oversized table and leaned toward McClure.

"Sir!" she chirped in a high-pitched, angry voice. "You would do well to overlook any small idiosyncrasies of Miss Wymore which you find either objectionable, or even downright annoying. You would do well to treat her with the utmost respect, right, Mendaleus?" She poked him sharply with her pointy elbow.

Mendaleus Moniker, startled by the poke in the ribs, looked as if his wife had just awoken him.

"Yes! Yes, indeed! Sorry, a bit tired, here, was working in the lab until late, but yes, Wassy, show the young gentleman what you obtained on their behalf, why don't you?"

Gingerly, Wassy Wymore set down the chalk and she held her head up high as she reached for the canvas bag she had hidden under the table. Pulling out two long, black leather cloaks, she reached her arm all the way to the bottom of the bag, extracting two large masks. The eyes were black, as were the large, conical bird-beak snouts.

"What the heck?" Phillip reached over to touch the matte leather. "I saw something like this at a co-splay convention, you know, 'Clure?"

"Yeah, I remember we were teasin' Claire that she should wear one like that since she was always sticking her nose in your business. I remember she didn't think it was funny, and she got pissed off. Wassy, where'd you come up with these?"

Wassy sighed, resenting his prying. "Well, youse babies, we has healers called Medicons here that comes around when people is sick. They dress in these clothes so people recognize 'em, and get outta' their way. Most of 'em are thought to be really spying on us for the Council. I know that two of 'em did a visitation on Miss Marabel, who thought she was comin' down with the gray-sky cough."

McClure huffed. "So now you got two naked healers running around the countryside?" He covered his mouth and stifled a laugh.

Lifting her chin and setting her jaw firmly, Wassy stared directly into his eyes and addressed him sharply. "They'll not be running anywhere again, so don't youse concern yourself with that! Someone told me they met with just a little bit of misfortune!" Her glance at Mendaleus was a dead giveaway. Maribel angrily whispered in her husband's ear.

Shocked by her accusation, he was indignant. "Absolutely NOT!" he insisted, as Maribel pressed him for an answer, then turned her fury on Wassy.

"Tell me you had nothing to do with this! Either of you!" Maribel probed, a deep furrow distorting her forehead.

"No, ma'am, Miss Marabel, I had nuttin' to do with anything dark, I swear. You know, I just found these clothes neatly folded, they was, outside the door to the cavern, you know, just like them Medicons was going for a little swim?

"Yeah," Phillip whispered to McClure, "I got a feeling what we saw floating in the underground river had some connection to this. Some little swim."

Mendaleus shook his head in denial. "Not a bit of idea what happened, not one bit. Whatever happened, Miss Wymore and I are totally above any suspicion of any wrongdoing. Why, we've been busy in the lab most all day, right Wassy?"

"Oh yeah, oh yeah, we been busy, we been trying to find a way to help these babies." Smirking, she turned and addressed the two boys, who looked shocked.

"Youse boys gotta' have a way to ride in my wagon tomorrow so's we can smuggle youse into the

'Ponics Institute, and this'en here's the safest way. No one gonna' question two healers that hitched a ride with me. I pickin' up a load from Hydroponics tomorrow to feed the workers in the fields. It's on me schedule. The 'Ponics lab is in the north part of the Middle Circle."

"Why not just take us right to Naji's shop and drop us off?" McClure shrugged his shoulders and shook his head. "Seems like a lot of intrigue for nothing."

"'Cause, you dummy, I got me schedule. The only way I's got any freedom is by sticking to the schedule. No questions asked. The Automats know where I should be, and it ain't at Najeem's tomorrow. Later next week, there's due a load of flour and 'vegebles' to the Octogon, so we can git you closer to the Town Center. Youse gotta" bide your time at the 'Ponics Lab till then, got it?"

"Yeah, we got it, it's just taking a lot longer than I thought to get to the shop." Phillip crossed his arms in front of his chest and turned to McClure as he continued, "We still have no clue about Mom, now, do we?" McClure patted his friend's shoulder.

"Look, I'm as worried as you. But, we gotta' be safe. That's our only chance, and we are her only chance. That is, if we can find her, right?" Phillip gave a big sigh and covered his face with his hands. Wassy shrugged her shoulders, and McClure shook his head in exasperation.

The Procession

Phillip and McClure stood in the atrium of the mill dressed in the black leather cloaks which reached to the ground and were belted at the waist. The costumes smelled old, musty, and were hot and itchy. Both boys avoided putting on the pointed masks and derbies until the last possible moment. They peered anxiously out the window waiting for Wassy as Mendaleus and Maribel stood on each side of them, protecting them until the last minute. Mendaleus spoke first, whispering softly into Phillip's ear.

"Remember, picture The Circles of this Realm on the map ye saw yesterday. Wassy has been driving long enough to know the boundaries by heart, and she knows the drivers of each of the routes. Trust her."

Interrupting him, Maribel elbowed Mendaleus out of the way and cautioned, whispering to McClure, "You must remember that you *cannot* go off on your own. Trying to get to Najeem's on your own, well, is a recipe for a disaster. Remember, there are strict rules on who may cross between the circles. Wassy is not permitted to change her schedule or she risks her life."

Mendaleus put his arm around his wife and chose his words carefully. "I know you are worried about your mother, and from what you told me, you have good reason to be. Please know we will notify our people the best we can, so more of us can be looking for her. You'll be safe at the Hydroponics Lab until our people can get you to the Inner Circle, where you can bed down in Najeem's shop."

Maribel added, "Lee Anna Loo has contacts on the Council and she can find out what they know about the disappearance of Pebby and Naji. We cannot have Pebby seen until we are sure she is safe. I know Lee Anna loves her and won't risk her safety." Rubbing Pebby's ears gently, Moniker held her face gently in both his hands.

"Be safe my littlest soldier! Linus will go with you to the Hydro Lab and then he'll return to the Octagon so as to not raise suspicion. Wymore has already sent a message to Deen Diggins to take him off schedule for a few days. Deen is sympathetic to our cause, and he is almost old enough to join us."

"Deen? Whose Deen? Phillip asked.

"Sorry, Deen is the Quartermaster of the delivery dogs. He's your age, and his mother works the bread line at the Octagon Bakery where Pebby was Chief Delivery Dog. You'll meet him soon enough, and he's someone you should get to know. He keeps his ear to the ground at the Octagon, and the more people we can get looking for your mother the better, right?" Phillip nodded, and McClure gave Moniker a thumbs-up.

Maribel turned to them both. "Quick! She's pulling up now! Remember what we practiced. Now, put on the masks! Do just what she tells you to do. Remember, *she will protect you with her life.*"

McClure nodded his head at Phillip, who looked terrified. "Com' on Phills, we can do this. We're doing it not just for us, we're doing this for Claire and Mom. We've got to stay alive ya know, and get us *all* home safely."

McClure could see the bird beak shaking in Phillip's sweating hands. "Just remember, stand tall, look proud, put on authority and the idiots will think we're healers. Com' on, let's go! Ya know, we just fake it 'till we make it, Phills. Now!"

Phillip bobbed his head 'yes' and slipped the pointy-nose mask over his face. The Monikers had stuffed the long curved black beak with fragrant herbs to make the wearing more palatable. Maribel quickly adjusted both bowler hats to just the right angle and gave both boys a quick hug, as she whispered to them, "I know your mother, wherever she is, would be proud! Be safe! Now go!" She blinked back tears.

Pebby and Linus were sequestered on a blanket in a straw chest, and Philip and McClure each took a handle. They marched out the front door, walking with feigned self-assurance. They stood together, silent, as workers in identical white jumpsuits lifted bags of ground wheat from a conveyor belt onto the snail-wagon. All around them, Automatons lined the sides of the driveway, inspecting each bag and monitoring the workers. Phillip and McClure glanced at, but dared not speak to Wassy, who stood at straight attention beside the driver's box of the snail-wagon.

As they planned, as soon as the loading was completed, she raised her hand high in the air. The boys quickly took their places on the rough-hewn wagon bench with the basket holding the dogs between them. The Automatons stood next to them, watching closely as they climbed to their seat. Wassy, not-saying a word, nodded twice and threw them a rope to tie over their laps. When she was sure they were secured, she climbed into her seat and started the engine.

The roar was deafening. Sooty steam puffed from the exhaust tubes, two in the rear, and one overhead. The wagon jerked and strained under the heavy weight of the ground wheat, as the Automatons stepped aside to allow passage. Rumbling down the dusty street, Phillip breathed a sigh of relief. It was McClure who spoke in barely a whisper.

"We did it Phills, we're on the way now, just relax a bit." Phillip, relieved, nodded in agreement.

It was after only about twenty minutes on the bumpy road that McClure noticed a cloud of dust arising on the road in front of them far off in the distance. There appeared to be a massive cloud of dust coming down the narrow road from the opposite direction. McClure jabbed his elbow sharply

into Phillip, who was starting to doze, his black beak
drooped down to his chest.

"What? What the heck?" Phillip jerked back and
shook his head from side to side. "Sorry, I didn't
sleep too good last night, ya know."

"Sshh! Sshh!" McClure admonished.

Phillip was awake now, and they watched in
amazement as a dust cyclone swirled up high into
the sky. They felt the snail-wagon jerk as Wassy sped
up and headed down the road a short distance, then
pulled far off the side of the road to make way for
the procession. She shut off the snail wagon, and
in the silence, they heard the drums beating out a
cadence, growing nearer and nearer to them.

"Holy Mother of God!!!" they both heard her in-
tone in a whisper. "Stay still! Stay very still!!!" Don't
move!"

Phillip glanced quickly back over his shoulder.
He saw her eyes, wide open, and a look of terror as
her head bobbled quickly side to side, almost as if
she was having a seizure.

"Turn around, *turn around* and don' ya be looking
here! Ye put ye's head down when they comin' by, ye
hears me? *And ye lift your hand right up beside youse eye
like we practiced!* Now don' move! *Youse just do what I
do!*" she said through gritted teeth.

Through the cloud of brown-gray street dust, came a large man riding something that looked like a chariot, but was pulled by a steam engine that puffed as if it was in pain. It seemed to strain as though it would burst open. From such a distance, part of his face was dark, as if he were a harlequin, but Phillip could not make out the details. What he saw caused him to stop breathing for a few seconds.

It was the same man he had seen through the crack in the floorboards from the basement hideaway in the Five Feathers Falconry. It was the same man who grabbed Norra's face and threatened Noah with the Terrible Wall. It was the same man, and he looked to be wearing the same hat and military jacket. But, it was what marched behind him that terrified them.

These were not the rattletrap crudely constructed Automatons Naji had described; not the square, poorly assembled rattleboxes they had seen guarding the front of the Falconry, and the Mill. These Automatons were much different. These were an army of precise, synchronous metal machines appearing more humanoid than Phillip had ever imagined. He sucked in his breath sharply and lowered his head as the army of machines passed in perfect cadence. Following Wassy's lead, he raised his hand to his temple, as did McClure, in a feigned salute of submission. He dared not move. The mask partially covered his eyes, but he could see the last row of Automatons all holding a towrope attached to a wooden platform.

On the platform sat a large square cage. Inside, four women and two men sat on plain benches, heads lowered. They were all dressed in simple muslin garb, and the woman had their backs to him. He started to shake violently. The leader had passed them without any response, barely acknowledging the poor calico clad Wassy, her load of ground wheat, and her two passengers, The costumed Medicons did not even merit a second glance. Phillip said a silent prayer. *Please God, not Mom in that cage, please, please, please!*

"It's not her Phills," McClure sighed deeply. "It's not her. Mom is not in that box."

"Poor fools!" said Wassy shaking her head. "They must'a been 'scapping and got caught. They's done for. They either gonna' cook 'em alive, or let the automats pound 'em in Scion Square, anyway, they is dead walkin' so com' on, we gotta' git to the Hydro Lab a'fore anyone misses them two healers. Hang on!"

She throttled the steam engine and pushed ahead while the boys peeked in the basket and saw Pebby and Linus lying perfectly still.

Then Phillip spoke, "That's the same guy I saw at the Falconry. Noah told me his name is Crashus, and he's the one that threatened Norra and Jeeson if they don't have the mechanical bird finished on time."

McClure shook his head in acknowledgement, all the while realizing that the chances were getting smaller that they would ever discover the whereabouts of Abby Weathermore.

"Phills, let's not worry, let's just keep with the plan, get to this lab, and find the quickest way to Naji's so we can find Abby and get the hell outta' here, ok?"

"Yeah, you're right," Phillip agreed. "'Clure, Mom's no dummy. I just bet she found a safe place to hide, and we just gotta' do what Naji said, get to the tailor shop, and start the search from there. Turning to look at Wassy, they found her bobbing her head to some imagined song that only she could hear. It was as if the sight of the doomed prisoners had not affected her in the least. Whether she had become immune to death and destruction, they could not know. Resigned to her control over their survival, they both leaned back and tried to breathe deeply through the uncomfortable masks. They felt the wagon lean precariously as Wassy turned down a side road and headed toward a massive, stone archway. They held on tight as the wagon jostled and lurched down a steep hill. They both felt a rush of cool wind as they passed through the opening. Suddenly, it was as if the world had changed.

They heard the deafening sound of falling water and saw two waterfalls grace the sides of a huge glass done that protruded from the mountainside. The honeycomb-shaped windows reflected the light and twinkled like jewels set in the mountainside. They heard a low growl coming from the basket and as they lifted the lid, Pebby shook out her ears.

"Oh, whoa," Phillip stared in amazement, "I can't believe this!" He took in the craggy mountain, the burnt but still surviving foliage, and stared as Mc-Clure ripped off his mask and inhaled deeply.

"I gotta' breathe! I gotta' breathe some air!" They were all but ignored by Wassy, who continued singing to herself, and turned down a cobblestone side road which snaked around the building. It was obvious she knew the way from previous deliveries, and the churning of the motor prohibited conversation. She blithely continued to sing as she headed for the massive metal delivery doors in the rear of the facility. Blowing her horn in two short and three long blasts, they watched in amazement as the doors opened silently. Slamming the basket lid shut to protect the two dogs, McClure quickly donned his mask and turned to Phillip.

"Ok," he sneered sarcastically, "let's make friends. Maybe we get lucky, and Abby found her way here, and we grab her and go. Forget the damn tailor shop, right?"

"Yeah, forget it all, grab her and go!" Phillip agreed. But, for the life of him, he could not forget the six strangers, heads down, riding in the cage pulled by the Automaton brigade. He couldn't forget the resigned look of desperation of the six strangers, riding helplessly along to their certain death.

The Lunch Date

Claire's feet were propped up on her mother's office desk. Bored to tears and lonely too, she strummed her fingers and chomped on a huge wad of gum. For the life of her, she could not believe that the grand adventure of a lifetime had passed her by, leaving her dejected and thoroughly disgusted at being left behind by the three people most important to her. It was *so boring* being an adult. Phills, 'Clure and her mother were gone and she had no way to communicate with them. Doctor Jarvis Jamison had seen her mother's patients this morning, and now, he was rapping on the office door for the third time. She grinded her teeth together and mustered a reply.

"Yes? What *is* it?" she intoned, frustrated at his repeated interruption of her daydreaming. She was sick and tired of paying bills and opening mail. She was fed up with being Abby Weathermore. "Just checking to see if I can take a little longer lunch break, I gotta' go to the bank. Is that a problem?" he asked softly, sensing her irritation.

"No, not at all," Claire replied, softening her tone and quickly taking her feet off of the desk as he opened the door. She pretended to be interested in the ledger books and schedule. "Ask Jaceena when the afternoon patients start, OK?"

"Sure," he replied. "Hey, wanna' grab a sandwich?"

"Uhhhh, not really, maybe some other time?" Claire felt her cheeks redden.

Jarvis tried to ease her embarassment. "Oh come on Claire, you gotta eat lunch, come on, how 'bout a quick sandwich? I'll treat. Come on. I have to talk to you about an update to the electronic records. I've seen how the system gets bogged down and crashes in the middle of my patient notes. For a fraction of the cost, we can have it updated before your mom comes home. She would appreciate it working faster, wouldn't she?"

He slid his white coat off his shoulders and folded it neatly over his arm. His white shirt and khaki pants were pressed to perfection. He was slim, not unattractively so. He was obviously fit and quite particular about his physical appearance.

Now, he had Claire's attention. She stood up beside the desk, straightening her black skirt which she had paired with black-and-white striped tights. Her long-sleeved lace top completed her outfit, and a black-and-white striped ribbon held back her ponytail. She was choosing her clothes more carefully since this young, attractive physician was paying her attention. Leaning on the desk with both hands, she tried to look the part of the young executive

"You really know tech stuff?" she asked uncomfortably, fumbling for something to say.

"Well, kinda-sorta. I started out as a gamer. It took the pressure off me when I was in med school. I started playing with a bunch of buddies, then I took some classes online. So then, I got a master's degree in game design just for the hell of it, then …" Claire interrupted him.

"Wait a minute. You got a master's degree in video game design for the heck of it while you've been working medical during the day? What kind of person does that?" Smiling, he winked at her. "The

kind of person you should go to lunch with, right?"
She smiled shyly. "Yeah...yeah, good idea! You got a
point there."

"Well," he continued modestly, "everyone's gotta
have a hobby, right?"

Grabbing her black and white shoulder tote, she
walked ahead of him as he followed her out of the
office, noticing her outfit in more detail.

"Say, what's with the black-and-white stripes?
You're not a *Beetlejuice* fan, are you?" he asked
sheepishly.

Claire stopped in her tracks. "OMG, you're a
fan? How many times have you seen the movie?"
she asked. "Probably ten times more than you!" he
replied curtly, raising his eyebrows. He pulled Abby's office door tightly shut. Claire scooted through
the lobby quickly past Jaceena's watchful eyes and
gave a little half-wave. Her mother's best friend was
straightening the magazines, tossing some wrinkled ones into the trash. Jaceena watched the two
of them exit the office and she shook her head in
disapproval.

Claire was changing since her mother left. Her
refusal to give Jaceena a phone number for her
mother was a source of concern. Jaceena imagined
Claire was afraid she would report on her new-

found interest in fashion, and the air of secrecy surrounding Abby's whereabouts. Jaceena was not so easily placated. She had been Abby Weathermore's best friend since her internship years and she was not about to abandon her now. *I got you in me sights Missy, so you can't hide anything from Jaceena!* Watching the two leave the office, she wondered when Claire had last spoken to Abby. Wouldn't there be a log of her calls on the phone bill? Jaceena wondered, making a mental note to find the phone bill.

Outside the office, the Florida summer sun made Claire catch her breath as she pulled on sunglasses.

"Sub shop?" asked Claire.

"No, there's a quiet coffee shop I found on the other side of the plaza, I'll grab my laptop from the car and show you some of my moves, I mean, some of my characters for my game. I'm on the tail end of the program, and I gotta design a short video game for my master's project. I'm set to graduate as soon as I turn in the final. I've been working on it the whole past year, and I'm anxious to get it done!"

Claire's interest was piqued.

"What's it called?"

"It's kinda silly, I'm calling it *Doctor Doomsday's Die-In.*"

Oh, that's rich. You gotta think of a better title than that. Don't you think it's a bit cliche?"

"Yeah, I guess you're right. The title is negotiable. But here's the thing. It's about a doctor, a cool one, of course, who's tired. He falls asleep at his desk in the hospital ... depressingly small office, of course. He wakes up, and when he goes to leave, the door is locked. When he finally pops it open, there are wild characters. Like, the patients have really turned into hideous, killing creatures. He's gotta fight his way out to a safe zone through the boss battles and dungeons. There is a nasty-pants woman supervisor on the security camera, and she's taunting him to just *try* and get out of the building, like it's a threat. She's his worst nightmare. She keeps turning the lights and alarms on and off just to taunt him.

"The patients are the villians too?"

"Yeah. They're monsters. Like, the worst of their traits come to life, kind of like caricatures of who they were. They're looking to eat him alive."

Claire laughed. "Sounds like you have nightmares about these patients? Huh?"

"Yeah, they eat up all my energy sometimes. Don't get me wrong, I love my work. But, it's exhausting, Claire. I haven't had time for much else.

The video games keeps my energy up. You know what I mean?"

Claire nodded in agreement, then added. "Yep, I know. I worked hard on my senior project, but it's not really finished. I'm trying to design an air purification filter that can work in the filthy factories polluting our air." He held the door for her as they entered the coffee shop and Claire followed him to a corner table, where he set up his laptop.

"Look, I gotta show you this." Claire sat close, and he pulled his chair even closer.

Booting up his laptop, he gave her a tour through his school files. She was impressed with the organization; each was neatly organized by course work and assignments. Finally, he opened the game he had worked on for over a year.

"I should warn you, I did the animation too," he confessed, "and some of it needs more work."

"Oh, this is insane! I love it, a robotic monster with a claw arm! What's the doc have, a syringe shooting blood that stuns the robots? That's cool. I love the background. Dark, like it's all underground. Is it a mental hospital?"

"Well, when he wakes up, the hospital has morphed into a creepy, dark place of slime and fog."

"Ooohhh! I love creepy!" Claire sighed as she took over the laptop and started working her way through the levels.

"Got'em!" she bragged as she blasted a hideous creature shooting at her from the confines of a wheelchair. As she moved through the levels of the game, neither of them noticed that it was time for the afternoon patients to be seen. The ringing of both their phones from the office number made them jump.

"Oh, God, Jaceena!" Claire exclaimed, downing the rest of her latte'.

"Hurry!" Jarvis urged as he slammed the laptop shut and quickly paid the tab. Claire grabbed her drink and made for the front door.

"Great game! Maybe we finish it later?" Claire offered.

"Friday night?" Jarvis requested shyly, holding the shop door open for Claire.

"Deal! My place, about seven?" replied Claire as she hurried toward her car, not wanting to face Jaceena twice in one day.

"You got yourself a deal Claire! Game night?"

"Game night!" replied Claire, smiling broadly as she happily waved goodbye.

The Clever Scientist

Pebby and Linus were scratching hard at the top of the basket trying to claw their way out. Reluctantly, Phillip and McClure unlatched it and the two dogs scrambled so hard that the basket tipped and they escaped. Phillip grabbed Pebby and McClure tried his best to get hold of Linus, but both dogs expertly wriggled away.

"Let them go you babies, let 'em go!" Wassy shouted. They been here a million billion times before, let 'em go! They's knowed this place better than youse! Now com' on quick, babies, I got'a schedule to keep! MOVE IT!"

Wassy gestured wildly with her arms, waving them down off the wagon. They had reached the loading dock of the Hydroponics Laboratory. Workers in green-and-white jumpsuits immediately began unloading bags of milled grain from Wassy's wagon. Suddenly, people were closing in closer and closer.

"Let's get out of here quick!" Phillip whispered. As they jumped off the wagon, McClure caught the edge of his long, black gown. There ensued a loud RRIIPP of cloth as McClure dropped to the ground and rolled over several times.

"Yowwwee!" they heard him scream as he grabbed his elbow.

"AAUGH!!!" Wassy screamed. "Fools! Youse babies gonna need these gowns and youse better take care of'em!.

"Com' on, Dude." Phillip offered McClure his hand and helped him up as blood dripped from his elbow. He whispered under his breath, "I'm so sick and tired of her laughing and yelling. Let's ditch her fast as we can, Phills."

Ripping off the sweaty bird masks, they ran across the short, cobblestone bridge toward the entrance. The dogs were trotting far ahead, making their way past two massive metal doors graced by decorative gears of different colored metals. Behind them, Phillip and McClure could hear Wassy tromping along after them, huffing, puffing, and cursing them under her breath. They couldn't make out exactly what she was saying, but they heard the word "babies" sprinkled liberally.

Suddenly, a pair of inner doors slid onto overhead tracks and swung upward with the creaking and turning of gears. They found themselves in a massive rotunda lit from the gigantic dome skylight. The room resembled the face of a gigantic clock, with exit signs marking hallways placed strategically around the clock like spokes of a wheel. The floor and walls were pristine white. Stretching as far as they could see overhead was a dome of honeycomb-shaped, faceted glass. Semilunar counters stood in front of each of the twelve doors as a staging area for supplies and deliveries. Hand trucks and dollies were in various stages of loading.

Wooden boxes held fruits and vegetables. some of which were unreconizable. There were purple mellons, and tiny orange heads of what looked like broccoli. There was round squash, and bunching onions that were big as baseballs. Workers in citrus-green and white jumpsuits could be seen entering through the twelve doors, pulling wagons and pushing carts loaded with produce.

All around the clockwork rotunda, an army of workers sorted and loaded items into wooden crates. Other workers loaded the crates onto dollies which moved outward through the same tunnel where Phillip and McClure had entered. Managers in lab coats holding clipboards were inspecting each load while they scribbled madly on the audit sheets.

Suddenly, without fanfare, marching through one of the doors came a tall, slender, dark-skinned woman outfitted in an immaculate high-collared white lab coat and sensible shoes. Multiple measuring devices and gadgets stuck out from her pockets, and her shoes were comfortable oxfords with thick rubber soles. Her heart-shaped face was covered with freckles, her nose aqualine, and her eyes the deepest turquoise. She held Pebby, who licked her face and at the same time writhed to get down. Phillip jealously and silently watched the scene.

"Come to Mamma, little baby!" Lee Anna Loo ordered, as she dropped to the floor, sitting beside the little scruffy dog and tousling Pebby's mop top haircut. "I thought you was a goner, and here you are! Ohhh ... baby girl, I've missed you so!" Pebby quickly threw herself upside-down on Leena's lap to get the perfect belly rub. Linus joined them, and before long, Lee Anna Loo was leaning backwards and toppled over with both dogs scrambling to get to her face. They covered her with licks. "Pebby!" Lee Anna laughed so hard that tears ran down her face. "Pebby! Gleena told me you were gone! Really, you gave me such a scare. Gleena was cryin' her eyes out! Who'd you bring to see me? What's going on here?"

Lee Anna Loo rubbed her eyes, and Pebby and Linus stood smartly at attention. As Wassy gave her a hand and helped her up, she addressed Lee Anna head-on.

"Miss Loo, do you remember me? *Miss Wascilla Wymore*, expert driver of the steam wagons, daughter of Wallace Wymore, Esteemed Director of the Wheat Fields? He has instructed, no, rather *ordered* me to bring these *babies*, I mean these *boys* here."

Moving closer to Lee Ann Loo, Wassy whispered in her ear. *"They's been sent from someplace far away by Naji Najeem, who couldn't make the trip. Naji gave strict instructions to them that they gotta git to the tailor shop, where he's left things for 'em with instructions, secret instructions, no less, to do his bidding here in Norwall. Miss Loo, you must keep this secret, even from all youse peoples! Does you get it? Can you keep this, you know, hush-a-*

hush?" With that, she chuckled loudly and clasped her hand to her mouth, then continued.

"Whoops! Maybe I said too much! I'm bringin' these babies to you to keep 'em safe 'til we can git 'em to the Inner Circle with no person takin' notice. We is figuring they kin ride with your next delivery down to the Groomerly, or Gearful Garment, where they can slip quite peaceably to Naji's shop and hide there. Can you agree to this? My father says if you cannot, I am to return these babies, I means boys back to Mendaleus Moniker for further instructions."

Lee Anna Loo listened carefully without saying a word. Then, she tilted her head and nodded in assent. She looked around her to see who might be listening and then she whispered.

"Wacilla Wymore. Now, I myself am worried about the loyalty of some of the laboratory captains. But, and I must say BUT! You know that I put great store by your father Wallace. If he says to keep a secret, then I *shall* keep a secret. *I shall keep it with my very life!* Hiding them could work, could work, but they'll have to agree to blend in with the workers. I don't have to tell you Wassy, that some of the workers here are scientists who were high in the old regime and they might be partial to Crashus and his cronies. They might keep contacts in the Council and have ties to the Eliticons. Our next delivery is in five days, so they can work 'til then, lay low, fit in with the crew. and we'll just keep Pebby and Linus too. I wouldn't say anything to Gleena just yet, we don't want word out on the streets that Pebby is back, too many questions will be raised. You know, it might stir up the idea that Naji would return and raise resistance against the Council, got that?"

Wassy, for once, was speechless, but nodded in agreement. Pebby also nodded her ascent. Phillip spoke up.

"Excuse me please Ma'am, but we came here, like Wassy said, under the direction of Naji Najeem, a new friend we met in our own land. We believe he came to our home by accident. But, then, our mother made the same mistake, coming to Norwall by accident. We believe she might be hurt, and we came here to find her and take her back home."

McClure interrupted, "Have you any information about a tall, brown-haired woman that might have come here in the last two weeks?"

Lee Anna Loo rose and stood up to her full height. Her curls bounced as she walked over to stand directly in front of Phillip and McClure as she addressed them. "First, I fancy myself a scientist and I keep my nose stuck in the lab, but I know Naji quite well. He was the governor of Norwall for many years, and he made sure I had the supplies I needed to run my experiments, no questions asked!" She ran both hands through her tousled curls, pulled her hair back, and swiftly tied it back with a green ribbon. She paced back and forth in front of the boys, her long white coat flaring out behind her.

"I never saw Naji do *anything* by accident. If he came to your land and found you, then I am *quite sure* it was not by accident. I am sure that he had every intention of finding you and sending you here for a purpose. Now what that is, is anybody's guess. We have got to get you to his tailor shop, if that is his wish. One thing you must understand, Naji loves the citizens of Norwall. No one would dare question his devotion to us. He would give his life for one of us, or for all of us, never doubt that. If he sent you, he knew *exactly* what he was doing.

Ignoring everything she had just said, McClure stood directly in front of her and repeated his question.

"HAVE ...YOU ... SEEN ... OUR ... MOTHER? You heard anything about a lost woman, someone new?" McClure stared right back at Leena, repeating his request slowly in a measured tone, as if he was speaking to a small child.

"No Sir, I have not. But, I have a lot of friends, and I can get word out through the Nautilus network, our secret chain of communication."

"We think she might be hurt, so we've got to find her as quickly as we can, do you understand?" Mc-Clure raised himself on tip-toe, to stare directly into Lee Anna's face.

"Well, I understand. I don't know anything yet, but not to worry! I'll mull it all over, like I said, put the word out through the Nautilus network, and we'll talk later! Come on, let's get you changed, and into the proper clothes. We'll store these costumes. Wassy, they are in good hands, so you best trot along and keep your schedule. It won't do to raise suspicions, now hurry on there, but first, give me the biggest hug, no?" Wassy ran to Lee Anna and threw her arms around her as Pebby and Linus stepped back.

"I love ya, Miss Loo, take good care of them dogs too. You know I mean to have Pebby for me own? I don't know why she cares about these babies!"

"Yes, I know, I want her too, but she is a free spirit, and we have to give her that freedom, Wascilla, don't we?"

Wassy shook her head in agreement as she picked up Pebby and squeezed her once more and nuzzled her neck.

"I love ye, little doggie, I love ye! Now be careful, and stay safe with Miss Loo. Don't 'cha be running off to do no deliveries!" She wiped her eyes and waved a quick little good-bye to the boys as she hurried down one of the dark hallways.

"Will we see her again?" asked Phillip.

"Oh, I don't think we're quite rid of Wassy Wymore," retorted McClure. "She's like a bad rash!"

They both laughed as Lee Anna Loo shook her head in amazement and led them through an archway at the four o'clock position on the rotunda. The followed her down pristine white-tiled hallways for a short distance, where she unlocked a stainless steel door, one in a long row of many. There were two tubular bunks mounted on the wall, and two small metal desks containing bookshelves and a writing tablet. A small adjacent bathroom with a steam shower and toilet completed the suite. Two small metal bureaus held folded uniforms, the same citrus-green and white they had seen on the other workers.

"Do you know anything about hydroponics?" Lee Anna Loo asked, flipping open a text book from the desk, and fanning the pages.

"No, Ma'am, but I'm sure we can learn," Mc'Clure offered.

"Well, most of the worker's have a background in science, so you better brush up on your didactics tonight. They will expect you to be the experts, and you might just get found out if you don't know anything! We'll try to pass you off as visiting scientists, and I'll assign you to some lower level jobs to get your feet wet, but you'll have to study hard! You can join the others for

supper in the dining quarters tomorrow, but you might be questioned, so be prepared. Tonight, you will eat supper here and try to study all you can about the science of it all. The dinner bell will ring in a few hours, ok?"

She smiled and pulled the door shut tightly as her white lab coat swirled around her. McClure had already plopped down into the straight-backed chair at the desk and was devouring the books detailing chemical reactions necessary to produce fruits and vegetables with only water. Phillip huffed, exasperated.

"Wadda ya want to bet the door locks from the outside? Wadda ya want to bet?" Jiggling the knob, his fears were confirmed. "Damn!" Why does everyone lock us in? I don't get it!"

"Yeah," McClure retorted, did'ja happen to notice that Pebby is on the other side of the door?"

"Crap!!!" retorted Phillip, slamming his fist down. "How'd we let that happen?"

McClure didn't answer. He just shook his head and kept speed- reading the text open in front of him on the desk, taking notes on his tablet.

The Table of the Elements

They stayed up late devouring the textbooks. McClure, always a quick study, made it through the first six chapters. Phillip, on the other hand, distracted by worries, methodically took copious notes on Chapters One and Two. His remorse was like a bad movie that replayed his misdeeds on an eternal loop. His mind kept drifting to how he had dreaded helping his mother maintain the plantings in the front courtyard and had scoffed when she forced him to smell various herbs to learn their names. He had stubbornly avoided her attempts to share her vast botanical knowledge. She had completed enough classes at the local extension service

that she had been awarded a Master Gardener cer-
tificate. He wished now that he hadn't brushed her
off, and better still, had paid attention.

Not only was the hydroponics textbook highly
technical with regard to plant cultivation, but it also
dealt with nutritional requirements of fruits and
vegetables. The chemistry was quite complicated.
Some of the Norwellian fruits and vegetables were
ones they had never even seen before. Nevertheless, he was determined to push through his shortcomings and understand the complex scientific
principles.

The next morning, McClure rose early and was
already at his desk, concerned he would unwillingly
be forced to converse with one of the scientists. He
cleared his throat and coughed loudly a few times to
wake up Phillip. Finally, his roommate stirred.

"Oh great! Just another day in paradise!" Phillip
said, as he yawned, stretched, and took his place at
his desk. Ten minutes later they heard a series of
chimes like the deep chiming of a grandfather clock.
The deep tones vibrated through to their bones. The
sound of the three short and one long sound, Lee
Anna had warned them, would herald food service
in the main dining room.

"Come on, Phills, I'm starving!" exclaimed McClure enthusiastically as he loudly slammed his book shut. Dust and pieces of wrinkled yellow pages flew out of the tome and landed on the desk. His dark brown cotton pants and shirt were too large and he set to work rolling up the cuffs and sleeves.

"Dude, you're swimming in that mess," Phillip chuckled. "I'm jealous! Mine's too tight, just look!" Flexing his muscles, Phillip heard a ripping sound on the left underarm seam.

"Phills, come on before you split it! Don't bend over or your butt will be in the open air and it's way too early for that. Now, let's head out for food!" McClure, frustrated with their confinement, sighed and shook his head. "This should be interesting," he remarked acidly.

They heard an automatic pop as the lock on their room door released. The door opened slightly with a second, even louder, "pop" sound. A long line of men in dark brown work shirts and pants paraded past silently, all of them staring straight ahead. Phillip peeked out, trying to avoid being noticed.

"Not a chatty bunch, are they?" he commented. "They look like freakin' zombies. Com' on let's just blend in, yeah?"

"We're blending into a perp walk of zombies?" McClure asked. "How is that alright?"

Phillip shrugged his shoulders, grimaced, and raised one eyebrow as they stepped out into the pristine, white-tiled hallway. Dozens of men, some their own age, passed them without acknowledgement. Each man had the same brown shirt and pants, same brown leather belt, same brown work boots, and same dead-ahead solemn stare.

"Creepy man, *real* creepy," McClure muttered under his breath. He walked, performing his favorite zombie walk, while Phillip put a hand over his mouth in an attempt to stifle laughter. Following the stream of workers, they headed back though the atrium and entered the tunnel located at the two o'clock position. The tunnel was short. It opened into a cafeteria lined with stainless steel tables and a buffet line manned by workers in brown and white pin-striped work-suits. It was clear that there was no selection as far as the food choices. All the trays were exactly the same, and held the same colored food cups. Phillip grabbed a tray when it was his turn and McClure followed his lead. Each tray was already loaded with food and they carried it to one of the stainless steel tables. The food was pureed. There were five compartments on the tray, and each compartment held a different color of food. Starving as they were, neither of them could find the courage to pick up his spoon.

Afraid to speak, they quietly sat next to each other. The silence in the room was eerily only broken by the clatter of the metal spoons hitting against the trays.

"What's this mush?" Phillip muttered, whispering under his breath.

"Crap! This is baby food!" 'Clure whispered back, gritting his teeth, careful to avoid being heard. Fifteen minutes later, they once again heard the chime: one chime, two chimes, then three in rapid succession. In synchrony, the entire line of men stood and carried their trays to a station in the corner of the room. It was then that they saw two Automatons standing guard over the conveyor belt.

They glanced at each other, then marched likewise, staring at the grimacing metal men watching the disposition of the trays and ensuring that no spoons were confiscated. They could not help but notice their vicious, pointy teeth. They winced at the angry faces and flashing turquoise eyes. As McClure caught his foot in the rolled up cuff of his pants, he stumbled and caught himself. It took barely a nanosecond for the robot to raise his left arm and point his weapon directly in 'Clure's face.

Phillip grabbed him by the elbow. and helped him regain his balance. Both boys froze and stared wide-eyed at the box-like metal robot that whirred and chattered his vampy teeth, all the while keeping his raised weapon ready to fire. The other men in the room ignored the standoff completely, as if nothing was amiss. McClure found his face inches away from the hissing box of metal, which rattled as steam extruded from the pipe on top of his head and his turquoise eyes flashed. The pointed teeth chattered a warning as a small stream of steam puffed from his drawn blaster. McClure felt the hot steam begin to scorch his face, but then the robot calmed, retreated a few inches, and slowly dropped the blaster back down by his side.

"Let's go!" Phillip whispered, spinning them both around and hurrying them away. As they exited the archway, McClure wiped the steam from his face.

"Let's head back to the room, ok? I'm kinda' spooked now by the garbage can man. Did you see that arm raising up? Did'ja see those teeth? That metal freakazoid was after me, man, I need a break! What the heck are those pointy teeth for? You tell me! Tell me Phills!" McClure gave a shiver and wrapped his arms around himself as if he was freezing cold.

"Yeah, I got it. I got it. You're safe now, just try and relax, man," Phillip said as he tried to calm McClure. "Look," he continued, "let's just not look back. Let's try and get through the next five days 'til we get a lift from here, and keep trying to find Mom. Keep focused, man, just keep focused, ok?"

"Yeah, well, you keep your focus now too, Dude, cause here comes a nightmare walkin'." McClure gestured as an extremely tall, emaciated man with spiky, gray hair sticking out in points from his head rapidly approached them. McClure noticed a wooden baton hanging from his belt. The man clapped his hands and pointedly shouted.

"Gentlemen! Gentlemen! You are needed in the microchem lecture hall! Come, chop chop, chop, CHOP!!!" He clapped his hands three times in rapid succession and pointed them to another archway located at the number seven position on the rotunda schematic.

"Hurry, hurry! Not to be late you know. Professor Loo has informed us that you've been sent by the Council to visit for several days, and I must say, I particularly *do* look forward to your take on our recent body of work!" Now clasping his hands and directing his bulging eyes upward, the skinny man looked for all the world like he was praying.

"Oh, I hope we are on track! Nothing like presenting our research for a fresh take on the herbology!" He motioned for them to hurry. "Come, come now!"

"O ... M ... G! He looks like a big praying mantis!" Phillip muttered under his breath, walking slower to let the man get ahead of them.

"I say we make a fast break!" McClure whispered. The man suddenly pivoted and stopped abruptly, as if he had heard them, his hand reaching for the wooden baton hanging from his belt.

"My apologies, gentlemen," he said, extending his hand. "Geoffrey Gilgorey, Second-Scientist-in-Command after Professor Loo. She instructed me to welcome you with the dignity and accolades that visiting scientists deserve! I find it unbelievable that you are so experienced at such a young age, but ... but ... genius is not to be questioned, correct me if I'm wrong?"

Turning back around and marching with fortitude in a stiff cadence, Geoffrey led them down another side hallway as his heels click-clacked on the white tile floor. He walked with purpose, his legs raised perpendicular to the floor on each step, as though he was marching. The boys glanced at each other. McClure's eyebrows were raised so high that Phillip could not help but try to suppress one of his demonic laughing fits. McClure put his fist up to his mouth and bit his finger. They quickly followed, and were led down another hallway deep into the bowels of the Hydroponics Institute.

"Should we be droppin' bread crumbs?" asked Phillip, stifling nervous laughter. Any sense of levity faded away as they were shown into a conference room filled with similarly clad men in brown work shirts and pants, all sitting quietly in straight-backed metal chairs, most of them silently staring straight ahead. Gilgorey motioned them to two chairs in the front row and took his place at the podium. He cleared his throat and began.

"Gentlemen! I am pleased to present two esteemed scientists sent by Council to review our current procedures and to give us an update on their research. Please give a warm welcome to Phillis and Clue McWeather! Let's hear first from our own Chee-Chee Chimone who will give us all a quick update on our progress for this week. Then, we'll give our visitors the floor, with a warm welcome from our own Hydroponics Institute Science Section!"

Robotic applause followed, as a slender, seven-foot-tall dark-haired man took the podium.

Without smiling, Chee-Chee launched into a robotic recap of the recent activities of the in-house scientific team. He detailed the recent discovery of the element carbon, which he boasted, can form bonds with four other elements! As Chee-Chee scrawled names of elements on the chalkboard, Phillip listened intently. McClure squirmed in his seat, glanced at Phillip and got a funny feeling in his gut. Holding his hand over his mouth to act as cover, he whispered to Phillip.

"Don't do it Phills, whatever you got brewing in that head of yours, don't do anything stupid!" Robotic applause heralded Phillip's introduction as he made his way to the podium. McClure covered his face with his hands for a moment, and inhaled deeply. Dropping his shoulders and grabbing the edges of his chair, he slowly shook his head side to side rapidly, trying to signal a strong "NO!"

Grinning modestly, Phillip took a deep breath and remembered the fun Friday afternoons with his family, where he took center stage and described his weekly progress. Was this so very different? He thought back to the infamous whiteboard Claire had propped in the kitchen as she helped him study for final exams in chemistry. He could see the picture clearly now, and he heard her voice loudly chastising him.

Com' on Phills, you silly, just look. If you were to fold this chart in half, you'd get it! The guy that invented this thing liked to play cards. He put the elements in rows like you put the cards in rows in solitaire. Look. If you fold the periodic table in half, the two sides show what metals bind with which other metals. Got it Phills? You got this? Yeah, YOU GOT THIS! The phrase repeated over and over and over like a stuck record in his head. As he took the podium, he began a soliloquy.

"Gentlemen! What if, ... and I say *what if*, we separate the metals by their weight, then list them, in order by their increasing weight? Would this not organize our work? Would this not enable us to see relationships, and to forge ahead, with purpose, with clarity, and with complete confidence in our abilities? Gentlemen, I give you the culmination of our work, our newest theory, one that we simply call, *The Periodic Table of the Elements!*" Thunderous applause erupted, but the audience still sat expressionless as they clapped in unison.

Raising his hands in the air to quiet the crowd, Phillip announced another revelation.

"And,... and,... what if, gentlemen, we pass currents through each of the sixty-three known elements and determine their weight? We call this THE ATOMIC WEIGHT! I tell you gentlemen; *Organization is the key! Organization is the key to being a leader!*"

The crown stood in unison as if prompted, and cheered even louder. Phillip beamed as he basked in the glory. *Oh, I sure wish Claire could see this!* McClure, still seated, was the only one not rising and cheering. His hand was pressed to the side of his head, as if he was nursing a terrible headache. He squirmed restlessly in his seat. He kept glancing at the Automatons, blasters half-cocked, marching back and forth outside the lecture room. Phillip was again raising outstretched arms in the air, motioning with his palms ratcheting downwards to quell the crowd.

"Yes, yes, fellow scientists, we place these elements in columns, ordered by ascending weight, and we organize them! Yes, ... Yes, ... *Organization is the key to being a leader, a great man once told me!*" Phillip took a quick bow and returned to his seat, giving a quick salute to the crowd. They continued applauding, while they rose all together, giving him a standing ovation. McClure covered his eyes and shuddered with fear.

The Threat of the Wall

Crashus dropped his head in his hands. The new prototype was causing more trouble than he'd ever expected. System failures and scarcity of the Titan turquoise crystals that powered the Automatons was causing frustrating delays in the schedule. He had promised the Council that he could produce a new prototype this year; an Automaton that actually looked and acted like a human. An Automaton so powerful and so unique, that one could hardly know that it was not human.

Still, in order to maintain absolute control, Crashus was faced with caring for the ever-increasing demands of the Eliticons. *Being an autocrat could be tiring*, he thought, and he looked up as the woman in the white coat breezed through his office door. Her pockets were filled with tools of her trade: an assortment of pen nibs, magnifying spectacles, and small rolls of twine. From her pocket, she withdrew the most luscious, pink, round fruit. Fuzzy skin protected the fruit, but not from Lee Anna's knife as she sliced it open on a small white cloth she placed on the desk.

"Try it, Crashi, com' on, try it! Grown just for you, and there's plenty more on the way. Com' on, you don't need to have your taster try it first, here, watch me!" She bit into the other half of the fruit still in her hand, and smiled generously as the juice dripped down onto his desk.

"Well, I suppose that since you haven't dropped dead, it's probably not poisoned, yes?" Crashus asked, as he bit into the luscious pink fruit and used his kerchief to wipe juice splatters from his face.

Lee Anna Loo smiled. The freckles that covered her face seemed more prominent., Her hair was pulled back into a series of neat, pretty braids which were decorated with green and white beads. Even though she was a scientist, Crashus found that she was not unattractive. But, she was not an Eliticon. She would never be an Eliticon. She was a worker, and she had always been, and would always be just a worker. Never an Eliticon. *A brilliant and beautiful worker, but a worker just the same,* thought Crashus, as he watched her devour the juicy fruit. *Providers. We call them "providers" because they provide for the rest of us. Wasn't it me that coined that term? How clever! Instead of calling her a botanist, or calling Gilgorey a brilliant taxonomist, we reduce their status to the common by calling them all one common name. Providers. We lower them by taking away their accomplishments and dropping them all to some bane, common level. Brilliant, Crashus, just brilliant!"* He said to himself.

"Tasty, no?" she asked as she also wiped her face. "All grown with hydroponics. Yes, water and minerals only. Of course, the fruit gets a little heavy, but we tie up the branches. What do you think, Crashi?" He stood up from the desk, and walked around to her, and quickly grabbed her by her chin.

"I think, Missy, I think, that I heard a rumor that several providers ran off from Wymore's wheat fields, and might be sheltering at your place. You heard about that? Any new recruits to your team?" Wide eyed, surprised and at the same time shocked at his crudeness, she shook her head.

"Uh uh," she tried to mouth as he continued to hold her by her chin.

"Well, Missy, you better be honest with me, and I do mean honest. My air fleet reported movement in the woods by the wheat fields last week, so come on, 'fess up now. I know you've got a heart of gold, but I'd hate to see you swinging from the Terrible wall, gettin' that pretty white coat all dirty. That'd be a shame now, wouldn't it?" He roughly pushed her backwards and she scrambled to keep from falling. Wiping her face, she shook her head.

"Nope, nothing. I mean I've heard of *nothing* like that. Of course, I'll keep watch. You know my loyalty is without question, Sir." She answered fearfully, afraid that he would find fault with her and terminate her on the spot. If she misspoke, he would surely send her to her miserable, torturous death in a heartbeat. He strutted and paced around the room.

"Well, let's keep it that way, Missy, remember, your value is in what you provide. Nothing more. All that knowledge, all that smarts in that pretty head o' yours, it's all nothing. What counts, and ONLY what counts, is what you can do for us. You and all the other hundreds of providers that think you are all so smart, you and that bird-lady Norra! *All just nothing more than the provider class! You all are nothing but pro ... viders!* You got that?"

"Yes, Sir ... Yes, sir. I understand sir, we are the *providers*, and we are at your disposal! Yes, sir!" Lee Anna exclaimed, as she shook her head affirmatively like a bobblehead doll.

"Well, just remember that, and remember that you serve and provide at our pleasure! Don't forget you are disposable, you and that big science brain of yours. Don't make me dispose of you, you and your other *providers*!" He snarled and shook his finger directly in her face as he thought of the new prototype, which would make her job obsolete. He imagined her hands behind her back tied with rope, and he smiled sardonically. The tattoo on the side of his face made him look even more grotesque, and Leena Loo cowered with fear.

"Off with you now provider, return to your lab, ... and PROVIDE!" He raised his arms widely in the air, as she scurried out the door and jumped in her steam wagon. It rattled loudly as she pulled away. He watched from his portico, laughed a few chortles, and cleaned the front of his desk where she had set the fruit. He muttered to himself under his breath.

"Filthy scum.... Providers ... brilliant move, lowering them all to one common denominator ... providers. *They give, and I take. They give, and I take,* he continued to mutter in a sing-song voice as he readied himself for another trip to the labyrinth of laboratories under his office. *The prototype is calling me. The prototype will never leave me, and the prototype won't ever expect a pat on the back for serving me,... the prototype will be per...fection,* he thought to himself.

Back at the Hydroponics Institute, Pebby was sprawled on the white tile floor in Lee Anna Loo's quarters. She was stretched out in what Phillip called full-t-bone formation, belly flat to the floor, stubby legs stretched out to the sides. She heaved a long sigh, exasperated and worried that she had not seen Phillip since their arrival at the Institute. She always thought Lee Anna was her friend, but Lee Anna had left for the day and Pebby was locked in her quarters. Why was she trapped here, and where were the boys? It all made Pebby nervous.

The plan was to get them all to Naji's tailor shop. But, what if Lee Anna Loo was keeping her here at the Hydro Lab? She wouldn't be much help to the boys if she was trapped in these quarters. They were all in unfamiliar territory. If Phills and 'Clure rode the transport, they would be dropped off in the middle of the inner city. The Automatons would surely recognize them as intruders, and Pebby couldn't bear to think of what would happen next. She *had* to be their guide; wasn't that what Naji wanted? His instructions echoed in her head. *Take them to the shop, Pebby, and show them the lab beside the stairs, don't let them come face to face with the Automatons, or they will be recognized and killed on the spot. You know every inch of that ole' clockwork town, so stay with them, please! You've got to!!!*

So here she was, trapped and useless. But Lee Anna *had* to come back sometime, and she would be ready. For now, she would explore every inch of the quarters. Nosing her way around the floors, she sniffed at every corner of the suite. While every inch was covered in white tile, the kitchen area had wood cabinets. The hand-carved cabinets were easy to open, and Pebby nosed her way into each and every one of them, searching hopelessly for an escape route. Instead, found a box of biscuits. *Didn't she deserve to eat?* Careful not to leave any traces of her handiwork, she made certain to leave no crumbs behind as she carefully nosed the cabinets closed. Hearing the front door of the suite open as the gears of the lock tumbled, she heard a familiar voice.

"Pebby! Sweetums! How's my favorite puppy? Did you miss your Lee Lee?" Picking up Pebby, Lee Anna nuzzled her neck.

"Well, well, well! Tomorrow's the day. Your boys are leaving for Town Center, and we need to wish them well! You know I always said you would be better off here than running around this old town, and I *know* we can be happy together!"

Setting her down carefully, Lee Anna took off her lab coat and continued.

"You know, *nothing* would make me happier than you settling in here, right? You'll have a chance to say your goodbyes properly tomorrow. Now, let's get you some supper!

Pebby nodded in assent, but the gears in her brain were spinning faster than ever. She wasn't giving up on Phills and 'Clure. Not now, not ever. Not on her life.

The Horrible, Terrible Mist

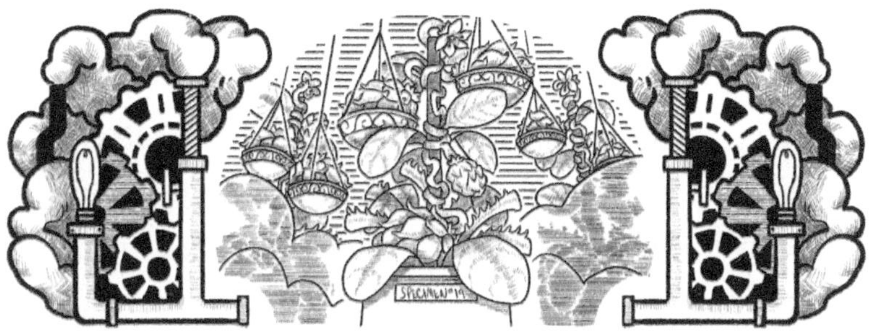

The presentation had come off without a hitch. McClure had reluctantly remained silent while Phillip expounded on the organization of the elements. His "B-plus" grade in chemistry had been earned by paying attention to the cram sessions in the kitchen, hosted by Claire. His bravado during his lecture had earned them a promotion of sorts. Instead of sharing meals wth the general population, they were summoned to enjoy meals with a select group of scientists who had access to the labyrinth of laboratories and environments housing the different classifications of vegetation. They typically began their day in the Macronutrient Lab, which housed the largest and the most proliferative selection of plants.

"Phills, concentrate!" McClure cautioned, as they pushed a wooden cart filled with test- tubes and chemicals. Phillip was overwhelmed by the magnificence of the room, with its high-domed glass ceiling and lattice work of support columns. Gigantic plants grew from long rows of white wooden troughs and wound their way up, supported on massive white trellises. The troughs were filled with the immense root systems, and the water refreshed every twenty-four hours. They could hear giant steam turbines pushing water from the two waterfalls that flanked the facility, inwards to the various laboratories. Their job was to check the acidity of the water and to add supplemental chemicals to neutralize toxins and as well as feed the plants.

"Yeah, Yeah, Yeah," Phillip replied, yawning, "I didn't sleep too well. I was trying to figure out the chemistry so I don't look like a fool, ya' know?" He looked up at the massive vines which were thicker than his waist. The monstrous leaves were as large as his bunk bed, and the luscious fruit hanging there had the rough shell of a cantaloupe, but was four times the size. From support poles hung string baskets which supported the giant fruits and kept them from straining the monstrous vines. McClure shook his head as he resentfully pushed the cart along, heading for the next feeding station.

"Yeah, well if you had kept quiet, instead of enchanting them all with your speech, we could've blended into the background. Now, they expect that you, and I mean WE, are expected to be the big brains with all the answers."

Phillip sheepishly answered. "Yeah man, I was just trying to blend in ya' know?"

"Blend in?" McClure was exasperated, but he kept his voice to a low whisper as he chastised Phillip. "Blend in? You got them putting us on a pedestal now. Here we are, trying to analyze the chemicals in the growing solutions when, hell, we got no idea of what's going on. Don't you get it?" He pushed the cart along the row, catching his white lab coat on a wooden railing and pulling it loose as he fumed, tearing the corner of his pocket.

"Yeah, I know, just try and blend in, can ya?" Phillip asked softly, as he dipped his test tube into the growing solution and put it back on the rack as he continued. "I mean, look at this! They got these massive plants outta this growth solution. Kind'a amazing isn't it? I sure wish Mom could see it!"

He looked up in utter amazement at the three-story green vines dripping with the tasty red fruit he had sampled yesterday. Pushing the cart to the next row and dipping his own sample, McClure agreed. "I know, I see it too. This is more than amazing. If we can learn how they are doing all this, we can take the information back and really have something new when we get home. I get it. But, the whole point of the trip wasn't scientific exploration, it was to find Abby Weathermore and bring her home. Let's agree to focus, OK, Phills? No more grandstanding. Let's get to the tailor shop, take our stand, and find Abby. That's all I want, ok?"

Phillip lowered his head. "Yeah, you're right, I got carried away in the moment, I guess. I kind'a liked being looked up to for a bit, you know. Mom always got so excited when I would shine. Kind'a like when I played the Star Spangled music at the assembly. Sorry if I looked like a show-off."

Now, McClure was the one to apologize. "Sorry, Phills, I got scared. We're not really free here, and I'm thinking that one wrong move, well, we could end up in that traveling cage we saw last week, and no one could save us. Remember, Claire and Naji aren't here, and we need to find Abby and get back home. Don't forget, there's lots of danger here that we haven't seen yet." Lots of stuff hidden here. Look!" Peeking through a partition in the wall, they could see three-story tall copper gears turning together and linking into each other. The gears moved gigantic pistons, and they began to feel a fine mist raining down on them as it watered the massive plants.

"Hurry, hurry, we're not done yet, we got, like, seven more rows to check!" McClure stumbled, pushing the cart along the basketball court-sized room. He nearly tripped, just barely catching himself. "Damn pants, why they keep giving me stuff that's too big, I'll never know."

Phillip hurried along to keep up with him. "Ok, ok, I get your point. But, look, you gotta' help me. I keep reading the manuals but it's not sinking in. You were always the whiz in chemistry. How 'bout helping me understand this stuff later?"

"Ok, I get it," McClure answered, laughing. "Now I'm supposed to play Claire and feed you the information, so you can be the grand wizard and have the glory raining down on you? Speaking of rain, are you itching at all?"

"No, wadda ya mean?"

"I mean Phills, the mist got some kind of chemicals in it, my face is itching." McClure wiped his face on his sleeve, and Phillip noticed that his eyes too were starting to itch. He grabbed McClure by the arm.

"Come on, exit this place, like now!" he whispered urgently. They pushed the cart, each grabbing samples from the last two troughs and exiting through monsterous doors which magically opened as they approached. Smiling sardonically, as he spied on them from an observation booth hidden underneath the dome ceiling was Geoffrey Gilgorey, who slid quickly down a slide chute to the main floor to greet them.

"Well, well, gentlemen, how are the water samples today? Everyone is still talking about your theory of atomic weight and the organization into that table. What did you call it?"

"Oh, you mean *The Periodic Table?*" Phillip replied, still brushing the water droplets off of his uniform.

"Yes," Geoffrey answered. "I found especially interesting your last statement, *Organization is the key to being a leader!*" I think I've heard that before. Where did you come up with that?"

"Oh, nowhere special, just from some old scientist, that's all," McClure gave a sideway glance at Phillip to silence him. The last thing we need is for him to mention Naji Najeem, thought McClure.

Phillip nodded, understanding the warning and choosing his words carefully.

"I think we are leaving here in a few days, and catching a ride to one of the factories, aren't we?" Gilgorey perked up and listened with interest.

"I thought you would be here for a few more weeks, that was my understanding. I suppose we have to talk with Director Loo to know for sure, she is the one who will decide the schedules. I myself was hoping for another enlightening conversation about the elements, no? Perhaps you can be persuaded to give another lecture before you leave, whenever that may be?"

Phillip stammered, now afraid he had given out too much information, but he continued anyway. "Yes, yes, I may be wrong, well, let's leave it up to our Director. And, of course, I would be glad to lead another discussion, we can ask Director Loo this evening, no?" Mc Clure winced at Phillip's offering, but remained silent.

Gilgorey nodded quickly, then motioned them to follow him as he exited the nearest cog-wheel door. They found themselves in the steam engine room, where two-story pistons powered by a twenty-foot steam engine provided energy to pump the water through the facility. The three-story copper-colored gears meshed seamlessly into each other, and the pumping of the pistons generated so much heat that Phillip and McClure started to drip with sweat. Gilcrest motioned to the lever controlling the gears.

"You see, I can stop it at any time, let's just take an example, say for example, one of our unfortunate workers tripped and fell, unintentionally of course, into the holding tank. I could simply pull hard on the lever, and the mechanism would stop, preventing him or her from being pulled into the mechanism of the gears and crushed alive. A fine safety feature, no?"

McClure, still rubbing his eyes from the burning contact with the watering supply, said,

"Yeah, but you have a wall there, pretty hard for someone to just fall in, right?"

"Well," Geoffrey added, "there are circumstances where, it just may happen that an unfortunate accident occurs, you know, like one of the staff tries to be a little too 'fresh' with ideas? You know, here we believe in conformity, above all else, and respect for authority of the superiors, don't we? We intellectuals have to keep on our own side of the road, right?"

"Oh, yes, I see that," replied Phillip, as he started to step back and forth uneasily.

"Even for those of use who are *organized!*" Gilcrest remarked, now sarcastically. "We must still respect the absolute authority of the Council, whether we are workers, scientists, or even Director Loo, do we not?"

With that, he blew three short whistles on the gear-whistle hanging around his neck. In an instant, three workers, men who Phillip remembered seeing at his lecture, marched forward, leading a man bound at his wrists and ankles. A rope encircled his neck, and they held it as if it were a dog leash. He wore a brown loin cloth tied around his midsection, but was otherwise naked. He stumbled along, and they dragged him as he writhed to get free. Then, they dropped a brown cloth bag over his face and lifted him as he continued to fight. They tossed him like a sack of potatoes into the mechanism of the cogs while wide-eyed, Phillip and McClure watched as he disappeared under the water.

The water turned cranberry-red for a few minutes as the cogs turned, moving the two-story pistons, which pumped and subsequently spewed water over the plants in the next room, and pumped more water into the trays housing the roots.

"Come, gentlemen, no need to worry, we test the water daily, so any pollutants are neutralized.

You see, we demand respect for authority, above all else!" Gilgorey chuckled, and motioned them on, past the pistons, through another gear driven door. *"Organization is the key, you say?"* I say organization without leadership and direction can spell your doom, no? I shall look for you at dinner. Now gentlemen, if you will excuse me?" He curtly turned and left them.

"Lordie, lordie," McClure opined, "that's why the plants are gigantic, they're grinding up people for plant food!" He shuddered. "What did I tell you, Phills, the place gives me the creeps!"

"Yeah, we gotta get outta here, but don't say anything to Loo. We gotta act like nothing is wrong. And, where's Pebby? I haven't seen her since we got here. I'm getting worried about her. Let's see if we can find Loo. Let's head back to the Atrium, she usually hangs out there in the afternoon when the shipments are going out, you know? She knows we're headed to Najeem's shop, and I'm nervous Wassy already gave away too much information, ya know?"

"Yeah," McClure added, glancing over his shoulder to see who might be watching them, "that wasn't our brightest move. Let's head to the rotunda now!"

Winding their way back through the halls, they remembered that the facility was in the shape of a giant clock. Neither of them could bear to walk through the gigantic vine habitat after the execution they witnessed. Winding through the hallways, they passed their room and found it unlocked. They hurried to the atrium a few doors down and found Professor Loo examining the produce harvested that afternoon. Sitting quietly beside Lee Anna Loo with her head down between her paws, sadly, was Pebby. She was wearing a small green-and-white striped kerchief.

"PEBBY!" Phillip spotted her, and broke into a wide grin. She sprung up and ran to him, wagging her tail wildly and lifting herself off the ground as she begged for him to pick her up, which he did.

"Hey, I've missed you! Where've you been?" She licked him wildly, covering his face with kisses. He rubbed his face in her neck and hugged her tight. "Oh, Geez, I thought I'd lost you!" He felt as though he could never let her go. Lee Anna Loo quickly interrupted their reunion. Putting her arms around both of their shoulders, she pulled them uncomfortably close and whispered.

"Well, ... I was just coming to find you! I've got a transport of produce shipping to Gleeful Garment tonight at seven o'clock sharp! I want you to be hidden in the transport, so you can have the best chance of traveling under cover of night! Gleeful Garment is not the tailor shop, but it will get you into the Inner Circle. So, let's get you ready! Pebby can't take the chance of being spotted, so she'll stay here with me. You can say your goodbyes later, but for now, head back to your room and change into your traveling clothes, gentleman!" She handed them each a tied bundle of fresh dark brown work clothes, and dark brown work boots.

"This will help you stay undercover! You must not be seen, and travel at night is by exception only, so you must stay out of sight! Remember, the Automatons will be watching. I'll tell Gilgorey that you were called back by the Council, so he won't be suspicious. Are there any other loose ends? I think that wraps it up nicely, don't you?"

"But we came here with Pebby, and we should leave with Pebby," Phillip intoned. "I can't leave her behind!"

"Oh, yes you can," Lee Anna insisted. "She belongs here, anyway. It's not safe for her to be running free any longer, even if it is to guide you around Norwall! Pebby, your home is here, do you understand?" Lee Anna Loo bent down and held out her hand to Pebby, who had not missed a word of the conversation.

Nor had her sharp eyes missed the fact that one of the delivery steam snails was just passing through the outer gear door. *Just passing ... just passing... and if I time it just right.*

She gave one last look at Phillip, and her eyes met his. She tilted her head to the side as she had done the first time they met. Their eyes met for only a second, but it was as if every clock in the universe suddenly stood still.

Phillip didn't say a word. He didn't need to. Quickly, he slipped her gear-vest over her head and it clicked into place. *I remember, very distinctly, the first day I saw her. Our eyes locked. She tilted her head slightly to one side and I raised my eyebrows and stared back. For me, and for her, nothing was ever again the same.*

He raised his one eyebrow and smiled his crooked smile. The tinydog gave one quick hop and skedaddled away, out through the crack in the massive gear door as it slammed shut behind her. She would do what she did best. Her ears flew out behind her, as she quickly broke into her characteristic, unbeatable, speedy run. *Go, go, a ....n ... d. ...GO!!!* She knew what she had to do. She had to keep him safe. She had to prepare the way for her boy.

The Cover of Night

When she escaped from the Hydroponics Institute, it was under cover of night. Nevertheless, Pebby did not take the cloak of darkness for granted. She made her way around the outer circle, staying just inside the border of the woods. The dusty road she chose led straight to the wheat fields of Wymore. She dared not go anywhere else, lest she be spotted by the Automatons. Airships were quietly cruising overhead looking for violators, but she kept herself invisible by skirting the edge of the woods.

Word on the street was that she and Naji had been vaporized at the park. If she was spotted, speculation would be that Naji might be alive too. News that the former governor miraculously survived would put the Council on high alert, which would put Phillip and McClure in even more danger. As she rounded the curve in the dusty road, she was breathing heavily. The dust made it hard to see, and she did not want to create a disturbance that would be obvious to the killing machines overhead. She felt a sense of relief as the stone cottage came into view. A rusty rattle-trap of an out-dated Automaton paced back and forth in front of the cottage, guarding the entrance.

The Habitron housing the wheatfield workers was shrouded in darkness, save for the flashing turquoise eyes of the Automatons. The rattling, rusty robots moved around the perimeter of the facility, each patrolling a straight path, intersecting with each other, and rotating to traverse the same path. Their steam blasters were prepared, should any worker think of escape. *Oh, I remember leading the boys to the cottage*, remembered Pebby. *That was so long ago, Naji would never believe it!* Pebby had an uneasy feeling about the Hydroponics Institute, and all her senses told her that the boys were in danger at that place. Scurrying out of the woods, dodging the gaze of the Automaton, Pebby headed for the round back door and started scratching frantically. Scratch, scratch, scratch! *Oh, please, Wassy, open up!*

The door opened, and there in her patched white nightdress, yawning, stood Wassy. Her signature braid hung down over her left eye, and she was barefoot.

"Pebby!" She opened the door just enough to let in the little scruffy dog. Pebby stood on her back legs, and although she dared not bark, dared not to make a sound, she shook her head back and forth and whimpered.

"Sunptin' wrong?" Wassy knew Pebby well enough to read her signals.

"Sunptin' gone wrong with them babies?"

Pebby nodded her assent.

"They still at the Hydro Lab are they? I never had no use for Lee Anna Loo, I thought some o' them folks like that skinny helper o' hers seemed like a bad egg and I ne'r trusted him, ya know? Dang. We can't take the snail wagon out this time o'night, we gotta lie low till mornin'. Then we'll head to Jevity's place, and he'll help us figure this out. I just bet you ran away from them, right?"

Throwing herself back down on her worn pallet, Wassy patted the space beside her.

"Come'on, you know yer welcome here, always welcome with me!" She squeezed the little dog tightly, and Pebby licked her face. Then, Pebby jumped up and trotted to the back door, where she whimpered pitifully.

"What's wrong girl, are those babies in real trouble?" Pebby pawed at the floor and pointed her nose at the door.

"They is moving those babies somewhere else? Is that it?" Pebby nodded.

"Then, there's no time to waste, we gotta move now, Automatons or not. Lemme get dressed. We got to get to Noah straight up now!" Pebby rested for a moment. When Wassy returned from the loft, her hair was pulled back tight, and dark paint covered her face and the tops of her hands. Her tight brown clothes were stained with dark green plant dyes to camouflage her in the wilderness. She removed the green and white kerchief Pebby was wearing and replaced it with a larger one the same camouflage color as Wassy's clothing. Pebby watched her fill a brown drawstring bag with a canteen of water, crusts of bread, and another shirt, which she rolled up tightly.

"Ok, let's go!" Opening the door, she inhaled the night air deeply, and quickly and silently made her way through the brush. Staying along the road, but at least six feet into the woods, Wassy and Pebby made the two mile trek to the Falconry. When Pebby tired, Wassy placed her lovingly in her drawstring backpack and carried her on her back. There was no time to waste. As they rounded the Outer Circle of the Realm they could see the filigree metal wings heralding the front entrance of the falconry. Moonlight from the three moons glimmered on the wings, casting beautiful, speckled, spotted shadows. The moonlight reflected colors onto the Automatons standing motionless guarding the front gate.

Wassy and Pebby dove deeper into the woods and circled around the back of the stone cottage, creeping stealthily, careful not to snap a twig and alert the guards. Tapping softly on the back door did not result in an answer. Wassy continued to tap quietly in code. Two short, Tap ... Tap ... and one long TTTAAAPPP. It was the code that she knew Naji had used when he was imprisoned early in the revolution, when Crashus had kept him standing in a tiny cell for weeks at a time. He had communicated the signal to the other prisoners, letting them know he was alive, and was fighting to survive, and still fighting for them. It was a signal not to lose hope.

Now, it was Wassy who was tapping that same code. TAP … TAP … TTTAAAPPP.

After what seemed like an eternity, the door opened. Norra, shocked, pulled Wassy and Pebby quickly inside. Whispering now, she wrapped her robe tightly around her.

"Wassy! What the devil is going on? Why and how are you here? You ran all the way from the cottage? Tell me, what's this all about? There must be trouble brewing somewhere, no?

"Oh, yes Ma'am, there's trouble all right. Best that I can figure from what Pebby can tell me, those babies are being moved tonight. Now, I don't think Lee Anna Loo would send a load of 'vegebles' through the darkness, and risk her reputation." Wassy began to pace back and forth, gesturing wildly with her hands as she spoke.

"I think that lil' weasel of hers, Geoffrey, is up to no good. If'n they movin them in the night, well, Lee Anna must know that they're in danger. I knows the other day on my run I passed Lee Anna Loo coming back from Council Quarters up north. She barely waved, and I could tell sumptin' was praying heavy on her mind. If Geoffrey knows them babies comin' with news from Naji, they probably sending them off straightaway to the Council, with the idea that maybe Naji is back. We gotta stop all of it. We gotta get those babies free. Where's Noah?"

Just then, the handsome teen appeared, clad in the same uniform as Wassy. A tight knit cap covered his hair, and paint, just like Wassy's, darkened his face and the tops of his hands. In his hands, there was a weapon that resembled one of the Trinitron Blasters. Wassy smiled knowingly. It was several months ago that Noah had let her in on his secret reconstruction of the weapon. One of the Automatons had run into the gate, and the arm dislodged. Noah happened to be riding by and was able to covertly salvage pieces just before the Automaton was carried away to the repair shop. Noah had shown Wassy his secret place under the house, where she marveled at his creativity in purloining parts from the construction of the clockwork falcon. Norra, eyes wide, shook her head side to side in disapproval.

"Noah! It's too risky! You and Wassy stay here, I'll wake Jeeson!" Noah raised his hand to interrupt her.

"Mom. It's my choice. I been gettin' ready for this for a long time. Every time I saw Crashus come here and threaten you, and intimidate us, I knew we had to be ready."

"But Noah," Norra whispered as she wrung her hands in exasperation. "You can't fight the Automatons with one Trinitron! Heaven's sake, I don't know why I'm whispering, but it feels proper to do so. *Noah, are you listening to what I am saying?* You cannot take on the Automatons with one gun!"

"No, Mom, I can't. But, I believe in Naji Najeem, and I believe that he sent Phillip and McClure here to help us. I believe that he felt the time was right to take back Norwall. We've got to save those guys and get them to the tailor shop. Naji told them everything they need would be there, and I believe he probably left a treasure trove of secrets. We can't let him down." Noah saw his mother wipe her eyes and look up at him with the saddest face he had ever seen.

"Take me with you, please. I can dress quickly. Please, Noah, I'll go too. Let me wake Jeeson, we have always adventured together. Now should be no different!"

Noah interrupted her. "No, mom. No. Simply put, no."

"But two of you against them?" Norra pleaded. "It cannot work!"

"It has to work, Mom, it just has to. Plus, there is a big part of you I *can* take with me. Come on, look!"

Noah quickly took Norra into the lab, as Wassy and Pebby hurried behind. As they watched in amazement, he lifted the secret panel and slid down the steps where weeks ago, he had sequestered Phillip.

"Look!" he bragged as he exited the staircase with a duplicate of the magnificent clockwork falcon up from the basement. He carefully placed it on the lab counter. "I finished it! I didn't want to tell you, until I was sure. I road-tested it last week, and it flies! Not for more than a few minutes though, 'cause I haven't perfected the power source, but IT FLIES!!! I didn't want to tell you, and have you offer it to Crashus. I was afraid he would term us and take the falcon for himself."

"Oh Noah," Norra sobbed openly. "I knew the wings were the key, and they are perfect!" She petted the metal structure as if it were a live creature. "I knew we could do it! But, why take it now?"

"Because, Mom, it's a weapon. It's a weapon against their injustice, against their tyranny, and against their taking away all we believe in.

"I built something I call a conduit into the strike light. The falcon flies, then when I strike the light, the door opens, and the muccoplasma extract from the plants drops on the Automatons and interferes with their mechanism. I'm not sure how long it lasts. I tried it on the two knuckleheads out front, and they didn't move for upwards of an hour. That's enough time for us to rescue the guys. Come'on, not a moment to waste. We gotta find them!"

Norra nodded. "But where will you take them? It's probably not safe to bring them back here, and probably not safe to head to the mill either. That place is crawling with Automats."

"No, you're right. We'll get them into the Town Center and try for the tailor shop, or maybe Groomerly Grooming, or Gearful Garment, wherever we can find a safehouse for the rest of the night." Then, he turned to Pebby.

"Pebby, I need you to get a note to Deen. We need Gleena's help to get settled in the Inner Circle, and she has contacts there. Get this note to her, but be careful! Best not to let anyone see you, Ok?" Pebby nodded her head in agreement, as Noah quickly scribbled a note, and safely tucked it into the pocket of her gear-vest.

"Ok, Noah," Wassy cautioned. Picking up Pebby and kissing her face, Wassy whispered in her ear. "Youse be careful, and listen to Noah. Don't be seen, and ye go straight to the Octagon now, and make the way for those babies, you hear?"

Pebby nodded her head in agreement, and waited only until Noah and Wassy loaded the falcon onto the velocycle. Norra hugged them both tearfully without saying a word, not knowing when she would see them again. She gave one last hug to Pebby too, as they silently pushed the cycle into the woods, away from the falconry. The clockwork falcon and the Trinitron rested in the sidecar. As Pebby watched them push it silently into the woods, she geared herself for the long run back to the Octagon. She had no time to waste. Everything depended on her making the way ahead of the boys' arrival. She would do what she did best. Her ears flew out behind her, as she silently, but quickly, broke into her unbeatable, speedy run. *Go, go, a ....n ... d. ...GO!!!*

Chapter 25

The Most Joyful Reunion

Without a doubt, the one person Pebby could trust was Gleena. Although the Chief Baker of the Octagon Bakery had friends in high places, Gleena's devotion to Naji and his regime was unquestioned. Pebby was sure that Gleena would know how to safely get the boys to the tailor shop, where Naji had said so many times, *Everything you need will be there!*

The road at night was treacherous, dusty, and dark. Pebby was tired and her paws were sore, but she fought fatigue and forced herself on. Thankfully, there were few Automatons in sight, and the ones she passed were dozing in sleep mode. But, as she approached the Inner Circle of the city, she noticed the Automatons on their usual patrol. She carefully waited at each intersection until they weren't looking, then broke into a silent, speedy run to avoid their gaze.

It all looked familiar now, the Gleeful Garment factory, where she had made so many deliveries, the Groomerly Grooming, where she had spent many afternoons with Treena. The little shop was totally dark now. It gave Pebby great comfort to know that Treena was sleeping in the habitron with the other groomers, probably still wondering about her. Pebby had no way of knowing that Treena still very much grieved the loss of the tinydog she loved so much.

Rounding the next block, she could see in the distance the tailor shop where she had spent so many nights resting with Naji Najeem. She hoped he was safe in Florida, and that Claire was looking after him as she had promised. As she sped around the corner, she could see the spires of the Octagon, and the cityscape was just as breathtakingly beautiful as she remembered it. She paused and felt sad at the beauty of it. For now, nothing was ever going to be the same again. It seemed so different now, since she had traveled the Parallax. It seemed like *that* part of her life at the bakery was a million miles away, now that she had a new life with Phillip. She had bonded to him in a magical way, from the very first time they met.

It was *that* life which she missed now, the feeling of belonging that she never had known before. Oh, she had belonged in a way to the culture of the Octagon, and to Deen Diggins, and to Treena Trembly, but it was the unique and special love from Phillip, and the giving of her devotion to him that she had craved all along. She had never known that kind of devoted, reciprocal, unspoken love before. Magical, it was magical.

She thought of him now as she scampered up the ramp of the loading dock. Jaunting past the other dogs, she heard them start to bay. Old Mavis stuck her nose in the air and gave the loudest, most raucous bay Pebby had ever heard. Linus, asleep on his pallet, started to whimper until she licked his ears. Lanky, golden-colored Willow came over and nosed the top of Pebby's head. Most of the dogs, surprised to see the return of their chief, started howling, barking, or a combination of both.

Instantly, a door slammed and out came Deen Diggins, Quartermaster and Chief Handler of the

Octagon Delivery Dogs. He rubbed his eyes, not believing what he was seeing.

"What the... whoaa!... Pebby, is it you? Is ... it ... really you?" He dropped down and sat on the cold stone floor as she jumped into his arms.

"Oh me ... oh my, ... oh my, my, my! I thought you was gone forever!" Wiping tears from his eyes, he squeezed her until she yelped. "Have ye seen Treena? She's not been the same since ye left. But where was ye? Come on, I gotta take ye straightaway to Gleena Glisson, or I'll never hear the end of it! Come on now, follow me!"

They cut across the bakery proper, and if she hadn't been so tired. and so intent on following Deen, Pebby might have heard the shoutout from a tall, chestnut-haired woman. The woman was pulling herself out of a gearchair, trying to stand, and she was grabbing onto a railing to pull herself up. When she saw the tinydog with the mop-top haircut and the long and silky silver ears, some memories that had been lodged deep in her brain flashed forward, producing a series of postcard pictures, as if she were flipping through a photo gallery.

The synapses that had so abandoned her when she tried to retrieve the pictures of the little boy and girl, now fired with expert precision. She could not remember when, and she could not remember where, but she knew, without question, that she definitely knew this dog. She turned to Evee Enock, her partner at the mixing bowls, tugged on her sleeve, and insisted.

"I just *know* that dog, I just do, I think sometime past, I walked her, yes indeed I did. Indeed I did!" she insisted as she shook her head back and forth. Evee laughed and also shook her head.

"Ye must be dreaming again. That there is Pebby, Chief Delivery Dog. Why, *everyone* knows her. She's the best dog in all the land, and she knows every inch of this Clockwork town!"

"Still, I know her, I mean I really know her!" Abby paused a moment as the dream and the dark-haired boy returned. He was holding that tinydog, and they were laughing. *I pet the long, silky ears* Then, quite suddenly without warning, the boy and the little dog froze into a still photograph. She clenched her teeth for the pain in her leg as the photograph faded softly into oblivion. Without any conscious decision to do so, she shouted quite loudly,

"Don't get any crazy idea about bringing that dog home!" Then, dejected, she sadly dropped back into the gearchair. Slapping herself on the forehead in frustration, she shook her head and began to cry.

It had happened again, and those around her smiled sympathetically at what they imagined was her dementia. The dream had faded so quickly, that the dark-haired boy and the tinydog disappeared without a trace. He's always gone without telling me his name. Always goes without leaving me a clear picture of his face. But the dog? Why, the dog was right in front of her, and Deen Diggins was carrying it up the spiral staircase to Gleena's suite. The times with the memory flashes made her sleepy. They made her believe that if she slept, and if she could dream, dreaming of him would pull him closer. And if she could only pull him closer, then maybe she could remember his name. It wasn't as if she didn't try. *Had* tried so many times.

Deen Diggens was out of breath as he climbed the twenty-one steps up the spiral staircase that led to Gleena Glisson's private quarters. It amazed him that, despite her bulky size, she made the trek every night. She told anyone who would listen that the sounds of the bakery machines lulled her to sleep. Besides, if there was an emergency, she could rush out onto her landing, and see the scope of the entire factory and most of the workers. Now, Deen rapped loudly on Gleena's door, as he heard her grumbling.

"Whose it? Tell me now, whose it? Devil be, what time is it?"

"Gleena! It's me, Deen! I've got something for you. Open this door!"

"Deen, you rascal, I'm in me night-dress! What the devil is happening? This better be good, boy, or I'll box them ears and move youse to the laundry division!" He could hear her groan as she dragged her large frame out of bed and shuffled to the door. As she flipped the latch and saw the tinydog sticking her nose in the crack, she screamed and jumped back. Deen pushed open the door and grabbed her before she fell backwards.

"No! It isn't! Bless my boots! Pebby, is that really you?" Gleena lowered herself to the floor, laughing hysterically as the tinydog crawled over her and stood on her stomach to lick her face. She licked and licked until Gleena's face was soaking wet. "Oh, You little traitor, where have you been? You see, I have your derby right on my nightstand! Oh, I can't believe it! Now tell me, quick! Is Naji alive?" Pebby nodded assent. "Is he here? Can you tell me?"

Pebby dropped to the ground and looked sad. Then she remembered the note that Noah had hidden in her pocket. Giving a short, quick bark, she pointed her nose at it. Grabbing it from the jacket,

Deen carefully unfolded it. Remembering that his reading skills were primitive, he timidly handed the note to Gleena.

"Quick, boy, retrieve my spectacles! They're on the nightstand, and bring me that derby! It belongs on the head of our one and only Chief Delivery Dog!"

Deen complied, and soon the derby was sitting at just the angle that Pebby liked. Gleena, relishing every word, slowly read the note out loud as Deen listened intently.

Naji is safe in another dimension.
He has sent two men to help us.
Everything they need is in his shop.
They have been discovered.
Wassy and I go now to rescue them.
Make a place to receive them shortly.
Noah

"Help this old lady up, Deen, we got lots of work to do!" Gleena dusted off her nightdress. Holding the edges, she twirled her huge frame and did a quick-step dance and sang a few notes.

"First, we crank this factory into high gear! That will keep the Automatons busy. We don't know when the men will arrive. Probably we should hide them either in the Gleeful Garmet or the Groomerly Grooming until we figure this out. We can't just break into the tailor shop. We've got to get them sequestered for the night and then plan. We've got to do it right, my goodness, right? Right!" She paced nervously around the room, talking to herself, as well as answering her own questions. Tossing off her nightcap and running her hands through her silver hair to fluff it, she addressed Deen, who stood at attention to receive his orders.

"Well, Groomerly is shut down for the night. Gleeful Garment runs a night shift, so you'll need to find an excuse to go there! Ask for Louis LaBouton, who's the manager on night shift. He's an old friend, took a liking to me way back in time ye know, so just tell him I'm callin' in a favor. Take this box of iced cinnis, and he'll know I sent ye. Tell him to keep a watch on the back delivery door, and add extra Automats inside the factory. Take the pressure off of the back entrance. Do what you can, Deen, and hurry! No time to waste!"

"Yes, Ma'am, yes, Ma'am! I am on it right away!" Deen didn't ask why a new box of iced cinnis was in Gleena's room, but he opined it was there for her bedtime snack.

"Deen, take my secret slide, it will put you right out on the street! Surely you can creep two blocks to the Gleeful now, right? Hurry! Get right back here, just alert LeBouton and return! Now go, ...and go quickly!" She opened a sliding door hidden in the wall, and a stainless tube shined in the darkness. Dropping down, still clutching the cinni rolls, Deen was whisked through a quarter mile of darkness, and he popped out onto the sidewalk. He chuckled, imagining Gleena trying to fit through the narrow opening. He quickly got his bearings and ran toward the Gleeful Garment Factory, staying well out of sight in the darkness.

Gleena quickly dressed into her bakery attire, resplendent in her white cap and a freshly pressed apron. Stepping out onto the balcony off of her room, which overlooked the entire bakery proper, she rang a large metal cowbell. The loud ringing always signaled an important message from the Proprietress of the entire bakery operation. This time, no words needed to be spoken. Gleena lovingly held the exhausted tinydog under her arm. Pebby, splendid in her beloved derby and gear vest, happily looked out on the crowd of bakers as the entire work-floor came to a complete silence. All the machinery paused. Even the Automaton guards were silent. There was an audible gasp, then more silence. Suddenly, more than one hundred white baker's hats flew into the air, accompanied by raucous cheering and clapping. Their beloved little vagabond had returned home.

Chapter 26

The Walk in the Park

Claire stood in front of the mirror in her mother's room. Jarvis was coming over in an hour or so, and she wasn't sure about her outfit. She had changed twice already. Jarvis probably would show up in a neat oxford button-down shirt, and she sighed deeply as she pulled off her t-shirt and replaced it with a black-and-white-striped tank. She tugged at her high-rise jeans as she looked at herself critically in her mother's mirror. Hadn't she lost a little weight? She turned sideways and pulled in her stomach.

After all, Jarvis had already graduated medical school, finished his internship, and got a Master's

Degree in game design just for the fun of it. Claire found herself a bit intimidated by him, but she thoroughly enjoyed the time they spent together. She found very few people that could keep up with her conversations about inventing and design innovations. Jarvis not only understood her rationale behind most of her designs, but he constructively and critically helped her think through some of her problem-solving. Most guys her own age didn't share her interests and they bored her. She smiled as she tied her hair into a neat ponytail and fastened it with a black-and-white-striped ribbon. He was a Beetlejuice fan just like her.

What fascinated her even more was his knowledge of the history and development of video games. He could recite for hours the historical development of modern game consoles and discuss the strengths and weaknesses of each of the systems. He was a fan of both *Traveler Tokki and the Mystic Woods* and *Legends of the Ligustrum,* two of her favorite games of all time. They could spend hours discussing the development of the storylines of the games, and like her, he never seemed to tire of either playing the games or watching game playthroughs by expert gamers.

Most of their time together had been spent in coffee shops and small bistros. But, more and more, they were spending time at Claire's house. Since Jarvis was on a temporary assignment at the Weathermore practice, his living accommodations were sparse, and he welcomed evenings at the sprawling, comfortable Weathermore house.

Tonight, he was picking up her favorite Chinese food. She heard the doorbell chime and Moushka bark a warning. Freddie–her mother's African Gray Parrot–mimicked the sound of the chime to perfection. Claire ran quickly to the front of the house, and pulling open the door, was pleased to find Jarvis holding a spray of summer flowers. Clad in a pinstrip black-and-white-striped oxford shirt and black jeans, he looked well put together.

"Hey! We match!" he exclaimed as he held out the flowers to her. Claire blushed. It was the first time she had been given a bouquet. *He's just too perfect!* she thought. Making his way to the kitchen, he set down the bags of Chinese food.

"Hot and Spicy Szechuan, just like you like it, with sides of egg rolls and fried rice! How's that for perfection?" He smiled at her. Then his eye caught the anxious dog in the big crate.

"Hey, how come Moushka hides in that crate?"

"I don't know," Claire replied. "Ever since Mom left, he hasn't wanted to come out much. He's scared of something, I don't know what. Even with the door open, he'd rather be in the crate than running free. Not sure why."

"Maybe he needs a vet visit? Look, let's take him for a quick jog down the street to the park and see how he does. Just a quick walk, so he gets some fresh air. You said your mom walked him several times a day. Maybe that's it. Maybe he misses her and you're gonna' have to walk him more."

"Oh, I don't know, I *already* walk him a couple of times a day. He just seems a lot more skittish. But, ok, let's take him on a quick walk before we eat." They leashed him and headed down the street. Jarvis was holding the leash as Moushka pulled hard in the direction away from the park.

"Man, this dog is strong! I can barely hold him!"

"Here, maybe he just isn't used to you," Claire interjected. "Maybe he'll be easier if I hold him." She took the leash herself but the big dog continued to pull. Walking at a faster pace, they tried to distract him, but he continued to pull with all his strength.

"Well, he **is** a Malamute, and they were bred to pull a sled, so what can you expect?" offered Claire sheepishly, embarrassed at the dog's behavior.

"Com' on, Moush, com' on!" she urged. As they approached the stone fireplace, she felt uncontrollable and unwanted tears well in her eyes. She remembered in absolute perfect detail that last time she had seen Phillip at this fireplace. He was dressed in all black, looking so mature, as he prepared to step into the unknown to save their mother. She couldn't bear to think of him on that fateful night, when he returned to the fireplace alone with Pebby to set off on the adventure without her.

"Hey! What's wrong? Did I say something? You look really upset. What's wrong Claire? Here, let me take Moushka. Are you ok?" Jarvis asked, as he took the leash from her.

It was at that moment that Moushka could no longer stand it. He had seen Abby Weathermore fall into the pink-gray smoke, and now she was gone, maybe forever. Something was very wrong in this place, and he could not, he would not, stay here one more minute, even if he was protecting Claire with his life. So, with one hard, sharp pull, he reared up, jerked the lead from their hands, and sprung free, trailing his leash wildly behind him.

"Hey wait!!!" Claire screamed. "Moushka! Moushka!"

"Come on!" Jarvis called as he set off chasing Moushka who was sprinting back to the house as fast as he could. Thankfully, there were no cars on the road, and they made it safely home. The minute they opened the front door, Moushka headed straight into his crate, and pulled the door to close himself in. Claire, sweating and huffing now, dropped into the kitchen chair as Jarvis washed his hands and started setting out the dinner.

"Well, that was a fail if I ever saw one!" he laughed. "I guess he really is a homebody! I take it you guys are not big fans of that park!"

Claire shook her head, still fighting back tears.

"Claire. Calm down. Nothing happened. I know you feel responsible for him with your mom gone, but he just pulled loose. He ran home, we made it home, and we're all safe, so no worries, ok?" He gently touched her on the shoulder.

"Com' on. He is just missing your mom. By the way, did you ask her about updating her medical records program? How's she doin'?"

"Uh, yeah, she's ok, guess I just miss her too." Claire regained her composure.

"Yeah, that's all normal!" Jarvis said in a comforting tone. "It's not like she goes away all the time. The three of you always seem to adventure together! Guess you aren't used to running the show like you have been, right?"

Claire nodded. "Yeah, usually she runs the show, and I hide in my lab, you know. I mean, it's like my own little space. I haven't been in there for a week or so. I had some projects sitting there and I just let them all drop!" He handed her a plate and took his place at the table.

"So. Before we get started on a game, and I mean a battle royale on *Ligustrum*, I want to see the lab! You've never shown it to me. I'd love to see the place where you bring your crazy ideas to life!"

She laughed. "Yep, crazy? Like how to remove the crap from the exhaust of a factory so that we don't all suffocate when the air is poisoned! You know, silly stuff like that, just saving the planet, one invention at a time!" She smiled as she launched into the plate of food, waving her chopsticks at him. "Maybe if the air was cleaner, it would cut down on some of your business, think about that!" she taunted.

"Now, that's something I would love to see! And if you figured it out, I could say, 'Oh yeah, I remember bringing her Chinese food, and upsetting her when I annihilated her in the Battle of the Century'!" They devoured the food, laughing and chatting incessantly. Finally, as they cleaned up, Claire was ready to show off her work.

"Okie dokie, move your butt straight down the hall! Follow me, for the grand tour!"

"Wow," Jarvis intoned, "this was worth the fortune the Chinese stuff cost me. You know how prices are going up? I expect a grand tour; I want my money's worth!" He pulled her close and gave her a warm hug, which did not upset her in the least.

"Com' on, don't get distracted," she giggled, fingering the buttons on the door lock. As she punched in the secret code, he laughed.

"Security locks? It's only your mother and brother! Who the heck is going to spy on you?" When the door lock popped, she tugged on the heavy wooden door, which always seemed to stick. Jarvis looked on in amazement. "Don't you think it's a little over the top? Do I need a retinal scan to get it?"

"Nope!" she retorted, "I'm getting ready for when some industry buys my patent, and I retire a trillionaire at the age of twenty-five!"

Claire flipped the light switch on and inhaled deeply, as she started to shake.

"No! No, no, NO!!!" She took in the destruction in the lab, and broke into tears. Her small prototype motors were smashed. Her whiteboard with her formulas was streaked and illegible. Her blackboard was cracked. Refuse was scattered over the worktop, and her soldering tools were bent out of shape. The items on the worktable were unrecognizable, and the wooden stools that she and Phillip had sat on for his lessons were splintered and broken into pieces.

"Claire, check the windows! Someone has broken in here! I think we need to call the police!" Jarvis exclaimed, as he tried to comfort her. Quickly he inspected the windows, which remained locked and unbroken. The wreckage was devastating.

"Claire, be honest with me. Has *anyone* else been in this house?" She shook her head as she sobbed.

"Is there any way, I mean anyway, that your brother could have done this before he left?"

"No, really, never ... no way," she sobbed, "It was fine the day after he left!"

"Then, what the heck happened? Claire, just tell me, please tell me? This is all very ... well ... strange!" Still sobbing, she sniffed several times and wiped her nose on her sleeve. She did not say a word as she pointed to the little robot who sat, motionless on the far end of the worktable. The metal man was silent, and Jarvis stared at him in disbelief and shook his head. Claire watched as Jarvis slowly approached the robot and reached out his arm. Claire watched as the turquoise eyes flashed once, twice, and a third time, as the metal mouth opened, flashing viscous teeth, and the disc on the front of the metal man began to flash.

"Claire, back up! Back up and let's get out of here. Let's just close the door until we think of what to do. Quick! Close and lock the door! NOW!!!" They both slammed the lab door shut and locked it. Nevertheless, the little metal man jumped down to the floor, and kept ramming himself forcefully against the lab door. They looked at each other in shock and disbelief at the relentless pounding, as the little metal man tried again and again and again to escape the confines of the laboratory.

The Ambush in the Woods

There was one golden moment, one very short golden moment, when Phillip and McClure could have looked at each other and realized that they were in deep trouble. There was one golden moment when they could have followed Pebby out the grand wooden door, run for the woods, and tried to escape. But, it didn't happen that way. As they watched the little dog slip through the doors, they looked at each other with resignation. Silently, they returned to their room.

"I think we're in trouble, 'Clure, I really do. I think Goeffrey picked up on the stuff I said about being a leader. He must have *known* that the phrase came from Najeem. I don't think we're going any-where near the center of town. I think we're being taken somewhere we don't wanna go."

"I'm scared, Phills. We can't use the tailor shop as our hiding place if Lee Anna is on the wrong side of this. We told her we were going there, so our hiding place isn't a secret anymore. I don't wanna be chopped into plant food. I say we take our chances, go along with the transport, and break free as soon as we can."

"Where do we go? We don't even know our way around!" Phillip sighed, holding his head in his hands, "I got a headache." Sadly, they changed into the brown work clothes. McClure was the first to speak.

"Let's go say goodbye to Lee Anna and scope her out, ya know?"

"Yeah," Phillip replied. "I think we can work our way back to Wymore, or Moniker. They'll have a better idea of what to do now. It's either that, or we just try to find the tailor shop on our own. Why would they have sent us here if they didn't trust Lee Anna Loo? Com' on, let's go see her now."

"Yeah, we need answers, like right now." McClure's voice was trembling.

Returning to the rotunda, they found Lee Anna inspecting a load of produce.

"Well, well, well, don't you look great in those traveling clothes!" She tossed her head back and laughed. "I don't know what got into Pebby! I hope she's ok."

"About that," Phillip began, "we're kinda' surprised to be traveling at night, you know, isn't it against that curfew they have here?"

"Well … well, yes it is. As a matter of fact, come here. I have a little going away present. I just was waiting to send you on your way properly, just a little gift from your Auntie Loo." She tossed her head back and laughed nervously. They saw her cut her eyes and look all around her. Then, in the instant Geoffrey's back was turned she slid two sheathed, carved six-inch daggers out from under her lab coat and quickly handed one to each of them. Whispering under her breath, she instructed them.

"It will fit nicely in your pants pocket, yes, there on the side. You can use it to slice open fruit if you need to along the way! Now remember, Geoffrey has friends in high places, if you know what I mean! *Now off with you,* before he tells tall tales on your Auntie Loo! Make your way, and make it carefully. *Take no prisoners!*"

She winked at them once, turned quickly and breezed away, her white coat flapping out behind her, as they heard Geoffrey call, "Gentlemen, over here, come now! You must leave as soon as possible!"

"Much as I didn't like her, I gotta say we sure could use the help of that Wassy now, don't cha' think?" McClure whispered, as they climbed into the truck and took their seat on a wooden crate of lavender-colored fuzzy fruit.

"Yeah," Phillip added, "I'm a lot less impressed with their fruit now that I know what they use as fertilizer, how about you?"

"Ditto," whispered McClure. "Wadda we do now? Uh ... oh, here comes nastypants himself. What do you think got him all stirred up?"

"I personally think he knows now that we have ties to Najeem, which of course we do, so I guess it was me shooting off my pie-hole about 'organization' that got us sitting here like a stinking bunch of fruit flies. No?"

"Come on Phills, too late now. Better think our way out of this box. Right now, it looks like it's gonna be us versus Gilgorey and three goon Automatons. Can we wait 'till we're down the road, and crawl out the back and head for the woods?"

"With two Automats bringing up the rear? Not a chance. I don't wanna be cooked by their heat-ray gun. Whadda' they call it, a *Triniton*?

"Yeah, a Triniton. Well, wadda you suggest?"

"I suggest we watch and wait. There's gotta be a time when there can be a diversion. Maybe we can start throwing fruit into the woods to make noise. When they start to investigate, we hop out the other side and run straightaway into the woods. If we're lucky, we find a safe spot to hide until daylight. Then, we get oriented and find our way back to Wymore, or the mill or the falconry, whichever is closer.

"Ok, I'm on board. I'll start quietly breaking into the boxes for ammo, huh?"

As the wagon lurched down the dusty road with Geoffrey at the helm and an Automaton sitting on the seat beside him, two Automatons followed behind the wagon, watching the boys, keeping their Trinitons aimed at them.

It was McClure who first started lobbing the cantaloupe-sized lavender melons into the woods. CRASH!! The first melon hit a tree and splintered with a thud. As the Automatons turned to look, he heaved another in the opposite direction. Oblivious, Geoffrey continued to drive the cart forward as the steam engine drowned out the distraction the boys were trying to create. They both lobbed several more fruits into the dark woods. Every time they crashed, the Automatons bringing up the rear swiveled and aimed their Trinitons at the noise. Then suddenly, after one forceful lob, a shout-out came from the woods. A familiar voice, barely heard over the roar of the steam engine, angrily admonished them.

"Ouch!!! Hey! Cut it out, youse babies!"

"What?" Phillip whispered, "that can only be Wassy!"

"Quick!" McClure instructed, throw in the other direction!"

They furiously lobbed more fruit to the opposite side of the wagon as the Automatons swiveled and headed in that direction. Two figures, dressed in camouflage gear and dark facepaint approached the wagon, motioning them to climb over the side. Relieved, they felt Noah's strong arms help them down as he motioned for them to be silent. The steam engine continued to move the wagon forward, as they headed for cover of the woods. Silent still, Noah pointed overhead as they watched the majestic clockwork falcon glide effortlessly through the trees and cruise at low altitude just ten feet over Geoffrey and the third Automaton.

Suddenly, they heard a horrific scream of pain as the steam wagon lurched to stop. The Automaton sitting beside the driver froze, as Geoffrey covered his eyes and put his head in his hands. He continued to whimper in pain. McClure and Phillip took one last look as the falcon glided silently through the brush and landed on Noah's outstretched arm.

"Com' on!" he whispered to the group, as he crouched and quickly led them deep into the forest. Crouching too, Wassy brought up the rear.

"Youse babies almost killed me with your fruit bombs, ya know," she said accusingly, as she swept leaves over their path to cover their tracks.

"Sorry," offered McClure. "Say, how'd you know we were in trouble?"

"Yeah," Wassy replied, "that tinydog made it all the way to me house, and she told me youse was in big trouble. Said it couldn't wait 'til morning. Then, we ran all the way to the falconry and got Noah too." Phillip touched Wassy lightly on the arm.

"Thank you *so* much. And, tell me Pebby is ok. Where is she? I couldn't stand it if she's in danger."

It was Noah that responded. "We sent her to the Octagon. She'll be safe with Gleena, and she can rest. That was a lot of road to cover tonight for that tinydog. By now, she should be safe with Deen and Gleena. They've looked out for her for years, so don't worry about that." He paused, and moved bristly branches away to uncover the velocycle. Securing Wassy in the sidecar and placing the falcon carefully in her lap, he motioned for them to follow. Suddenly, however, they heard an airship cruising toward them.

"Hide! Hide! Hide!" Noah whispered furiously, pulling branches back over the cycle and looking around quickly for brush to cover himself.

"Com' on youse fools," Wassy exclaimed. "Come here!" She pointed to a downed, rotten tree, and threw branches over them as they flattened themselves. She scurried up a dense tree and buried her face in her arm as she blended seamlessly into the foliage. Searchlights shined around them. They all kept their faces down and held their breath as the light shined near them. The airship cruised over at least four times as they froze, unable to even move, lest they give away their position.

Finally, they heard Wassy slide effortlessly down the tree and softy land. Roughly, she pulled away their cover.

"Com' on out, it's all clear!" She smiled and offered her hand as she helped them each stand and brush off their clothes.

McClure looked down sheepishly. "I'm sorry for what I said before, you know, you saved us."

Wassy blushed. "It was really Noah, he's the one. He got us here quick, he knows the Rastadon inside and out, don't 'cha Noah?"

Smiling now, pulling the velocycle out from its hiding place, Noah laughed. "You might say this was always my playground. I've been hiding out here for years, mostly from my mother, but she was wise to me after a while. She knows the lay of this land better'n me. She can flush me out, and she can run faster too!" He laughed.

Phillip was curious. "But, where did that falcon come from? I thought you were still testing the metal birds?"

"Well, it came from the same basement you hid in the day Crashus came. I've been

working on this prototype myself. It releases a nerve liquid that stops the transmitters on the Automatons, but unfortunately, OR fortunately, it has the bad effect of burning the human eye and causing temporary blindness. So, you see, Geoffrey didn't see you escape. He can only lay on the bench and cover his eyes for, oh say, about the next six hours. He's not going anywhere. That's if the crabmetals don't find him first. But, more about all the mechanics later, let's head on. Com' on. I sent a message to Gleena to prepare for you, so we gotta long trip tonight, and we gotta make it before dawn. Got it?"

Wassy laughed. "Com' on youse babies, let's see how tough you really are! We gotta move, but we can take turns riding on the cycle. I'm first!!!" She laughed again as she strapped herself into the seat and held the clockwork falcon gingerly on her lap. Noah took the driver's position, and motioned for them to follow.

"Com' on, follow me! We can't use the engine, it makes too much noise. We gotta move the old-fashioned way. Com' on!" He led them out of the wooded area, to a leaf-covered dirt path.

"Hey, wait a minute!" Phillip asked. "Isn't that the mill in the distance? How come we didn't use this path the last time we fought our way through the Rastadon? We didn't know about this?"

"Well," answered Noah slyly, as Wassy laughed out loud "We didn't like you much then!"

"Yeah youse babies," Wassy sassed back, "we didn't like you much then!" She crinkled her nose, threw her head back, and laughed out loud as Mc-Clure and Phillip looked at each other in amazement.

The Middle Circle

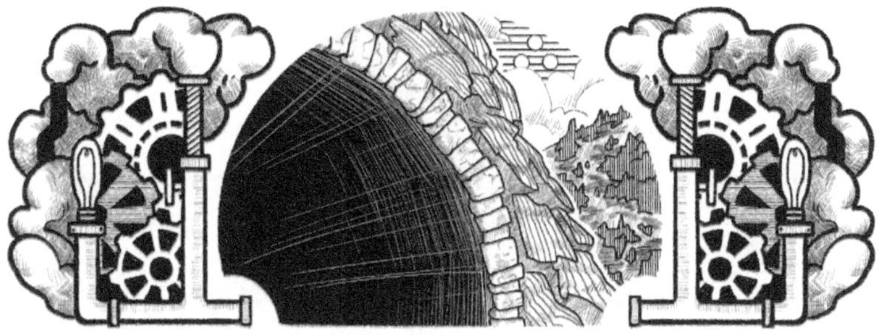

This time, their trip through the Rastadon Woods was quite different. They didn't miss the rough terrain, nor the acid rain that had poured down on them during their first trip through the woods. Wassy and Noah expertly guided them along a path that they had masterfully prepared over the past few years. The underbrush had been stripped away, and a three-foot-wide pathway cleared of debris. The cover of the tall deciduous forest interspersed with dense pines gave them cover from the frequent passage of the guardian airships cruising overhead. The diameter of the Outer Circle of the Realm was heavily patrolled. Phillip admired the pathway as the team plodded along.

"Wow! You guys made this trail? Why? Why would you go to all this trouble?" Noah, a bit out of breath from peddling the velocycle, quickly answered back.

"We had to have a means to get to Moniker's Mill quickly. We hoped that Mendi, with his laboratory and knowledge base, would be the one to unite us after Naji became ill. Unfortunately, his memory is failing. As much as he may want to, he's no substitute for Najeem." Noah shook his head sadly. McClure, now riding in the sidecar, lightly touched his shoulder.

"I get it. You've kept the hope that his resources and knowledge could be combined with your mother's, and maybe you all would be stronger together, right?"

"Yep, we had our hopes. Unfortunately, that hasn't happened. We keep starting over, and Crashus keeps making stronger and more intelligent Automatons, more and more of them, while we fail miserably at any attempt to match him." Noah turned to Wassy.

"Wassy, take over the cycle, I've gotta stretch my legs." Phillip was breathing hard too, having kept up admirably with the velocycle. Wassy, rather than taunting him in her usual way, saw his distress and changed her demeanor.

"Hey, youse. I kin see youse tired, here, sit in the sidecar." She motioned McClure to get up. It was at that point that 'Clure noticed Phillip weaving and blinking his eyes rapidly, as if he might faint.

"Com' on Phills, sit down right now!" McClure urged as he leaped out of the sidecar. Wassy and McClure grabbed Phillip's arms and guided him into the sidecar seat. Wassy gingerly placed the clockwork falcon in his lap. Then gently said, "Now, you sit a bit whilst I move us, no?"

Embarrassed, Phillip relaxed in the worn leather seat as McClure walked alongside. Noah led the expedition, carrying a brass walking stick. "Keep moving forward everyone. Com' on!" he urged. "We need to make the crossroads well before daylight!"

"Why are we looping so far to the east?" McClure asked, wanting to learn the lay of the land.

"Because there's only one safe way to cross the Middle Circle." Noah continued, "And that's a little east and south of Moniker's. There's a tunnel that crosses that circle, a tunnel that is heavily patrolled. But, we have prepped a separate pathway *outside* the main tunnel. It's covered in thick brush, and we shouldn't be seen. We *can't* be seen, if we want to get there alive!"

McClure shuddered. "So we're looking for this path to split, and if we stay straight on it, we run right into Moniker's, right?"

"Exactly!" Noah replied. "But we're going to veer off and take the western limb which will give us a straight shot to the Octagon. Depending on when we get there, if it's dawn, we'll hide out until dark, then move on to Gleeful Garment, where we'll wait for darkness again, when we can make it to the City Center and Naji's shop."

"Sounds like you've got the plan, Noah," Phillip said gratefully. "I'll feel a lot better when we get settled there. Then, we can see what Naji meant." Phillip kept hearing the words over and over. *Everything you need will be in the tailor shop, and this little dog knows the way.* But what did that mean? Everything we need for what? To find Mom, or is there some other purpose to the old man's words? As Phillip breathed deeply and relaxed in the seat, he wondered.

McClure trudged alongside as Wassy peddled furiously, the velocycle becoming harder and harder to navigate as the underbrush became more dense.

They had to keep stopping to remove brush from the wheel spokes of the cycle.

"OK, let's stop here." Noah advised. "We'll ditch the cycle, and walk the rest of the way. Here's our turn-off."

Wassy motioned them to be silent. "Susshh, youse babies," she whispered, "We gotta unpack the stuff! Here, gimme' a hand."

McClure watched incredulously as Wassy opened a compartment under the sidecar seat and lifted out two Triniton Blasters, not unlike the ones he had seen attached to the Automatons arms; not unlike the ones held by the guards in the Hydroponics kitchen.

"What? Where did those come from?" he asked, watching Wassy sling one over her shoulder.

"Our little secret, guys," Noah added, as he picked up the other Triniton and likewise, shouldered it. "Com' on! No time to waste!"

"I *still* don't see how you knew this was the right turn," Phillip said. "I'm trying to get my bearings on these circles. How do you know this is where we change directions?"

"Look!" Noah pointed to a rock ledge at least twenty feet above them. Phillip could see a ridge extending along the summit. Before he could even blink, a long line of turquoise eyes flashed not once, but three times in rapid succession. Phillip watched in amazement as Noah took a strike-light out of his pocket and held it high above his head. Flicking it once, all four of them turned their attention upwards to the ridge where a long line of crabmetals stood at attention, right-front pincers held up to their faces, in a salutary greeting. Noah saluted them back. They responded by flashing their eyes three short blinks, followed by one long blink. Noah smiled the first smile they had seen on him for hours.

"Ok, com' on, give me a hand, guys," Noah asked, as he pushed the velocycle under a rock ledge and hurriedly covered it with brush. "We gotta go, or that tunnel will be crawling with Automats once day breaks!"

"Gotcha covered!" McClure answered back as he collected larger branches and helped Noah.

"Got this, we got this!" whispered Phillip, as he too picked up loose branches and covered the cycle.

"OK, babies, let's move!" urged Wassy as she crouched down and started to push her way through the branches, carelessly letting one snap back which cracked Noah square in the face. "Sorry!! Really, really sorry!" she intoned, shrugging her shoulders. As he muffled his cry of pain.

"Com' on, be more careful!" Noah retorted, motioning the boys to go ahead of him. "I'll bring up the rear!"

Moving hurriedly through the dense forest, Phillip kept yawning to try and stay awake. Truth be told, he was exhausted. McClure too, was rapidly fading. After an hour of struggling through the dense, scratchy vegetation, they emerged to find themselves on top of a ridge. Below them, a tunnel. The large, arched, stone structure was at least two-stories tall, and as long as a city block.

Far off in the distance, illuminated by the three yellow moons, stood the cityscape of Norwall. Never had he seen anything so beautiful, yet at the same time so mysterious and foreboding. In the distance tall metal spires reflected the yellow moonlight. Most of the buildings were roofed by metal domes topped with spires. The metal shimmered like the pink reflections of the Florida sunset on the water when he had watched the sunset from the southernmost pier at Key West. The reflection of pink from the rooftops was in stark contrast to the dark, gray fog cover over the streets and buildings. There was a noticeable lack of lights, or signs of life in the city,

save for an occasional gleam of lights from what appeared to be a factory. Massive airships dotted the
sky, and gray smoke rose from the factory towers,
giving an even more eerie look to the horizon. As
Phillip was lost in the beauty of the view, he felt Mc-
Clure's elbow gently nudge him.

"Wadda ya think of the size of the tunnel? I've
never seen stones lined up this way, have you?" Mc-
Clure asked.

"It's the oldest structure in Norwall." Noah whispered. "It connects the Middle Circle of the Realm
with the Inner Circle, and it will be crawling with
Automats real soon!" Phillip and McClure watched
as a platoon of Automatons patrolled the roadway.
Coming through the tunnel was an array of steam
engines: small vehicles, chariot-like, transporting
one person; larger vehicles with a driver; and a wagon fitted with comfortable bench seats, carrying
four and five people, all of them dressed in elabo-
rate Victorian clothes. Noah kneeled down below
the brushline, and Phillip and 'Clure followed suit,
hanging onto every word from Noah.

"See, you've got the Eliticons coming into the Inner Circle to browse the shops selling goods from
the factories. They'll take merch from the shops,
and goodies from the Octagon storefront shop back

to their homes. The Town Center is their own little warehouse. Goods are cheap, 'cause the labor is cheap!" Phillip nodded.

"So what do we do after we pass the tunnel? How we gonna' keep from being spotted?" Wassy, now coming to kneel beside them, replied curtly, "We got'cha covered! After the tunnel, there is a wee patch o' woody land. It backs to the Habitron of the Octogon. It's a solid brick wall, so not much patrolling by the Automats. Around the side, there be the loading dock for the Delivery Dogs. They don't start to line up until eight o'clock sharp, so, …"

McClure interrupted, "So we better get there now. Right. Com' on, we've got maybe two hours before we're plant food. We better move now. Com' on Phills, one last push, then you can rest." He offered Phillip his hand and pulled him up. Phillip shook his head and tried to revive himself, but, despite the excitement, couldn't keep himself from starting to doze.

"I know, I know, I'm trying!" he exclaimed as he slapped the sides of his own face.

"Gotta wake up!! Com' on, com' on, baby!" Wassy urged him as she poured water from her canteen into his cupped hands and he splashed his face.

"OK, I'm ready now! Let's go!" Phillip straightened up, nodded his head, and pulled all his reserves together. He gulped, and gave one last look at the cityscape. *Somewhere Mom, I hope you're out there.* McClure seemed to read his thoughts.

"I know Phills, I hope that somewhere she's out there too, and she's ok. At least we're on the way now, and soon we'll be in that tailor shop and we can focus on finding her, right?" Phillip nodded in agreement.

"One last push, 'Clure, one last push! Let's go!!!" Phillip urged, as he followed behind Noah and Wassy, who had unroofed a small opening on the side of the mountain. It took Phillip and McClure a moment to realize it was the entrance to a slide. They watched incredulously as Noah and then Wassy, dropped to the ground, inched into the opening, and slid out of sight. They followed immediately after.

When Phillip and McClure emerged from the long slide, Wassy and Noah were there to grab their hands. Wassy motioned them to be silent, holding a finger to her lips. Stealthily, they ran the perimeter, careful not to disturb the brush. Once, they flattened to the ground as an airship passed overhead. Phillip's face was covered with dirt and he was shaking with exhaustion. Noah motioned them to hurry as the three suns started to rise. The sky gave off a pink glow, as in the distance, they could see the four-story brick wall of the rear of the Octagon Bakery Habitron.

They could not stop to admire the chrome spires, nor could they notice the puffs of gray smoke that emitted from the smokestacks. As Wassy promised, the rear of the building was windowless, and no Automats were in their way. They skirted the edge of the building, as Noah approached the corner first. He motioned for one of them, and McClure stepped up. He dashed toward the loading dock, and crouching, made his way into the waiting arms of Deen Diggins, who motioned to Noah to send the next person. Wassy made her way, likewise crouching, skillfully, silently making her way to safety. Deen hugged her close, and moved her to the side. The suns were rising now as Noah grabbed Phillip by the hand and shoved him around the corner. Noah's voice shook uncontrollably.

"Hurry man, hurry!!! GO!!!" he whispered, following closely behind Phillip, realizing that Phillip's exhaustion was getting the better of him. Grabbing Phillip's arm, Noah dragged him up the ramp, just as the first platoon of Automats rounded the corner and proceeded to the loading dock and their watch positions.

Phillip, unable to go another step, dropped down to the floor inside the loading area, as McClure and Noah pulled him by the legs and sequestered the entire group in a closet reserved for the delivery dog kibble. Sitting down beside him on a large bag of dog food, Wassy poured her canteen water into a cup and wetted his lips. McClure rubbed Phillip's arms, trying to keep him warm.

"He's nearly done for, it's been a bit much for 'im, give me one of those blankets," she pointed to a shelf and wet a cloth from her canteen water and placed it on Phillip's forehead. They heard a scratching at the door, and as Phillip fluttered his eyes, Noah opened the door a crack, as Pebby nosed her way in. Phillip opened his eyes and smiled. She licked his face with reckless abandon, as the little group breathed a sigh of relief.

Chapter 29

The Talwin Tunnel

Wassy Wymore shook Phililp so hard he woke up to feel his brain rattling inside his skull.

"Hey!" he retorted as he swatted her hands away. "What's going on? Wait a minute, where are we?" He rubbed his eyes and sat straight up. Beside him, McClure stirred.

"What the heck?" 'Clure rubbed his eyes too. They had slept the entire day. They were lying on scratchy dog pallets in a closet in the dog quarters of the Octagon Bakery, hiding there until they could move under cover of night.

"Com' on youse babies," Wassy whispered. "We gotta go in a few minutes. Com' on! Noah is out there talkin' to Deen. They working out our way to Gleeful Garment. We gonna hide there, and tomorrow make it to Naji's. But, we gotta go now. It's just comin' nightfall and the Automats is changing shifts. Now is our best chance of avoiding 'em. Come'on, hurry!"

Standing, shaky on their feet, exhausted from the past few days' journey, Phillip and McClure stood and stretched. The closet door opened a crack as Noah slipped in. He was still dressed in camouflage clothes, his face covered with black paint marks to help him hide in the brush.

"Guys! We gotta go in a few minutes. Here, have a snack." Noah pulled out a small bag from his pocket, and offered them each a slice of sourdough bread dripping with sweet margarine. They made quick work of it, and just in time. Next, Deen Diggins opened the door quietly and handed in several paper cups of cleote-spice tea, a Norwall specialty.

"Com' on all of you, finish up, we gotta' get on the move! I made arrangements with Sam Standerfast to open the back gate in about an hour. Any later, and we put him at risk. We'll travel along the back wall of the Octagon. Stay at least six feet apart so we can fade into the background, keep flat as you can against the brick walls. The Automatons are programmed to sense movement. So, if you see one, flatten and FREEZE! You got it?" Just then, Deen felt a cold nose push against his ankle.

"Oh, well, she *insists* on coming along!" Through the crack in the door nosed Pebby, resplendent in her gear-vest and her favorite velvet black derby, placed *just so* on her head.

"Pebby!" Phillip exclaimed as he bent down and picked her up, hugging her tightly. "Don't you look fancy!" He gently touched the black velvet derby, positioned just so on the head of the tinydog. He took in the deep-violet ribbon band and the solitary deep-rose flower. Her vest was spotted with gears of colored metals. He held her close as McClure rubbed her ears. Deen laughed, and Wassy crowded in to kiss the tinydog.

She cautioned Phillip. "Don't you babies touch the hat! She's real particular 'bout it. Only *one* Chief Delivery Dog, and that would be Pebby. And, *only* the Chief can wear the hat, right Pebby?"

She nodded her head as Phillip carefully set her down. *I promised Naji I would get them to the shop, and I gotta do what he said. I know this ole' Clockwork town better than any of 'em! I knows every nook and cranny and side tunnel, so's I even know it better'n Deen ever could!*

Deen knelt in front of her.

"Now, Pebby, don't go gettin' fancy on me. Just get them to Gleeful, no further! Take them around the back, near the garbage pits, but watch out! Ground is soft there, but shouldn't have Automats at this hour, right? This is when they change shifts and get their recharge, so you gotta go quick, but safe." Pebby nodded, and steeled herself for the trip. Deen continued. "I'm gonna tell Treena you're back, and Linus is due for a grooming. So, I'll have a chance to get him over to her. Old Merry McGuttchen ain't been feeling so well, so maybe Treena can sneak out to see ya, ok?"

Pebby nodded, then looked up at Phillip with trusting eyes. She thought back to the first time they met, at the Adventura Mall on that crisp, sunny Florida morning. He looked at me over the top of his glasses. The morning sun was in my eyes, but we stared at each other forever, as if every clock in the universe suddenly stood still. I knew then that I would protect him always.

Now, he stared at her once again and gently shook her paw. She gave his hand a quick licky-lick.

"We'll be right behind, don't you worry," he reassured her.

"We ready?" Noah asked. "Wassy, you follow behind Phillip, then McClure, you behind her, I'll watch from the rear. Everyone got it?"

"Yep," McClure replied. "Wassy, I'll stay back, but I'll never let you outta my sight!"

"You got it, baby," she answered curtly. "Just you keep a look back at Noah too, make sure he's ok, and signal me with three fingers if'n he needs help. You got it?"

"Yep!" McClure saluted her in a mock show of respect, knowing that their life depended on their camaraderie. Phillip laughed.

"Com' on, let's go!" He carefully set Pebby down, and she braced herself. *Ain't no reason to go to that stupin Gleeful. I knows the shortcut, and the passage through Talwin Tunnel, so like Naji ordered me, I gonna git 'em to the tailor shop! Ain't no one knows this Clockwork town like me, and we gotta make it before those suns come up!*

Not one of them, not even Deen, would have suspected that Pebby had changed the route. Noah and Wassy had never spent time in the Town Center Circle, so they were not alarmed when Pebby trotted carefully down the loading ramp, and made a sharp left turn.

Phillip followed six feet behind her, careful to keep her in his sight. He flattened himself against the brick wall of the Octagon, and he hardly had time to look at the engineering marvels in front of him as he traveled in the shadows. The sky was foggy with gray-fog pollution from the factories, so he could not see more than half a block in front of him. The three moons had arisen high in the sky, and they generously gave them enough illumination to see the dangers, but not enough to give away their positions. Occasionally, Phillip faithfully glanceed back to make sure Wassy was following. She, in turn, kept watch on McClure, as Noah brought up the rear.

Carefully, they followed Pebby down the mildew covered sidewalks, flattening themselves against the side of buildings. The town was creepily quiet. Phillip noticed that most of the buildings were deserted. The three moons lit up the cobblestone streets, and the tall brick buildings cast enough shadows to cover their slow but steady progress. Pebby kept watch to keep them in the shadows, as she carefully turned down a side street to head for Talwin Tunnel. She crept along slowly, so as not to make a sound. Airships constantly patrolled overhead, shining searchlights on the vacant buildings and empty streets, looking for any sign of movement.

Noah was puzzled. It was supposed to be about a thirty minute trip, but it was taking much longer. Their circuitous route worried him. *It seems like we're going in circles*, he thought. On the next street corner, Pebby raised her nose high in the air and shook her head, motioning Phillip to take cover. Clattering down the dark, black-tinged cobblestone street, came a giant copper-colored snailwagon, tall as a one story house.

Phillip's eyebrows raised in amazement. A middle-aged, angry man in a black waistcoat, derby, and goggles perched on the wooden bench seat. He frowned sourly, and his long, pointed nose gave him a bird-like appearance. The wagon he pulled was loaded with firewood, and the giant snail was powered by a noisy steam engine. The man's chubby hands could be seen grasping a toggle stick which directed the vehicle.

If Phillip had not been so frightened, he might have laughed. As it was, he froze in the shadows and glanced back quickly to make sure Wassy was doing the same. The bird-man did not look their way. The noise of the steam engine would have obscured their movements anyway, but they remained frozen against the dark walls. After he passed, Phillip motioned to Wassy to hurry along. Pebby ran past rows and rows of three-story wood and brick buildings lining each side of the cobblestone streets. It did not escape Phillip's attention that they were vacant. There were sad signs of the previous inhabitants' life: an overturned tricycle, several deflated balls from the children's playtime, and a rusty wood and metal scooter.

Pebby turned to look at Phillip, and she caught his eye as she pointed her nose toward a vacant house. On the corner sat a tall, gleaming six-foot tin-and-brass-colored box, covered in gears of all metals and size,s was, an Automaton. Their activity had triggered attention and the large copper and brass gears on its back started to spin against each other, grinding, softly spinning and whirring. The mechanical man started to move toward them in jerky, stop-gap motion, as the Triniton Blaster rose from his side to point in their direction.

A brass colored front panel slid open to reveal a sinister face with gleaming, turquoise eyes. Pointed teeth protruded from each corner of the frowning mouth, and the head snapped from side to side, scanning its surroundings. His arms flew up in a defensive mode and the machine's all-directional wheels started straight toward Pebby.

Unafraid, she walked slowly toward it, as it aimed the Triniton directly at her face and relayed her demographics back to Council Command via its internal radio system. Phillip and Wassy held their breaths and did not move. Unaware of what was happening, McClure and Noah froze in place.

As the tinydog courageously stared straight into the face of the Automaton, it validated her as a worker. Despite her several-week absence, she still maintained credentials permitting her to navigate the streets at such an early hour. Steam puffed from a short, stainless tube at the back of its head, emitting three short, smokey, gray puffs. Noisily, it spun on its base, turned, and headed in the other direction.

At the intersection, Pebby gave a sharp turn to the right, and ahead, Phillip could see an arched stone tunnel. It was covered in vines and the ground wet and slippery under his feet. The smell of mold and mildew was overwhelming; it was clear that Talwin Tunnel had been abandoned for years. As they passed through, Phillip glanced back to find Wassy entering the tunnel as well. He could hear the sound of running water through rusty metal grates in the floor. The underground river smelled of decay and death, as if something had rotted there. He could see nothing in the blackness, and he dared not light the strike-light.

As he emerged into the open air once again, what rose up in front of him was definitely *not* the Gleeful Garment Factory. What emerged, unexpectedly, was Town Center, a strip of dark, closed shops and emporiums. Following Pebby, still keeping to the inner edge of the sidewalk, they moved more quickly now. The three moons were still high in the sky, and there would be several hours before the suns rose. Phillip thought it odd that the moons were aligned in a perfect triangle. The golden streaks of the moonlight were a beautiful luminous yellow, splattered with gray. The moonlight gave the deserted wood and stone buildings an eerie glow,

Phillip watched Pebby stop, raise her nose in the air, and sniff at a small aperture, a semicircle, only large enough for a tinydog to fit through. Looking up at the signage, gasping, he thrust his hand in his pocket. The widget he had carefully carried all this time had never left his pockets. He clutched it, and motioned for Wassy to hurry as he unlocked the door on the side of the building. Breathlessly, Wassy motioned for 'Clure and Noah to hurry as the adventurers, exhausted and worn-out with *every last bit* of their courage and fortitude spent, *finally* found themselves in Naji Najeem's tailor shop.

The Lost Labyrinth

"Oh ... no ... no! There's nothing here!" Phillip moaned softly, as slowly, in the darkness, he wandered around the abandoned tailor shop. It sat just as Naji had left it that day, when he took Pebby to Favingsham Park, not knowing he would never return. Phillip bent over and picked up a tape measure lying on the floor and carefully draped it over one of the dressforms where, a few months ago, Naji had pinned the pieces of a man's waistcoat.

"It's in centimeters," he remarked under his breath. McClure was exploring as well, but came closer to look at the marks on the tape measure. Wassy and Noah took a seat on stools at the worktable, and they watched curiously as the boys explored the small shop.

"Phills, there's not the *everything you need* we were promised. I'm thinkin' we've been pranked, and I mean this has gotta be one big time prank!" McClure said sarcastically, as he fingered the rolls and rolls of navy and black pinstripe fabric stored on the carved wooden shelves. He pulled up a stool beside Noah and Wassy and rested his elbows on the long, marble-topped worktable, his face ashen.

"Would ya' believe it, Phills? *Everything you need?* The old fart is probably snickering at us right now, sending us all the way back here to retrieve a picture. Unbelievable! What do you make of it?" Phillip paced from one end of the shop to the other. Pebby sat motionless, watching his every move. She gave a low growl by the back exit door which led to the foyer where a wooden staircase led to Naji's small quarters.

"Look," Noah said, "there's *got* to be more. Naji is a straight shooter. He wouldn't have sent you both all the way here to grab Hannah's picture. We've *got* to be missing something."

"Yeah," Wassy chimed in, "maybe there is stuff in the upstairs? Seems like Pebby wants to explore. Look, she's itching to get out the back door!"

"Ok, ok, I'm coming, I'm coming," Phillip answered curtly. "Let's go see this picture that he wants so badly. Com' on, let's go!"

Begrudgingly, they trudged up the steps, led by Pebby, who would not stop whimpering.

"What is wrong with you?" McClure asked impatiently. "Maybe she's gotta go, if you know what I mean."

Meanwhile, Phillip used his key to unlock the upstairs apartment door. All four of them stood frozen, staring at the dirty, dusty small space. Cobwebs hung from the ceiling corners, and a little square red-and-black plaid blanket lay on the floor at the foot of a wooden rocking chair. A small alcove served as a makeshift kitchen, and a small ceramic bowl decorated with flowers sat empty on the rough-hewen wooden floor. Pebby immediately laid down on the blanket. Phillip pumped water from the sink, cleaned the bowl, and filled it with fresh water for Pebby.

"That was your bed?" Phillip asked. "So there it is, the picture of his wife," he continued, as he retrieved the photo from the fireplace mantle. "Looks like the woman in his pocket watch, remember?"

"Yep," McClure answered. "I'm just, ... well, I can't believe we came a universe away just to retrieve this picture? I guess I'm well, ... I'm kinda' in shock." Mc-Clure ran his hands through his hair and pulled at it, as he always tended to do when he was baffled. Just then, there was a soft tapping at the downstairs door.

"Who's there?" Phillip asked, making his voice deep and husky, trying in vain to sound authoritative.

"Guys, it's me! Open, quick!" they recognized Deen, even though he was whispering. Running down the steps, and pulling the door open quickly, they admitted him and his companion, a very pretty young girl dressed in a yellow striped pinafore apron over soft gray pants and shirt. The pinafore had ruffles on the shoulders, and her blonde ringlets were tied back with a soft, yellow-striped colored cloth. Pebby bounded down the stairs so fast she slid the last few steps on her belly as she landed. Without hesitation, she jumped up on the new arrivals. The girl lifted her up, and Pebby licked her face with wild excitement as the girl threw her head back and giggled.

"Pebby!!!" she exclaimed, tears forming in her eyes. "Where ya' been?" The girl's shoulders shook as she sobbed, and she wiped her eyes on her sleeve. She cuddled the little dog lovingly as the group looked on in amazement. It was Deen that made the introduction.

"This here is Treena Trembley, best dog groomer in town! She be Pebby's groomer!" Deen offered.

"Pleased to meet ya!" Phillip nodded his head, more than a little jealous at the obvious affection between Pebby and her long-lost groomer.

"Yeah, likewise!" McClure added. "She keeps whimpering, kinda like she doesn't like it here. You got a clue what's goin' on with her?"

Treena wiped her eyes, setting Pebby down gently for a moment.

"She's trying to tell us something," Treena sniffled. "Come up to Momma, Pebby, you tell me what'cha want, ok?" Pebby jumped up once again into Treen's arms. The tinydog began to bark uncontrollably at the staircase, as the entire group gave a loud, collective "SHUSSSHHH!"

Treena carefully carried Pebby, and headed up the stairs in the direction that Pebby was pointing. As they approached the half-way point, the little dog again began to squirm excitedly, shaking her head and whimpering.

"It's the clock!" McClure exclaimed. "She's pointing to the clock!" He rushed up the stairs, gently

moving Treena out of his way as he leaned precariously over the railing.

"Ok, it won't come off the wall," he announced. "Hey, it's got no glass on the face, and it's not the right time anyway. It hasn't moved since we got here. It's still stuck at seven o'clock. What the heck is up with that? What time is it? I'm gonna reset it and see if it even works." He began to play with the hands of the clock to reset the time.

"Shushhh, everyone! I'm hearing something!" he motioned for quiet as he continued moving the hands. The group was silent, including Pebby, as a distant clicking sound could just barely be heard.

"Keep going 'Clure, keep going!" Phillip urged, as he put his ear to the wall under the clock. Mesmerized, Treena set Pebby down and the little dog ran to take her place by Phillip. She put her nose on the wall by his legs, and as the hands of the clock met at the twelve o'clock position, the clicking sound changed into a loud meshing of gears, a turning of wheels and a sequence of pulleys as the secret panel slid up, revealing a narrow, short staircase.

"Whoa!" Phillip called out. "Com' on guys!" Pebby was the first to go, as the entire group quicklyfollowed down the stairs. There was a collective gasp of surprise all at once, as they found themselves in a massive underground labyrinth full of curiosities, lab tables, bookcases, and dusty old collectibles. Noah dropped the heavy backpack that he had shouldered, where he had hidden the clockwork falcon, having disassembled the wings for transport.

"Naji, you old buzzard, you been fooling us the whole time! Ya been sewing clothes, and working a side-gig in your basement! Old fool, always thinking of his next move!"

"Yeah," Wassy chimed in, "he been workin', that's for sure, I bet he and Mendi were cooking up the revolution, layin' groundwork, but Mendi was gettin' forgetful. Naji was all alone, and his lungs started given' out from the gray-skies. No one to help him." She shook her head side-to-side sadly.

"Tell all of us everything you knows about Naji again, will ya?" she requested, as she came and stood beside Phillip. "Maybe something will click, like them gears, ya know?" Tell us what you kin, ok?" She put her hand gently on his shoulder.

As Phillip told of his chance encounter with their much-loved governor, McClure wandered away to explore the underground lab. Naji had thought of everything. There were tools, lab equipment, and drums filled with chemicals. There was a fresh-water underground river filled with fish, the likes of which 'Clure had never seen before. Naji had prepared this underground labyrinth as a laboratory, as well as a fortress and communication center for what he believed would be his return to power. But, his declining health and gray-sky lung disease had crippled his plans. McClure heard Phillip approaching him, and he gave a deep sigh as he turned to face him.

Phillip put his hands on McClure's shoulders and looked him square in the eyes. "You know what this means?" Phillip said solemnly

"I'm so afraid of what it means, Phills," McClure dryly answered.

"What do you mean by that?"

"I mean, this is not about Abby Weathermore anymore, is it?"

"Look 'Clure, it is. It really is. It's all about her. Look, Mom's smart. If she survived the Parallax, she's probably hiding somewhere. She's no dummy. She's a survivor. She might be anywhere right under our noses. But, I know what she'd want us to do. And, so do you. She'd want us to help these guys. She'd want us to step up to the plate and step right through our fear. I can't give up on finding her, you know that, don't you?"

"I know you want to take a break from looking for her, and lead a rebellion now, that's what I think! Well, I'll never abandon Abby Weathermore, not for any cause, not for all the rebellions in the world!" McClure answered back, turning his head to hide his emotion from Phillip.

"I'm going for a walk, ok? Gonna explore a little," said McClure as he hurried off. His eyes were teary, his disappointment in Phillip painful, as he lost his balance and stumbled down a set of wide stone steps into the hidden recess of the laboratory. While Phillip explored the side-cave offshoots, McClure made his way to the underground river and plopped down on a stone bench to take in his surroundings. His thoughts drifted to Abby Weathermore. He didn't understand the emotions bringing tears to his eyes. The thought that her own son was forgetting that she was lost to them was breaking his heart. What was it that triggered such feelings in him? He wasn't sure. But he was sure as he was sitting there, that she knew his favorite color was green. She knew his favorite candy, and got it for him without him having to ask. She kept a fresh toothbrush at her house for him, and a comb, in case he forgot his.

It was just that, he reasoned. It was a million little things she had done for him, without being asked. It was the million little things that no one would ever notice. He doubted his own mother knew his favorite color, or knew what he liked to wear. Abby had given him a soft black hoodie for Christmas, just the perfect size, that quickly became his favorite. He had worn it that night when he slid into the Parallax, and he had carefully carried it with him the whole time. Taking it out of the messenger bag they had given him at Moniker's Mill, he hugged the hoodie, as if hugging it could bring her back to them.

As he inhaled deeply and took in his surroundings, he saw that this was more than a lab. This was an outpost; a communication center; a sanctuary filled with preserved food, dried vegetables, and a generous supply of fish. They could survive here for some time. Naji had planned for everything, except his own physical decline. Serendipitously perhaps, or perhaps on purpose, Naji Najeem had come through the Parallax and selected Phillip to carry on the redemption of his beloved city. He had sent Phillip back with the instruction that "everything you need is in the tailor shop!" Sure, thought McClure wryly, everything was here to support a rebellion against the autocratic dictator. But, there was nothing here intended to help them locate Abby Weathermore.

McClure missed her more than he would ever admit to anyone. When he had begged his own mother for a shred of affection, she looked at him with an indifference that broke his heart. Abby's kindness and caring ways had left her mark on him. Best of all, her love was unconditional, and freely given. He vowed to continue to search for her, no matter what the cost. No matter what Phillip chose to do.

Then, something across the cavern caught his eye. Something silly, a stupid toy, but where had he seen it before? He couldn't remember. Approaching it slowly, he tried to recall where he had seen that toy before. The little robot stood about two feet tall. The scowling mouth and the dull eyes looked familiar, and as he reached out to pick it up, it buzzed. The eyes suddenly flashed turquoise, and a small disc, centered over the lower right torso, started to flash and spin. There, on the robot's left arm, was a toggle switch. He flipped it once, twice, and the power died. When he rebooted it, he found he could control the flashing on the small round disc on the robot's belly by pressing another disc on its shoulder.

Silly piece of trash, some kid's flashlight. Just then he heard Phillip approaching from behind.

"What's keeping you?" Phillip asked. "They're all asking about you 'Clure, don't be shy, you've got to be there 'Clure, I can't do this without you!"

"Ok, Phills, just taking a breather, you know me, I'm a background kinda' guy! Hey look what I found, creepy kid's toy. Where have I seen this before?"

"'Clure!" That's the robot from my room at home! Gimme that!! No way! This one lights up. Lemme see!" Phillip tried to grab the miniature metal man, but McClure laughed and held it at arm's length.

"Watch this Phills!" And Mc'Clure flipped the switch again, and pressed the buttons.

DOT DOT DOT … DASH DASH DASH … DOT DOT DOT … DASH DASH … DASH

"I don't get it. Why is the brother to this thing sitting in my bedroom at home? Just leave it, we'll think about it later, com' on, back up to the group. They're all wanting to hear more about the time we spent with Najeem."

Putting his arm around McClure's shoulder, Phillip turned, and led him back over the slippery stone floor to the atrium, where the assembled renegades waited for their newly ordained leaders.

"Do we really have to do this, Phills?" McClure asked, not ready to hear his answer.

"Yeah, we gotta do this 'Clure, for Claire, for Naji, and most of all, for Mom," Phillip replied, without hesitation. "You see, if by chance they have her, we gotta find her, and if she is already captured, we are the only chance she has to be rescued." McClure nodded, then thoughtfully answered. "I got your point. If it's for Abby, I'm all in. All in."

"'Clure," Phillip answered, "We're not just kids anymore." He turned and looked straight into McClure's eyes. It was then that he noticed Pebby standing straight and tall beside them.

"Clure. We are the resistance. We are the best that they've got. I'm not afraid anymore. I know my mother, and I know she would want this."

McClure resolutely nodded his head. As he trudged up the narrow stone steps behind Phillip, he remembered his history class, always one of his favorites. He remembered the melody that had stuck with him when they studied the antifascist rebellion in Italy during the Second World War. Soon, with a little coaching from McClure, the group was standing in a circle, holding hands. The soft refrain they sang acapella echoed through the caverns, as if in prayer. Their voices, more sure with each refrain, parroted the words that 'Clure taught them, some of the phrases in English, some of them in Italian. Softly, quietly, they sang the Italian song of freedom, of rebellion, and of resistance to the Fascist Regime and the Nazi Occupation during the war. They sang, with all their hearts, the "Bella Ciao." Pebby the tinydog, nose raised in the air, bayed softly to the music, as she stood proudly between Phillip and McClure.

Una Mattina, I woke up early,
Oh Bella ciao, Bella ciao, Bella ciao, ciao, ciao
Una Mattina, I woke up early,
E 'ho Trovato e'in vasor

O partisano, take me with you;
Oh Bella ciao, Bella ciao, Bella ciao, ciao, ciao
O partisano, take me with you;
Che mi Sento di morir

E sei io muoio, da partisano
Oh Bella ciao, Bella ciao, Bella ciao, ciao, ciao
E sei io muoio, da partisano
Tu mi devi seppellir

E Seppellire, up on the mountain.
Oh Bella ciao, Bella ciao, Bella ciao, ciao, ciao
E Seppellire, up on the mountain.
Sotto l'ombra di unbel fior

Y la gente, che passeranno
Oh Bella ciao, Bella ciao, Bella ciao, ciao, ciao
Y la gente, che passerranno
Mi diranno che bel fior!

It is the flower del partisano
Oh Bella ciao, Bella ciao, Bella ciao, ciao, ciao
It is the flower del partisano
Morto per la Liberta!

Epilogue

Meanwhile, in a universe away, Claire and Jarvis, embroiled in an aggressive videogame match, stopped and stared as the little robot they had tied and bound with bungee cords to a straight backed kitchen chair suddenly got their attention. His turquoise eyes lit angrily, as the magenta disc on the right of his torso flashed a series of lights. It looked for all the world as if he was trying to break out of his restraints and inflict serious injuries on someone.

"He's having a seizure!" laughed Claire, as she moved closer to him.

"My dear," Jarvis intoned seriously, "that's no seizure." Wide eyed, he also approached closely, but still kept a safe distance from the angry robot. Claire was intrigued now.

"Well, if it's not a seizure, then ...what ..."

"Claire," Jarvis quietly offered in amazement. "Claire, I'm no hero, but I'm a Boy Scout from way back. That's S.O.S. Claire, someone's sending you a distress code."

He saw her mouth drop open, and he grabbed her, just before she dropped to the floor.

The Clockwork Adventures continues with Part Three, Lost in the Labyrinth, coming summer of 2024

"Bella Ciao" is an Italian folk song, a song of protest. It was first sung by workers in Italy who labored long and hard weeding the rice fields. They mainly labored in the summer, when working conditions were harsh, and the pay was very low. During World War II, the song was modified slightly, and it became the theme of the Antifascist movement in Italy. The citizens were protesting their own fascist government, as well as the occupation of Italy by Nazi Germany. The song is almost hymn-like to Italians, many of whom lost loved ones to the brutal fascist government and the Second World War. The song was brought back to popularity when it was featured in the Netflix show The Money Heist, where the main characters were protesting the perceived tyranny of the government of Spain.

The theme of the song is a story of rebellion against tyranny and oppression. The song says:

Take me with you, and if I die fighting the tyranny, as a soldier of the rebellion, bury me high on the mountain, under the shade of the beautiful flowers. Let all who pass by say, "There are the beautiful flowers. They are the beautiful flowers of a soldier who died fighting for freedom!

The Story Continues...

The Clockwork Adventures continues in
Part Two: Circles of the Realm. Let's learn
about how the story evolved!

So continues the story of the feisty fiercely
independent tinydog. But now, the family and the boy
that she has become devoted to are split widely apart,
divided by time and space. Pebby has been asked to
switch roles once again. Just when she was ready to
give up her independence and spend her life with the
Weathermore family, she is deputized into serving as
Phillip's guide in a world unlike anything he had ever
experienced before. She is asked by Naji to return to
Norwall and get Phillip safely to the tailor shop.

When we left our characters at the end of *The Search
for Norwall*, Abby Weathermore was alive, but could not
even recall her own name. Her ankle is now encased
in a series of gear splints, and we find out through
her caregiver that it nearly had to be amputated. She
is immobilized and confined to a bed. Her head is
wrapped in bandages, and she sees a tall metal "statue"
standing in the corner of her room, with menacing
teeth and a frightening countenance.

Meanwhile, at the end of *The Search for Norwall*,
we found Phillip, McClure and Pebby running from
gigantic overhead airships as they tried to find a place
to hide. Pebby, acting as guide, directs them to their
first safe-house, Wymore's Cottage. There, coming out
from the shadows, they encounter Wascilla Wymore,
better known as Wassy, a tough, sarcastic teen who
cannot resist the urge to fist fight, and also torments
them by referring to them as "those babies". Wassy
would soon become part of their team, and many times,

their safety and wellbeing would be in her hands.

At the same time, Claire, who turned in for the night, awakens to find that her brother is missing. She does not immediately realize that her brother has gone without even so much as goodbye. Worse, he has taken his best friend McClure with him, as well as the tinydog Pebby.

So, in all fairness to Claire, *Circles of the Realm* had to begin in the Weathermore family kitchen with Claire's realization that she had been left behind on the adventure of a lifetime. Of course, it does not take clever Claire long to realize that the survival of the family depends on her. The house, the peculiar, particular, persnickety pets, her mother's business, and the terribly ill Naji Najeem will look to Claire for guidance and strength. This "cold-water-in-the-face" was necessary to allow steep linear growth of her character arc. The abrupt shift in her life forces her into responsibilities, which, for better or worse, have previously been shouldered by her mother.

The prologue was designed to showcase the feelings that will lead to her transition, as will subsequent chapters, where she "was awfully tired of being Abby Weathermore", in other words, tired of becoming an adult. She realizes that her education and high intellect may not be enough to navigate the treacherous world outside of her mother's protective armor.

Phills and 'Clure, as *Circles of the Realm* begins, quickly realize that they must develop a broader skill set to survive. Their teasing and jovial teenage pranks are out of place now, and their survival depends on their learning new ways of not only problem solving, but relating to people as well.

As the story evolves, we meet characters of all ages from all different backgrounds and experiences, who play an integral role in the storyline. Wallace Wymore,

Mendi Moniker, Gleena Glisson, and Lee Anna Loo, are just a few of the adults that Phillip and McClure meet. Each of these adults have their own set of problems. These adults are not like any persons they have interacted with in their previous lives. These are people who carry tremendous burdens of loss, hardship, and struggle to survive against unsurmountable odds. This is more than a story about two lost teenagers. It became a story about relationships and trust across people of all ages. Phillip and McClure have entered this new world with no idea of whom they can trust. Their sheltered background has in no way prepared them for the skills that they need to survive in Norwall.

They do know, from the start of their adventure, that their only reliable friend is the tinydog Pebby. "Her sincerity has never been questioned." The adults that they meet, may or may not have their best interest at heart. While McClure may have dealt with dysfunctional adults in his home life, Phillip has been relatively protected. In *The Search for Norwall*, we saw that Abby Weathermore would not allow Phillip to go to McClure's home. It was implied that she suspected all was not quite right there, which was her reason for including McClure in the family activities. It was as if she welcomed McClure as a brother to Phillip.

The relationship between the boys has always been close. They become even closer in *Circles of the Realm*, as the backstory of McClure's love and admiration for Abby Weathermore becomes clear. Can Phillip share his mother? Can McClure move past the poor relationship he had with his own parents and find his way with the Weathermores? Is there a price he pays for making that trade?

As we accompany Phillip and McClure on their quest to locate the tailor shop of Naji Najeem, we remember he told them, *Everything you will need is there*. We raise the question, what will they really need? What could they really need, to not only find their mother, but to lead the cause to save the republic, and to perhaps return home safely?

We have to ask the question, "What was Naji thinking?" Was he so sure that these teenage boys could manage to do what the citizens of Norwall could not do, that is, to take back their country? Could he really expect that they could accomplish something that he, as governor, could not?

The perilous journey through the Circles of the Realm will test Phillip and McClure in a way that nothing else ever has. The assumption of her mother's duties, both professional and personal, will challenge Claire, as she confronts the attentions of a new romantic partner and looks forward to college in the fall. Abby Weathermore, who barely remembers her name, will confront her own demons as she tries valiantly to remember her life before Norwall.

In *The Search for Norwall*, we asked the question, how is this book different? We discussed the development of the characters and places and the worldbuilding. In *Circles of the Realm*, we have kicked off the adventure. These multidimensional characters are drawn into the adventure of a lifetime. As Noah tells Phillip and McClure;

This is no longer about finding your mother. It's no longer about getting you and your friend home, and it's no longer about keeping thi tinydog. It's bigger than any of that. It's about finding the people that need you. They need you to step up and bring them together. This is your calling Phillip, and Naji sent you for a reason. He saw something in you that you cannot deny.

Why is this story more than just a teenage adventure? It is the story of a democracy, and as in the Washington post motto, "democracy dies in the darkness," so Norwall has fallen. It is the story of people who were not paying attention to their leaders. It is the story of a people who lost their moral compass. It is the story of the taking down of the intellectuals, and the making of them into a commodity, used only to provide. Do we not see that currently? Listening to some of our elected officials reinforces the idea that everyone is an expert in everything. The internet would seem to be the answer to all questions, but perhaps we need to be asking different questions. Where are the intellectuals? Mostly in hiding. We are all aware of the malicious comments directed at intellectuals during the pandemic. In the Clockwork Series, the intellectuals are termed *providers*.

Where have we heard the term *providers*? it's commonly used in the medical profession to describe anyone that provides care. Some highly trained intellectuals might find that insulting. We have also seen marginalization of minority groups, and loss of compassion and kindness in our society. There will never be a time when the story of Norwall is more relevant. Why not drop two relatively sheltered teens into a dystopian land riddled with exciting flying machines, Automaton robots, and tortuous penalties for civil disobedience? Could someone like Councilman Crashus dominate our society? We will see where the story goes, so enjoy the journey!

Like a winding spring on a watch, winding tighter and tighter, the characters as well as the readers, are drawn into the adventure within the *Circles of the Realm*, in a story that only becomes more complex and more intriguing as it progresses.

Character Development

Get a more in-depth look at some of the cast of **The Clockwork Adventures, Part Two: Circles of the Realm!**

~ COUNCILMAN CRASHUS ~

Every villain needs a backstory, and by all means, Councilman Crashus is no exception. Crashus, or as Lee Anna Loo disrespectfully calls him, "Crashi", has a complicated backstory extending back twenty years. We first see him as a brilliant inventor, developer of the Automaton, husband to Catrianna, and father of a toddler. In order to adequately develop his rise to power, it became necessary to understand how the Republic of Norwall, a peace-loving city, came under his spell. To this end, we found it first necessary to appreciate the steps by which a free people can fall under the spell of an authoritarian.

Some of the references we used detailed the rise of authoritarian governments in other countries, and explained the similarities that one sees when an authoritarian takes control of a population. As we discovered, it is sometimes, in the beginning, quite insidious. Looking at not only the history of Nazi Germany, but also Yugoslavia and several South American countries, we patterned the decline of Norwall after countries which had the will of the authoritarian replace the will of the people.

We traced the rise of his anger and bitterness, and developed a story detailing just how he accomplished total control of the population of what had formerly been the Republic of Norwall. We hear his ruminations, self-congratulatory, explaining how he grabbed the freedom of the people and twisted it into the dark death of their freedom.

We planned, in developing the character of Crashus, to find an inciting event in his younger years for his hatred and need to control. We traced his issues back to the exodus of his wife. After his mistreatment of his toddler daughter, she left in the middle of the night and he was never to see either of them again.

Unanswered questions include the hinted-at relationship between Norra Jevity and Crashus, the relationship he has with Lee Anna Loo, and the speculation concerning his henchman, Geoffrey Gilgorey. We see Gilgorey spirit the boys away from the Hydroponics Institute, and we have to ask, where was he taking them, and is he involved in the rise of the new Automaton championed by Councilman Crashus?

~ ABBY WEATHERMORE ~

Abby Weathermore is portrayed as a strong but kind woman in *The Search for Norwall*. Her devotion to her family and her career is unfailing. Her main flaws, her persistence in redecorating, her pressure on Phillip to do well, and her overlooking of Claire's faults all make her more human. However, they are never bad enough to make us, or Phillip, not like her. In fact, her character had to be especially likeable enough that McClure would prefer her to his own parents. The relationship between them was crucial to explaining McClure's absence to his parents when he unexpectedly left for Norwall to follow Phillip and Abby. Their relationship could not compromise the love for her own children either. Her character had to be written so that it was believable that both Phillip and Claire loved and respected her enough to risk their lives to try and find her.

In Circles of the Realm, we see her incapacitated. The dizzy spells that overwhelm her are secondary to her head injury when she fell into the fireplace in the park. Research on head trauma and recovery was done to make her recovery as close as possible to that of a live patient. The "visions" or dreams that Abby has when her memory starts to regenerate happen in real locations in Florida. The colored panes of glass she visualizes in the old mansion are indeed real, and can be seen in the Mediterranean Revival House, Ca' d'Zan, the winter retreat of John and Mabel Ringling, American circus moguls. As she recovers, watch for more locations in Florida to be featured!

~ WASCILLA WYMORE ~

From the time we see Wassy step out from the shadows, she is written as a strong, central character. She comes out with her fists clenched, not afraid of the intruders. In fact, we don't see Wassy afraid of anything. That is, until one night, when Pebby interrupts her sleep to tell her that "those babies", as Wassy refers to the boys, are in trouble. It is crucial to her character that she is tough, but also a softer side. She, of course, wants to keep that tinydog for her own.

There is an "easter egg" in *The Search for Norwall*, when Pebby is arriving to Wymore's Cottage with a delivery. We see Pebby wait in the distance until she sees Wassy drive away, because Pebby does not like Wassy squeezing her too tight. That's our first sighting of Wascilla Wymore. Her dialogue is written distinctly different from other characters, so look for her unique patterns of speech.

Wassy is also a bit strange, singing to herself after she has seen a wagon carrying condemned prisoners to their certin death, or chastising McClure after he tears his Medicon disguise. She is clever, too. Having lost her mother at an early age, she has grown up fast. She is a basket of contradictions. She is a tomboy. We see her in camouflage while she is part of an ambush. We see her twirl her skirts in Moniker's Mill laboratory. We see her rapidly deny any involvement in the brutal dismemberment of the murdered Medicons. Yet, there is a part of us that believes she might be capable of just that. That's the beauty of her character!

~ NOAH *Jevity* ~

At first glance, Noah appears to be a brooding, dark-haired, black-eyed older teen with an asymmetric smile. He has unquestioned devotion to his mother, and, like her, he is a scientist. Caught in the intrigue of the sketchy relationship between his mother and Councilman Crashus, he was spared placement in the work-house prisons. He tells the story of his parents' persecution as intellectuals, and he boasts of his mother's accomplishments rather than his own. She is one of the most decorated scientists of her generation. However, it is Noah who first enlightens Phillip on the story of the downfall of the Norwellian civilization.

Noah educates Phillp in an important monologue in which he describes in detail the dying process of their democracy. People weren't paying attention, and there grew a moral vacuum. He describes the change in Norwall as the rotting from within and we come to know that Noah himself is not only a brilliant scientist, but is also quite insightful. Although he works tirelessly for his mother, we find that he has his own secret agenda. He and Phillip share a common ground, both trying to protect their mothers from a deadly fate. Although there is animosity initially between Noah and Phillip, we see them both maturing and realizing that they are fighting for the same ideals and purpose. Noah has tremendous perceptiveness about people, mature insight, and a vicious protectiveness for those he cares about.

~ LEE ANNA LOO ~

In *The Search for Norwall*, we were first introduced to Lee Anna Loo, Chief Scientist of the Hydroponics Institute. She loved the delivery of hot, fresh baked goods transported to her by Pebby, Chief Delivery Dog for the Octagon Bakery. Even more than that, we see Lee Anna Loo anxious for the tinydog to call the institute her home. We meet Lee Anna again in *Circles of the Realm*, this time, in an ambiguous role. We see her meeting privately with Crashus, and this raises suspicion that she may be more heavily involved with the political schema than previously thought.

Who is she really, and where do her loyalties lie? This offbeat madcap scientist, not unlike Doc Brown in the *Back to the Future* series, follows the rules, but is not above breaking them. She is smart, but also very careless in pretending that Phillip and McClure are something they are not. Presenting them as visiting scientists pressures them to re-invent themselves just when they are trying to get their feet on the ground! Her ambiguities are purposeful, and inject some comedic relief into the tense situation.

However, the ambiguity of her visit with Crashus is deliberate. Did he summon her, or did she meet with him only to entice him with a new fruit? There is more ambiguity in the gruesome execution that takes place in front of Phillip and McClure. We are left to wonder :does Lee Anna Loo knows about this? Or is this the work of Geoffrey Gilgory, her second in command?

~ LINUS ~

We were first introduced to this small, white fluffy dog in *The Search for Norwall*. When we see Abby Weathermore fall through the Parallax and lie injured in a field, Linus is the one to rescue her. We wanted the bloodprint on his bandana to tie him to the "scene of the crime". Later, we placed the bandana in Wassy's pocket to protect Linus from questioning. The irony is that Phillip and McClure are there when Wassy discusses the print, not knowing that it is from the very mother they are searching for.

Years ago, Pebby and Linus, who are siblings, had been taken to the Steam Station, where unwanted animals are taken to be euthanized. When Gleena Glisson arrives to pick more delivery dogs, she tries to take Pebby. But, Pebby refuses to go without her brother. She clings to him and faces death rather than separation. This scene is written in order to portray Pebby's extreme devotion and loyalty. We see her demonstrate this not only to Phillip and Linus, but also, later, to the entire group of resistance fighters.

The Places of Norwall

In this section, you'll get a deep dive into the some of the places in **The Clockwork Adventures, Part Two: Circles of the Realm!**

THE Norwall CITY SKYLINE

Norwall is described as a Victorian Steampunk town. It is a city full of domes, spires, and industrial design elements. We see it flavored with cogs and gears, thin smokestacks, pipes and various mechanical devices. Steampunk style is a marriage of the industrial revolution with ornate Victorian style. Add robots, inventors, and unusual flying machines, and you have an idea of what the Norwall cityscape would look like.

In *The Search for Norwall*, we see the city through the eyes of Pebby, and we are shown the Outer Circles of the Realm and the Inner Circle shops such as Groomerly Grooming and the Octagon Bakery. In Circles of the Realm, we are given a more accurate view of a city under siege. The once bustling town center is devoid of all but a few chosen shops. The streets are cobblestone, dusty and poorly kept, and are patrolled by a crew of rattletrap Automaton robots. When Phillip sees the majesty of the city from the hillside, he sees the combination of nature and technology that makes Norwall unique.

~ THE OCTAGON BAKERY ~

A bakery that uses a delivery-dog team to bring fresh baked goods to patrons? That would be the Octagon Bakery of Norwall. Pebby, Chief of the Delivery Dogs, was the one delivery dog authorized to wear a black derby and a vest decorated with gears. She pulls a wooden delivery wagon loaded with fresh pastries. We featured other dogs on the delivery team, such as old Mavis the corgi. Fans have asked for other breeds to be featured, and we plan this for future books in the series. The bakery floor proper is a gigantic octagon, and is manned by hundreds of workers who answer to the Chief Proprietress, Gleena Glisson. The design of the bakery combines the clean lines of the industrial revolution with the ornate decorative frills of the early Victorian era.

The interior of the bakery consists of the bakery proper: mixers, ovens, and conveyor belts.

The living quarters of the staff, the Habitron,is actually inspired by the tubular environment that small pets are given. The area in the rear of the facility is the area where the delivery dogs live and sleep, with small cubicles, and a separate quartermaster responsible for their well-being. In the basement, laundry workers toil day and night to clean the uniforms and clothing of the workers.

The actual design of the exterior of the Octagon Bakery was inspired by the design of The Toothsome Chocolate Emporium & Savory Feast Kitchen, at Universal Citywalk in Orlando Florida.

~ THE RASTADON WOODS ~

One of the most dreadful places that Phillip and McClure encounter is the Rastadon Woods. As the world was constructed, a gigantic map was used to show the areas of interest as well as trace the path that the boys would travel. To the east of the city, between the Falconry and Moniker's Mill, was a densely wooded area known as the Rastadon Woods. Unbeknownst to Phillip and McClure, there was a three-foot wide path through the woods. But, Wassy and Noah did not reveal this path to the newcomers, but instead, gave them a few rations and sent them out to navigate the woods on their own. Later in the story they admit their treachery!

The horrors of the woods are designed to show how the characters react to each other under extreme stress. We see them protect Pebby at all cost, and we see them care for each other when injuries occur. We see them face a rainstorm, but the rain is actually acid falling from the sky. We see them at their worst, as they ration their food, and crawl on their bellies. We see them face one hundred crabmetals, horrifying crawling crabs with snapping pincers. The crabmetals were designed to have their base at Moniker's Mill, and are actually there to lead the boys out of danger. They were designed to be friends, not foes.

The dense woods, vines, and hazards are inspired by the woods of the middle eastern section of Florida near Weeki Wachee Springs.

~ MONIKER'S MILL ~

The boys were ready to give up in the woods. The rescue came from the most unlikely source: a line of crabmetals wih turquoise eyes and snapping pincers. Aside from the majestic clockwork falcon at the falconry, this is the first time the boys meet metal creatures that will continue to be a part of the world of Norwall. Luckily, these are friends, not foes. Their interaction with Pebby reveals that she has known them before. We see her communicate this to Phillip, and the boys run for cover.

Why do these creatures disappear back behind the Mill? Moniker's Mill holds may secrets. Not only is it a place to grind grain, but it houses a secret laboratory, where the crabmetals have been invented. We see Moniker, Chief of the Mill as a Victorian Santa, but Santa Claus he is not. He is a benevolent second in command, but has a memory that is failing, and cannot lead the rebellion in Naji's absence. We see him almost delusional, still waiting for orders from his esteemed leader.

Moniker's Mill is inspired by The Old Mill in Sevierville, Tennessee. In Circles of the Realm, the giant waterwheel and rough-hewn wood floors are combined with industrial architecture and Victorian flourishes to create this masterpiece of construction, complete with a river running through it. The river deep in the mill that the boys stumble on accidentally is meant to horrify them when they see an arm floating by. Later, they learn about the missing Medicons, and they are left to wonder, who did it: Wassy or Mendi?

~ THE OFFICE OF CRASHUS ~

In *Circles of the Realm*, we finally get to see more of the Town Center. Previously, we saw the Octagon, and near it, the Groomerly Grooming Shop. This Central Area is where officials in the previous government of the Republic were permitted to work in small shops rather than be subjected to the horrors of living in the habitrons. It seemed fitting that Councilman Crashus would want to keep close watch over this area. In this particular illustration, we see him looking out his window onto Wenderling Way, the main thoroughfare. His desk more resembles a map such as one would see in a war room, with buildings and flags that represent Automatons throughout the city.

This room was intended to be his lookout over the city he has conquered. We notice that he is always by himself, and always in uniform. Below his office is the massive factory where he has designed and built the new prototypes of the Automatons. There would be modifications through the years, and the rattletrap machines that once served people, would now be ready to control the human population. It is here that we start to see the scope of his evil and the depraved depths he will go to satify his urge to control.

Of note, is that his office overlooks the area where the tailor shop is located. So, How will the boys come and go? How will Treena Trembly and Deen Diggins continue to be part of the team and avoid raising suspicion?

~ NAJEEM'S TAILOR SHOP ~

What a disappointment! All this way, and they come to the tailor shop, only to find nothing there that could help them find Abby Weathermore, or help them assist the enslaved citizens. If only Pebby could talk! At the shop, the group is finally assembled. Treena, Deen, Noah, Wassy, Phillip and Mcclure are all together. The secret of the tailor shop, is a secret labyrinth hidden below. This was constructed to be the headquarters and command center. When Naji said, "Everything you need will be there", he didn't mean just the supplies. He meant the tools to begin the rebellion. In the labyrinth laboratory, we have yet to discover *all* the inventions and secrets that the governor has left behind.

As McClure explores the lab, he finds... the same toy robot that was in Phillip's room? Remember the phrase on the bottom of the robot? "Your story begins here." While the meaning of the phrase may not be clear now, remember it: you'll see it again.

So, is the team complete? Not yet. Who is missing? What about Claire? It really could not be her fate to stay home alone while the adventure of a lifetime passes her by, can it? When McClure activates the robot, and flippently transmit an SOS signal, (which is the only Morse code he knows), the robot tied to a chair in Claire's living room picks up the signal. Her new friend Jarvis, a Boy Scout from way back, realizes it's a distress call. He does not know why, but the clever Claire instantly realizes that the distress signal could be only from either Abby, McClure, or Phillip. Overwhelmed, she faints, as our story breaks!

The Art Of Clockwork

Get a behind the scenes look at the illustrations of **The Clockwork Adventures, Part Two: Circles of the Realm!**

This *Artist's Edition* features chapter illustrations and a vintage Victorian cover. In these special behind the scenes pages, you can get a glimpse at the development of the art behind the book! In the Artist Edition of *Part One*, we showed you how *The Clockwork Adventures* came to be. This time, we'll show you how the chapter illustrations are made!

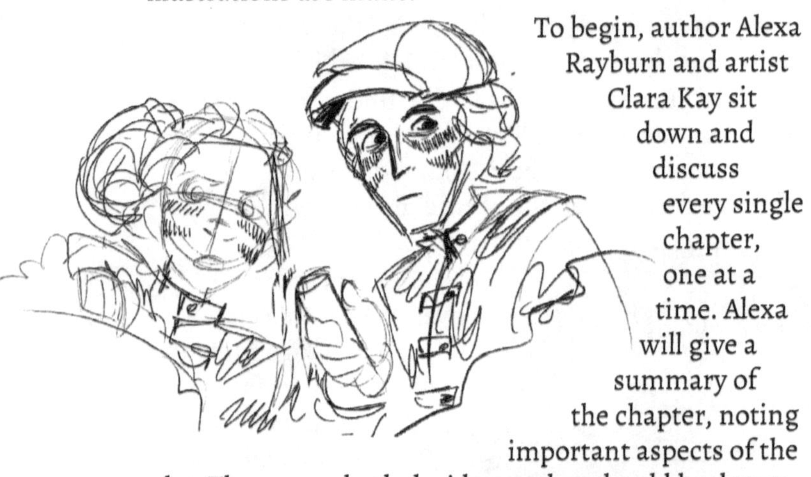

To begin, author Alexa Rayburn and artist Clara Kay sit down and discuss every single chapter, one at a time. Alexa will give a summary of the chapter, noting important aspects of the plot. Then, once both decide on what should be drawn to best represent the chapter, Clara asks questions about the scene. What do the characters look like? What are they wearing? What kind of setting are they in? How are they feeling about what's going on?

Questions like this are important to decide what poses the characters will be in, what expression they're making, and how they are framed on the page. Some sketches end up more refined than others: Clara had drawn Wassy before, for Chapter 1, but this was her first time with Noah, so he looks more refined here.

As Alexa and Clara discuss, Clara will take notes of details that stand out to her that she believes would make for interesting illustrations. Its important to be consistent throughout the book as well, making sure characters don't mysteriously have different clothes than they do in the book, or that they don't look different than the last time we've seen them. With the above illustration, you can see Clara's notes. One of them says, "like in Artist Section." This was to make a note that Naji should wear the same outfit he wore in the very first drawing

she ever did of him, as an "easter egg" for our long time fans! See also how she included a picture of his drawing from Part One, so that she would draw him consistently.

Sometimes, Clara will make notes such as camera angles as well. Notice in the second image, the drawing of a camera angles up at Claire. "Worms' Eye" is written beside it. She wanted readers to be looking at Claire as if they were the little toy robot. So spooky!

For this book, Clara had many locations to draw.
With our heroes finding themselves in the Victorian
steampunk city of Norwall, it was important to illustrate
this strange new world. Researching old machines,
finding pictures from other steampunk creators, and
reading about interesting landmarks that seemed as
if they'd jumped out of the pages of this book is where
most of the inspiration for these illustrations came
from.

Packing in so much detail on such a small scale is
difficult, though. The illustrations in this book are only
about 1.5 inches tall, after all! Choosing what sort of
details should be included, versus what should be left to
the reader's imagination, was a difficult balance.

Sometimes, the final version of an illustration (the
one that ends up at the top of every chapter) differs
from the sketch. In this chapter, Pebby was initially
drawn standing up. However, Clara flipped the
direction she was facing, and had her sitting down- just
like how she was drawn when *The Clockwork Adventures*
was going to be a picture book!

Sometimes, the final drawings stay very close to the initial sketch. The scene of the bakery above is almost exactly how it appears in the final, with Pebby looking up at the giant factory-like structure. You can see the same domed work building, the ramps leading up to the loading docks, and the octagon shaped window. Industrial pipes billow smoke into the sky.

However, sometimes the drawings end up very different. While an idea might seem perfect in the sketching stage, it might have all manner of issues as it is finalized. For the tailor shop illustration below, the final chapter, the layout in the sketch felt too flat. Clara wanted the deep emptiness of the tailor shop to feel more like a cave, and so the final version of the illustration has a greater sense of perspective. Many objects also became far more refined as she researched Victorian furniture and old-fashioned tailor shops to be accurate to the steampunk aesthetic. This final chapter is intense- the illustration needed to be, too!

Meet the Author and Illustrator

Nan Kopitnik is a Board-Certified Addiction Medicine Physician. She cares for vulnerable Florida citizens who suffer from addiction disorders.

She authors children's books under the pen-name Alexa Rayburn. She is the author of four children's books and The Clockwork Adventures, a young adult science-fiction series.

Nan has published articles in medical journals, lectured at national meetings on addiction, and counseled countless families. She loves to weave relationship issues into exciting adventure stories.

She also authors humorous stories and scripts, which can be sampled on her website. From the age of seven, she was a great fan of the novels of Patrick Dennis, which she read under her covers with a flashlight. She has recently authored Shy Sam the Wolf-Dog, an educational book featuring the true story of one Florida family's remarkable and humorous integration of a wolf -dog into their family structure.

Her latest achievement has been completing the Master of Fine Arts Creative Writing Degree Program at Full Sail University in Orlando, Florida. She is an annual vendor at MegaCon Orlando, where she sells books and merchandise from her company, Tinydog Books. She is the keeper of toy robots, and one remarkable tinydog. She is the handler of five large rescue parrots that bite with reckless abandon.

Information about her books and novels can be found at: **https://nankopitnikwrites.com** and **https://www. tinydogbooks.com**. Her books are available on Amazon Kindle, as well as Barnes & Noble Bookstores.

Books and merchandise can also be purchased at **https://etsy.com/shop/TinyDogBooks.**

Clara Kay is an illustrator, concept artist, and 3D animator located in Central Florida. She has a Bachelor of Fine Arts (B.A.) in Character Animation from the University of Central Florida.

Clara is a Florida native. She enjoys horror media and challenging modern storytelling techniques. Illustration and concept art are her passion, and she loves designing worlds and characters with intricate stories. She has been writing and illustrating for her own stories since she could hold a pencil. Her passion for art and design comes from growing up playing video games. She has participated in dozens of online fan-made art anthologies called "fanzines," being an active member of the zine community. She loves tabling at conventions like MegaCon in Orlando, and enjoys presenting her work to the public.

You can visit her at **https://linktr.ee/clarabellumsart** to see more of her work!

Visit our LinkTrees to see our websites and stores!

TinyDog Books

Clara Kay

Check out our other books!

Nasty Cat

Moushka: The Big Dog That Wanted to be a Tinydog

The Plucky Parrot

Shy Sam the Wolfdog

The Mayhem and Medial Mischief of Dr. Olivia Day

The Clockwork Adventures, Part One: The Search for Norwall

www.TinyDogBooks.com

www.ingramcontent.com/pod-product-compliance
Lightning Source LLC
Chambersburg PA
CBHW021412310726
48971CB00005B/1312